Montana Son

By

Alek Leslie

Copyright © 2015 by Alek Leslie

First Edition

Designed and edited by Theresa Leonard

Maps - State of Montana Map 1881 ©iStockphoto LP
Cover Art - ®Bigstock, ©iStockphoto LP, ©Shutterstock, Inc.
State of Montana Map 1866 – Mitchell's New General Atlas
(Philadelphia: S. Augustus Mitchell)
Pryor Mountains and Bozeman Trail courtesy of www.demis.nl

Printed in the United States of America

Published simultaneously in Canada by
Rowe House Publishers

Leslie, Alek
Montana Son : a novel / Alek Leslie

ISBN-13: 978-0-9938600-1-0
ISBN-10: 0-9938-6001-X

Montana Son

For my spouse, my strength

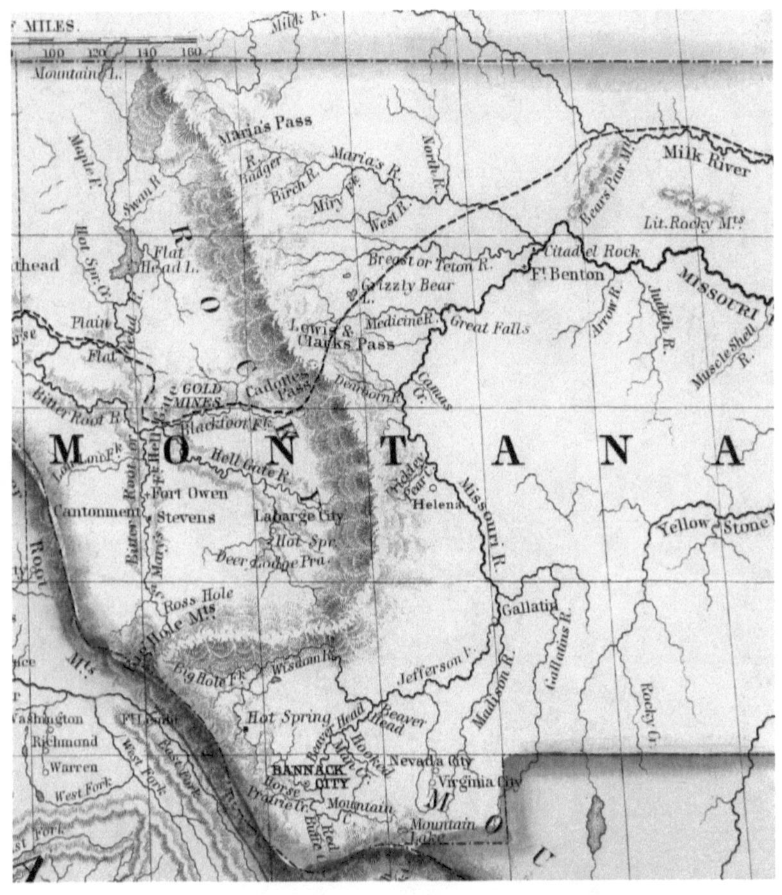

Source Citation: Mitchell's New General Atlas....
(Philadelphia: S. Augustus Mitchell, 1866), 44.

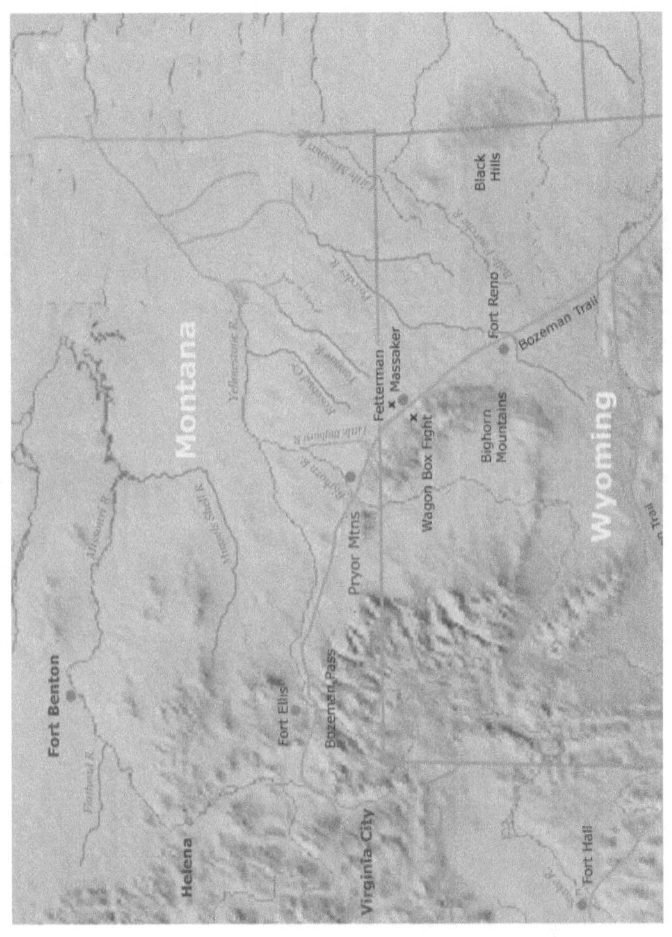

Pryor Mountains and the Bozeman Trail

Source Citation: "Bozeman01" by Nikater
Background map courtesy of Demis, www.demis.nl

Part 3

A new name

Chapter 1

Fast moving clouds were rolling over the Montana Trail when Bill Sullivan glanced up. Winding along the wagon road, he hoped to see the Elkhorn Mountains through a brown haze, but what emerged stopped him dead in his tracks. Raising a hand, his five companions and a long line of wild mustangs came to a halt.

A slew of papers were twirling in the wind or flapping in the boughs of the evergreen trees. Jimmy Donnelly dismounted and snatched one skipping in the dust.

"Tey be music sheets, Bill."

Jimmy pursued the pages of lines and notes past tall pines. Bill and Strong Bull soon followed until they found Jimmy kneeling, shoulders sagging.

"What is it?" Bill commanded.

Looking up with great dread, Jimmy stammered, "It's a boy and his mother, I believe."

Bill's steps quickened towards his friend while Strong Bull disappeared beyond the wagon. The sight of the boy, whose livid skin was swollen and scabbed in parts, over a woman staring blankly at sky, was deeply disturbing. Bill's hesitant hand was poised to turn the boy around when he found a weak pulse.

"He's alive!" he said with much emotion. "Jimmy, call the men over and get some blankets!"

Strong Bull approached. "Two men dead. Arrows snapped, guns gone, horses gone."

Bill's frustration fused with anger when Trey Stewart and Andy Grant approached.

"What the hell went on here?" Trey hollered.

"Trey, grab Andy and Strong Bull. Bury those men!"

"But…."

"Do it now!" Bill snapped as he climbed into the wagon. His frantic search ended when he grasped small clothing to cover the child.

When Jimmy returned, his eyes took in the red shirt.

"Leave me two blankets and clear some room in that wagon for him. Be quick about it!" Bill bellowed, "We have to hitch two horses and get the hell out of here!"

"Bill, ye don't tink it's White Bear's kin."

"I don't know what to think. I just want to get this boy somewhere safe and warm." His voice spoke with urgency while his hands gingerly wrapped the small, inert body in a woolen blanket. "We're going home! There'll be no stopping in Helena!"

Bill was set to climb in the wagon when Jimmy held out his arms.

"I'll take te child and care for him like he was me own. Ye need to get us home, Bill."

Mike O'Leary appeared, carrying a disheveled pile of papers.

Bill scowled at his dimwitted friend, stealing them away. "Mike, wrap the woman in the last blanket and put her in our wagon. Be quick with you now! I'm not interested in losing the horses we just rounded-up!"

Mike nodded somberly, unable to take his gaze from the pretty woman's face, eyes so blue around skin so white, flawless. He swathed and carried her as if she still could still feel life.

By the time horses were hitched to the prairie schooner, the last shovelful of dirt was filling a shallow grave.

The journey to the Sullivan ranch was a slow and solemn one. Bill couldn't shake the sight of the boy and his mother from his mind. It brought back a flood of painful memories.

Jimmy's heavy body throbbed and knotted as he absorbed every bounce of the rickety wagon, the child held warmly to his chest. If the frail boy was to die on this day, Jimmy would not allow it to be under Bill's watchful eyes.

A soft orange hue filled the night sky as the ranch came into sight. After the wheels stopped rolling, Jimmy clambered out of the wagon with eyes focused on the bunkhouse until Bill blocked his path, arms outstretched.

Mary looked up from the kitchen table as he entered.

"Bill, my God, what have you there?"

He walked to a bedroom right of the kitchen and placed the boy on a small bed. A quick examination of his arm brought relief because the wound was small, the blood dry.

"Do we need a doctor?" Mary asked with concern.

"No, just clean water and cloth," he replied.

When Mary returned, she watched as Bill sat on the edge of the bed, dabbed the graze, and wrapped it in an old torn cotton shirt. After the small, leather boots were unlaced and gently removed, his still frame was covered. Sheets and a soft quilt were snugly placed around a florid face, warm to the touch, but so haggard and listless, Bill's eyes watered.

Walking Mary to the kitchen, he spoke in a hushed tone, "We found him south of Helena. He was laying over who I believe is….was his mother. She's in the wagon….already gone when we found them. I thought maybe we could bury her. I thought we, we could…." Rubbing his temple, he swallowed.

"I know, Bill. That'll be fine," Mary spoke softly. "How old do you think he is?"

Bill figured he was eight or nine years of age. Considering he was a normal weight, clean and well-manicured, Bill surmised the boy wasn't penniless and couldn't have been long on the journey.

"He's been harmed, Mary. Not today, but not long ago, either. He has a number of scabs on his back," he voiced grimly.

A sick feeling overwhelmed her. She put a hand to her mouth in alarm. "How could anyone hurt a child of God?"

Bill tried to think of something that might calm her. "Why don't you prepare some food? When he wakes up I imagine he'll be hungry."

******

The first time I opened my eyes, the room was dark. I heard familiar sounds: walls creaking, someone snoring, the wind howling outside, so I felt relief believing I was home in my bed. That comfortable feeling didn't last long. I lifted my arm to see it tightly covered and sore when I pressed on it. How did I do that? Just as that thought fled my mind, another one crept in.

"No," I said sadly, realizing this wasn't my bed. I looked around the room as my eyes adjusted to the darkness, not recognizing anything. Fear swept over me like a cold breeze. I curled up in a ball, squeezing my eyes shut, praying for sleep to come. I rocked my body from side to side, shaking and resisting all of the images that wanted to keep me awake. Sleep finally came. Sweet blackness seeped through my mind, clearing any thoughts with it.

The next time I opened my eyes, daylight shone through a window. A strange man entered the room and I quickly turned to face the wall. I heard dishes and could smell food.

"I'm William Sullivan, but everyone calls me Bill."

He spoke to me very slowly and very calmly, but in an unfamiliar way.

"My wife is Mary. You're in our home and you're safe."

I didn't move except for the trembling I couldn't control. My eyes fixated on a spider that was crawling up and down the planked wall.

"I've brought you some food and water. It's on the bedside table. Please try to eat something. We'll be just outside the room if you need anything."

The man lingered, and I wished he'd just go away. After the footsteps left my room, I breathed a sigh of relief. I felt made of stone, was so tired, and had no hunger. The smells of food began to make me feel sick. All I wanted was for Momma to come and scoop me up in her arms.

Watching that spider crawl to the corner of the room and build its web, my eyes became so dry and heavy that I succumbed to sleep once more.

I awoke to more daylight, unsure whether minutes or hours had passed. I checked on the progress of my spider and the web was finished. I was still curled up with blankets around my head when light footsteps filled my ears, and the aroma of food filled my nose again.

A woman cleared her throat, getting my fearful attention.

"I'm Mary…Mary Sullivan," she said in a soft spoken voice. "I brought you some food. I'll leave it here on the table for you. I've got porridge, some dried apple, warm biscuits and water."

I heard strangeness in her speaking, too.

She stepped closer. I felt her presence over my shoulder, eyes looking down on me. I hoped she wouldn't touch me. I only wanted Momma to comfort and hold me.

"If you need anything, please let me know."

She lingered a moment, but I didn't move.

I heard her leave, and the sound of dishes in water soon filled my room. The kitchen must have been right outside my door!

My eyes focused on the spider in the corner, though I couldn't make out if it had caught anything in its web. I pondered how long it took to starve. I decided I wouldn't eat. Wasn't hungry, anyway. If anything, I'm just thirsty.

My body felt so heavy, it wasn't hard to be still. I weaved in and out of sleep with short dreams… dreams I wished were real. I dreamt I was with my cousin, Patricia, and she was trying to find me. I could hear her voice as I hid behind a spruce tree. Eventually, I jumped out at her and she ran. I followed her as she weaved around the trees. She seemed so fast and I seemed so short of breath. I crouched, hands on my knees, peering up to see she had vanished.

Around suppertime, Bill came in from the barn.

"Smells good, Mary," he said, placing a kiss on her forehead. "Any movement from our guest?"

She looked over with worry. "No, Bill. He didn't touch his food. I couldn't take it if he, if he…"

He put arms around her small fretful shoulders.

"Every time I see him he's staring at that wall," she sniffled, the frown lines of her forehead deepening. "I just want to turn him 'round Bill…..get him to eat."

"He seems to be in a melancholy way. It's just unnatural to see a boy his age feel that way. If he doesn't eat by tomorrow, I'll call the doctor."

I heard heavy footsteps and a man's sigh, but stayed facing that spider's wall.

"Mary has made some supper and would like very much for you to join us at the table."

I didn't move and prayed he wouldn't force me to.

"Feel free to join us if you change your mind."

I thought I heard him mutter, "This is your last chance, child. Tomorrow, we will have to do things my way or you'll perish, and I won't have that in my house."

"I'll bring him more food," Mary said, rising.

"Wait, just wait," Bill pleaded with a reassuring hand on hers.

I could hear Mr. and Mrs. Sullivan talking quietly to each other. The sounds they made were soothing, relieving some of the loneliness and isolation I felt. They talked for a long time and never raised their voices to each other.

As I closed my eyes, I saw Momma, took her hand and, she led me to Willowtree Creek. It was spring. The leaves were new and fresh. She had a blanket laid out and I put my head in her lap. Her gentle fingers ran through my hair. It was a good memory. One that led me into a deep sleep.

I slowly came out of my slumber lying on that soft blanket of pale yellows and pinks, but Momma wasn't there. I moved deeper into the forest, walking along the bank of the creek, but she was nowhere to be found. Panic and worry were creeping in as I called for her and heard no response. My search became frantic until I bolted up from my pillow, eyes wide awake.

It was dark in the room, though I could see and smell food still atop the bedside table. There was such a brightness peaking around the curtains, it made me curious. I pulled myself up from the bed feeling dizzy and very weak, but determined to get to that window. When I pulled the curtains back, the big full moon lit up the stable. I saw movement to the right of the stable. It was horses, their backs glistening in the bright light. There were so many of them. Eager to take a closer look, I quietly moved across the room.

As I opened the door, I could hear the sound of snoring…a man's deep sleeping which gave me confidence to leave the bedroom.

My eyes scanned the silent kitchen through the soft light of two small windows. A table and six chairs filled the middle of the room. There was a stove, a washing stand, and cupboard of dishes on the far wall. To my right were four doors, one slightly ajar. A large fireplace divided the doors, two on each side.

This house didn't appear to have steps to a second floor. I moved through the square light of one window to the door, my hand on the round metal knob. My footsteps made no sound, but the door creaked open and shut.

The air's coolness gave me a burst of strength to step off the porch toward the corralled horses. The grass was damp, and the choruses of spring frogs were filling the night's silence with their peeping sounds as I glanced at the stable to discover two more buildings to the right of it. As I reached the high fence, the horses began to stir and snort. I became nervous of their movements and sounds so I changed course for the stable. When the heavy door finally gave way, a shiver ran down my back rocking my body as I thought of the last time I was in a barn with my grandpa.

I cautiously entered, the moon's fullness providing just enough light through the windows to see seven, maybe eight, horse stalls on each side. The first horse I approached was light brown in colour and looked at me as I timidly held out my hand. I could see the reflection of the moon's light in its gentle eyes.

The horse's velvety nose nudged my palm. I smiled, stretching to touch its silky hair. The horse didn't flinch, inching closer to me. I saw a wooden stool and dragged it over. As soon as I could, I buried my head in its warm neck, curling my fingers through its tangled mane. As I wrapped my arms around it, tears came quickly, stinging my dry eyes. I whispered what I did and how much I missed and loved my momma.

I felt aware there was someone watching me. My soft whispers and little sobs ceased as I turned nervously to the stable door. A dark shadow lurked towards me, and it became almost lifelike until the cool night air passed through it.

A wave of tired hit me, and I whispered good bye to the gentle horse. I used the last bit of energy I had to close that stable door and drag myself back to the bedroom. I was so thirsty I drank all of the water, then tried to take apart one of the biscuits, but it crumbled in my hand. I felt like one of those chickadees back home eating crumbs. That brought back the memory of Willow-tree Creek, and I felt so sleepy and alone. I put my head on the pillow and deep dark sleep came, quickly wiping that memory from my mind.

Chapter 2

The next morning, Bill came in from the barn to find Mary cooking over the cast iron stove. His strong arms wrapped around her small frame as eggs were effortlessly cracked from shell to hot pan.

"You aren't going to get it any sooner," Mary smiled.

"Don't rush," Bill replied with a kiss to the top of her head. He then peered at the bedroom door contemplating his next move. After what he saw last night, he wondered whether it was his horses that could do more convincing. He knew wallowing any longer in that room was not an option.

"Why don't we serve breakfast right here this morning?" he suggested, pointing to the table.

Mary turned around. "I don't know that he'll leave that bed."

"We have to try," he said, thinking about last night. "I'll go and talk to him."

Heavy footsteps entered my bedroom, but I was already safely facing my spider's wall. The man called 'Bill' cleared his throat.

"Breakfast is ready. It'll be served at the kitchen table. After that, I'd like to introduce you to our wild horses, all fifty or so of them, plus the tamed ones in the barn," he announced while glancing out the window.

I lay there a few minutes unsure of what to do. While still horribly weak, I was very curious about those fifty, did he say fifty or so horses? Well, maybe I could take one more look. I just had to get past breakfast with those strangers. Taking a quick vow of silence, I was not to speak no matter what 'till the day I died.

They were already sitting when I slowly entered like a mouse creeping towards a chunk of cheese. My eyes remained staring at the floor.

Bill offered a chair at the end of the table, where he said, "Porridge, dried fruit, and thick slices of buttered and toasted bread are waiting to be eaten."

With eyes centered on the bowl, I sat down and pushed the spoon into the porridge.

Bill and Mary ate quietly, though I felt the man's eyes on me until he finally spoke again.

"When you're finished breakfast, take the dishes to the basin, put on clean clothes and meet me in the stable. Your clothes are in the dresser."

I timidly peered up at Bill and Mary for the first time.

Bill was very tall and solid looking, his arms the size of small tree trunks. His dark, thinning hair was speckled grey. When he looked my way, his eyes were a pale blue that seemed to stare in a friendly manner. I shot nervous eyes at his hands, relieved to find they weren't large, just average.

Mary had a soft smile on her round, pale face. Her dark red hair was tied severely in a bun. She had green eyes. I had never seen green eyes before.

Just then, someone knocked on the door and I resumed looking down and eating my breakfast.

Bill opened the door. "Hello, Jimmy. Come in."

"Hello, Bill…Mary," he said cheerfully. As soon as Jimmy saw me, he came right over. "Ah, yer up and about. It's good to see!" he spoke with tremendous enthusiasm.

I just stared at him.

"Our guest is not up for talking yet," Bill advised with lightness in his voice.

Jimmy laughed. "Well, he mustn't be Irish ten. No worries. Spend time with te likes of us and ye'll be yelling, not talking!"

I had to lower my head because a smile was starting to form. Jimmy was robust, had a twinkle in his eyes, and a jovial smile. He spoke like Bill and Mary, but his manner of speaking was even stranger, almost confusing.

"Well Bill, the men be anxious to get started."

"I'll be along shortly." Turning to me, he said, "When you're finished, join me at the stable." His eyes stayed on me until I nodded.

"Take your time, love," Mary exclaimed softly. "There are plenty of horses to be broken in."

Once I was finished, she said, "You're excused. You may go."

I hastily removed the red flannel shirt that was Momma's favourite and pushed it under the rest of my clothes. Maybe if I didn't see it anymore, it wasn't really there. I focused on getting dressed and out to that stable, eager not to anger the man by taking too long.

As I was leaving, a wooden chest at the end of the bed caught my eye. I was curious about what was inside, but that would have to wait until later.

I slithered my way around the kitchen table and was just about to open the front door when Mary touched my arm. Timidly, I turned to see her standing with a small wide-brimmed hat in hand.

"To shade those blue eyes from the bright sun," she smiled, cautiously perching it on my head. "Perfect fit," her voice trembled. "Stable is just off the porch to your left."

She opened the door, and I stepped into a world of farm animals: cows to my right and horses to my left. The cows made me shudder. Even though they meandered about, covered in familiar hides, their long and bony horns stretched wider than their tummies.

The horses put my feet on a curious path away from the safety of the covered porch. The pasture seemed full of them, some clustered by tall pines, some darting from one end of the fenced walls to the next, kicking up dirt and pounding the ground. I was in wondrous awe when Jimmy quietly approached.

"Bill is waiting for ye in te stable just over tere," he pointed.

I snuck another glance before my footsteps headed for the wooden building.

In the daylight, the stable looked bigger; but it was still smaller than my grandpa's. Bill had fourteen horses in their stalls. I was motioned over to the far end where I was introduced to the stallions, Samson and Goliath. The geldings were Moonlight, Midnight, Blizzard and Legend. I held my gaze on Moonlight and Midnight as they touched noses, one a creamy buttermilk against the other, a shimmering black.

The yearlings and two year olds were Murphy and Stewart, followed by Elsinore and Walker.

The broodmares were Maggie and Ginger. Bill said that the broodmares were the breeding mares. The last two mares were named after Bill's favourite aunts, gone but not forgotten, Rosie and Shannon.

Bill stopped at Ginger. "She will have a foal, soon. Go ahead and pet her if you like. She's the gentlest horse we've ever had."

I eagerly stretched a hand along her neck and body, silently asking *do you remember me?*

Bill's eyes never left me as I pushed away bits of straw and dirt with my hand. He grabbed a brush and offered it without saying what to do.

I paused a few seconds before instinctively grooming the horse.

In a commanding voice, he said, "I've a few rules you must abide by in this stable."

I thought back to my grandpa's rule, 'Stay out of my barn!' and jumped.

Bill figured it was the tone in his voice that caused the startling, so he calmly said, "Rule number one - stay clear of Samson and Goliath. They are moody and can bite. Stay clear of the yearlings and two year olds as well, for they will also bite. Rule number two - never leave lamplight unattended. Number three - put back any of the tools that you use. Number four"…and he continued with a few more rules.

"And the final rule is never to be afraid to pick up a shovel," he grinned, but I just peered at him with a dull and somber face.

"I mean, never be afraid to pick up a shovel and clean the stable," he repeated with a light smile. "As you can see, we name our horses. Speaking of names, we must have one for you."

I returned my attention to Ginger.

"I'll not be calling you boy!" Bill spoke adamantly.

Upon hearing those words, I stopped suddenly. That name stung like a slap to my cheek. Bill could watch me 'till day turned to night; my name would not pop out of my mouth! No sounds would ever come from my mouth again!

"Well," he continued, "why don't we call you Patrick? He's my favourite saint."

I thought 'Patrick' was much better than Henry, or boy, or bastard, and resumed grooming Ginger.

"Saint Patrick, as we call him, was taken from his family in England when he was young to become a slave in Ireland. He was a slave for many years and was very sad. One day he decided to escape. Nobody ever escaped Ireland in those days. It is surrounded by treacherous waters and sheer rock. Amazingly enough, Patrick did. He returned to his home but not for long. He decided through his deep faith to return to Ireland to teach Christianity. He had to have been very strong and brave."

Bill paused a minute. "So, can I call you Patrick?"

Pondering it, I didn't understand why he spoke so much of this Patrick; but it was better than being called…Henry. I hated that name. So I accepted my new name with a nod, though my eyes still felt sore with sadness that I couldn't hide or deny.

"Let me give you a walk of the ranch before I introduce you to the men."

Bill took long strides out of the stable and into a small pasture. There was a chicken coup in the corner of the stable and barn. We peaked into the white-washed small building.

"This is where we get our eggs," he said. "Do you eat eggs, Patrick?"

My head bobbed up and down, watching the noisy chickens squawking and pecking the ground. A few of them shuffled their feet across the coop like they ran the roost.

"Good, because when you want eggs, this is where you'll get them."

Along the opposite corner was a sty with four messy pigs playing in the mud.

"Do you like bacon, Patrick?"

I was so mesmerized watching one pig screech and storm away from his siblings, obviously upset about some muddy problem, that my absentmindedness settled the quarrel in favour of a greasy breakfast.

"Good because this is where you'll get your bacon. They're not so easy to catch, so you'll leave this dirty job for one of our ranch hands."

Bill opened the doors of the barn to reveal cows to his right, and farming equipment and hay to his left. He walked over to a brown and white speckled cow in the corner of the barn.

"This is Iris, our milking cow. Ever milk a cow, Patrick?"

This time, I was quick to wag my head.

"Well, we'll remedy that really soon."

I was soon out of breath, following Bill's big steps to the third building, which began at the end of the barn and was directly across from the stable. It was the bunkhouse and this was where the ranch hands slept. The three buildings formed a U shape with the small pasture in the middle.

Bill didn't open the door to the bunkhouse. He didn't care for giving reprimands if it wasn't clean enough to his liking. The men had more important work to do in the corrals.

I hopped to the stable pasture just to keep up, where Bill pointed out two corrals with high fences.

"This is where we tame horses. If you like you can watch," he offered before summoning the men. "These men need to know you're around, and you need to know who they are."

Jimmy, who I met at breakfast, was Bill's oldest friend. He shook my hand and said "Patrick" with a wink.

Trey was the youngest and had the firmest handshake. He was tall like my cousin, Tommy, but with sloppy blond hair and a grim almost menacing smile. His blue eyes stared too long, making me feel very uncomfortable.

Mike was stocky, looking the strongest of them all.

He mumbled, "Cead Mile Failte."

I didn't understand a word of it, and I didn't see any teeth in his mouth either.

My baffled look caught Jimmy's attention. "Oh lad, nobody understands Mike," he chuckled.

"Jimmy," Bill sighed. "Mike says welcome in Gaelic. Mike, English please."

Not that it would have done any good. Mike's words were lost through lips that curled around empty gums.

Lastly, there was Andy, who was very short, though agile and quick. He never stopped shifting from one boot to the next the entire time I stood there. He was the first Canadian I ever met and looked just like an American.

The stable pasture was divided into two sections. Bill told me that all of the horses in this section were wild mustangs taken from the High Plains. The other pasture was for the horses in the stable, mostly thoroughbreds. If I wanted to, I could watch the men begin breaking horses.

Bill explained that it would take several patient weeks taming these creatures so that they could be ridden safely by Cavalrymen and cattle rustlers.

I watched as Andy came in with a mare that was a golden honey, white star atop her head. As the strong horse moved wildly around the corral, Andy waited patiently while looping his rope. I watched in awe as he triumphantly lassoed the mustang on his first swing. Then I jumped in fear as she hoofed at air, whirling her head, while Andy firmly held the rope. The small man never flinched despite the horse's erratic aggressiveness and dreadful, ear-piercing noises. Once she stopped rearing, Andy's confident hand moved along her neck and barrel.

As he led her around the corral, I peered at the other corral where Trey was already atop his black mustang. The horse wasn't saddled but Trey managed to stay on despite the horse's kicking and plunging. I started to feel queasy as Trey's body was tossed and twisted in bone-breaking ways with the horse's sudden jerky movements.

Within seconds, Trey had that horse loping smoothly around the corral. I couldn't shake the queasy feeling so I took my tired body back to the house.

Mary was at the piano playing a parlour song. She was good but nothing like Momma. Momma floated her fingers across the black and white keys, her timing of the notes unforgettable.

Mary glanced my direction and I immediately fled to the bedroom. I was about to assume my favourite position when she walked in.

"Can I get you something to eat?"

I shook my head, yawning.

"Looks like you need to rest. That's fine. Your books are on the desk, and I've also laid out a journal for you to write or draw in if you like," she smiled warmly.

I nodded politely.

"Have your rest. I'll call you when it's time to eat."

I couldn't be woken up by Mary despite her repeated attempts at noon time. My deep slumber would remain until supper time when I heard a loud bell that sounded like it rang over my head. I entered the kitchen rubbing sleepy eyes. Bill was just coming through the front door with a bucket of water in hand. The food was already on my plate as I sat down.

I had my fork in hand when Mary calmly said, "We say grace before our meals."

I shyly held out my hands, bowing my head. My eyes should have been closed but the food was too irresistible. I didn't even hear grace; was too busy drooling hungrily at the roasted beef, dark thick gravy with brown onions, mashed potatoes, carrots, pickled beets, fresh peas and warm crusty bread with melted butter.

My stomach growled angrily as Bill said, "Amen."

"Patrick, start eating," Mary encouraged.

I recollected hearing her say that I looked like a Patrick, and that she couldn't wait to see Patrick smile.

I devoured my food, never looking up. Figured I ate even faster than my grandpa. As I wiped my lips, the sounds of my chewing were replaced with the sounds of Mary and Bill talking to each other. They didn't fight. I figured they were saving that until I was out of the room.

After I put my fork down and eyed my empty plate for too long, an uncomfortable silence began to fill the room.

"Patrick, would you like any more to eat?" Bill asked.

I shook my head with eyes staying on the gravy-stained plate.

"Well then, you may leave the table."

I went directly to the journal on the writing desk. As I cracked the spine of the leather bound book, I dipped the pen in ink and printed as neatly as I could *Patrick Sullivan*. I described my first day on the Sullivan ranch, completing a whole two pages before I became so tired printing so neatly.

Turing around, I remembered the chest that hadn't been explored yet. Bill and Mary resumed their talking as they washed dishes together.

Gingerly opening the lid, I was very happy to discover toys. I pulled out a wooden rifle, followed by a small smooth round object that spun around on the floor.

My most curious discovery, though, was a long wooden box. I slid the cover open to find it filled with smaller wooden pieces. Painted on both ends of these black pieces were white dots ranging from just one to six dots.

Bill's voice startled me. I jumped back in surprise.

He knelt. A smile crept across his face as he picked up one of the dotted pieces.

"Dominoes, Patrick. You can play them as a game and match the dots or you can place them on their sides close together."

He did as he explained and knocked them over with a slight touch of his long finger.

I wanted to touch the toys but my body remained strangely still until Bill said that they were now mine.

"Goodnight, Patrick," he said before leaving the room.

I lined up those dominoes and knocked them down until I could no longer keep my eyes open.

Bill must have scooped me up sometime afterwards because my last memory of that night was clinging to those wooden toys like they would be gone the next day.

Chapter 3

It was Sunday. I found out it was Bill's day of rest. I came out of my room and he greeted me with a smile. The kitchen felt cosy from a fire in the hearth of large pale stones that ran the length of the dining table. Bill told me that he and Mary slept in the room closest to the right of the fireplace. Two more bedrooms were on either side of the stone hearth.

Bill said water was being warmed for my bath, which explained why a towel was on my bed.

After breakfast I would be asked to take off my dirty clothes, wrap myself in the towel, and join Bill in the fourth room farthest to the left of the hearth. It was called the keeping room.

Eating hurriedly, I couldn't remember the last time I had a bath and was anxious to get clean.

Though my back was still sore, gone was the burning pain. Thankfully I had no idea what it looked like or it might have felt worse than it did.

Mary was leaving for church when I returned. She pointed me in the right direction and waved goodbye.

Bill was waiting for me. This was where the piano and sitting chairs were. On the far wall was a cabinet full of books and in the corners of the room, a strange looking thing lurking across from a familiar one, a small Conestoga wood stove. I peered up to find Bill holding scissors, asking to see my arm. Gently, he cut away the cotton to reveal a tiny, healthy scab. When he motioned for me to turn around, my body stiffened.

"I just want to make sure there isn't any sign of infection, and then I'll leave you to your bath," he spoke softly.

My foot clumsily tripped over the other as I tried to figure out how he knew about my wounds. I felt so nervous and fidgety until Bill said that everything was healing well.

He came around and said I could go in the bath. But my feet felt like they were nailed to the planked floor despite jittering limbs until Bill said he'd be in the kitchen should I need anything. Soap and a washcloth were on a nearby chair.

When he was clear of the room, I entered that tub of tepid water and felt much better. I loved taking baths and hoped I wouldn't be rushed out of this one. This tub was much bigger than the basin I used to have to squeeze my legs into and wash carefully as not to get so much water on the floor. This tub was so full of water I could hold my breath, go under, and count to thirty. I imagined swimming in a big lake floating like a duck along the rim, almost forgetting to scrub my body clean. It wasn't until my fingers were wrinkled that I decided to get out.

When I scurried through the kitchen, Bill asked me to get dressed and bring my Bible to the table. It was atop the desk tied with string to other books Momma had carefully chosen for the voyage north. I wriggled the book loose and noticed something sticking out from its pages. It was the letter Momma had written to my father. His full name was on the envelope.

I forgot about the letter she had written. I forgot about my promise to her. How would I ever find my father now? My thoughts were disturbed when Bill entered the room.

"Patrick, are you ready?" I threw the letter in the drawer of the desk and followed Bill to the kitchen table.

"Can you read?" he asked curiously.

I nodded, my eyes still fixed on the floor.

"Right then, come and sit at the kitchen table." Bill thumbed through the Bible. "Romans one to eleven."

His eyes were upon me as I flipped through The Holy Book, finding the scripture quite quickly. In fact, he never turned away as I read and turned the pages and read again. When finished, I peered up, relieved to see a smile on his face.

"Patrick, point to the part where David kills Goliath," he said, scratching his chin.

I shot Bill a perplexed look before searching for the passage, stopping and starting again, until I got to it. When I finally found Samuel seventeen, I pointed to the page.

"Very good, Patrick. I think that's enough for today. Let's go for a walk."

On the way to the stable, Bill asked if I could ride a horse. I nodded trying not to show any enthusiasm.

"You'll ride Legend," he advised, "legendary for taking it nice and slow."

Under his breath, he said the gelding was more interested in eating oats than leaving the stable. As I watched Bill, his hands seemed so nimble, bridling and cinching the horses, and leading them out to a dirt path.

After he tightened the cinch on both horses again, his hands were cupped for me to climb onto Legend. My stirrups were adjusted before he handed me the leather reins and walked us along the passageway that ran between the stable and cow pastures.

My gaze stayed fixed on the horses along the fence's edge as they lazily grazed on tall grasses, their tails swishing and barrels quivering as flies nipped at them. Bill approached Legend once more and adjusted the cinch again.

"Legend likes to inflate his belly."

Before climbing his horse, he showed me the proper way to hold the reins and instructed me to tug on them gently if I ever needed to stop.

We went through a forest of soaring pines before we arrived on a hill overlooking water.

"Patrick, this is the Missouri River. Winding its way like a slithering snake up to Fort Benton, it's surrounded by limestone cliffs as high as twelve hundred feet. After that, it continues east through the Northern Plains and into Missouri. The gates of the mountains make it a treacherous descent to the river. Good for fishing, though, with trout as long as your arm."

Glancing at me, Bill asked, "Have you ever gone fishing?"

I nodded eagerly, maybe too eagerly, so I hastily looked away.

"Next time we come here, we will fish in this river and bring home supper."

We headed south, then east, and soon were surrounded by walls of rock.

"These jagged formations have been here many years," he advised. "They are a breathtaking site to behold, aren't they Patrick. This mountainous terrain stretches throughout all of western Montana, beginning from the north in a country called Dominion of Canada, and ending to the south in a State called New Mexico.

I'm always in awe of the natural landscape….makes me grateful to be alive." His chest puffed with a heavy breath of cool, moist air.

I gazed at the canyon threaded in pink and green hues, to the mountains that towered into sky, so familiar that it almost felt like I was home. Memories of Momma started flooding my mind until Bill interrupted my thoughts. He told me that we were a few hours north of Helena and a few days ride from Fort Benton.

My somber eyes passed over Bill before returning to the tree covered mountains. As he gently guided the horses to the Sullivan homestead, I stayed transfixed on the tall peaks wondering how far we were from Virginia City.

Bill shook his head in frustration. Maybe it was because I remained so quiet after he mentioned the two towns. Maybe it was because my eyes went so sad at the sight of the unforgettable mammoth rocks.

****

Over the next few weeks, a routine was established for me. Bill got me moving in the morning even though I always got out of bed feeling so tired. He said that all of the work I would be doing was important work and that I would be given lots of opportunities to learn. He felt it necessary for everyone to have a sense of purpose and importance.

My first important tasks were in the barn milking Iris the cow and scooping up enough eggs for breakfast. After breakfast, I scurried over to the stable where I would feed the horses their hay.

By mid-morning, Mary had me reading and writing while she made a noon meal or prepared a tasty dessert for supper.

In the afternoon, I watched the men bring the untamed horses into the corral. On one of those warm and sunny days, I heard Bill arguing with Trey in the stable.

"I want you to saddle 'The Grey' again!" Bill commanded.

"I've already saddled her five times! She's ready!" Trey snapped.

"I'll tell you when she's ready! Saddle her again!"

A few moments passed before Bill stormed out with bridle, saddle, blanket, and Trey at his heals.

"Dammit, Bill!" Trey stammered.

Bill called for Andy to bring the mare into the corral. She was speckled black in spots reminding me of a grey moon. Bill mounted that horse and loped around the corral without any fuss from 'The Grey'. Trey stood beside me, his face full of smugness.

All seemed calm until Bill started making loud, boisterous noises with his voice and his whip cracking ground, which spooked The Grey. She started bucking and kicking, nearly knocking Bill to the ground. He got the horse loping again, but even when he yelled out, "WHOA," the horse bolted again.

After Bill jumped off of that horse, he was sweating and fuming as he thundered towards Trey. I felt it a good time to return to the house.

The kitchen was empty, so I headed for the keeping room but was distracted by a picture of Bill and another man on the wall.

The door flew open. Bill came in and stomped to the stove for a cup of coffee. While pouring, he glimpsed my way, anger subdued, but with narrowed eyes.

He walked over and took the picture from the wall.

"My brother, John," he said with a light smile. "Have a seat. I'll tell you all about him while I cool my temper."

A plate of oatmeal cookies sat in the middle of the table, and he casually slid the plate to me. I wasted no time taking a cookie as Bill said that they were born and raised in Cork, Ireland. John and Bill had worked as stable hands for a wealthy family with many horses. Their father taught them how to tame and care for horses. The owner liked their gentle ways, and they were very much respected for their hard work and dedication.

He took a deep breath and turned gloomy. "My father passed away in 1850. Around that time, there was a great famine in Ireland. Cork was inundated with catholic Irish and immense poverty followed. Everyday there was less and less to eat."

He spoke of how, one day, John was staring into his paltry soup and said 'Let's go to America.'

Bill's lips curled at the recollection. John had heard stories about America where horses ran free across the plains, and he kept saying 'Let's go to America, capture wild horses and build our own ranch' with a sparkle in his eyes.

Bill sighed. "I didn't have a dream at the time so I decided to follow his. My brother looked down at his paltry soup and ate it with such fervour."

Their father left them money that they used to buy passage. Bill was only sixteen when he left on the big boat across the Atlantic Ocean, his brother, three years older. John was boat sick most of the time, so Bill stayed on deck most of the time.

He laughed. "That's when I met my Mary. I told her of John's wild dreams which were my dreams, and she told me hers. We felt we could make our dreams come true together. We landed in America with hundreds of other immigrants. Started out in New York City and discovered that the Northern Plains were two thousand miles away! We had very little money left so we had to stay and find work. Found a tiny, dingy room in a boarding house. It was miserable. Just as Mary and I had some time alone, John would walk in singing, drunk. Some nights I wanted to squeeze the life out of him."

I expressed fright at his unkind words.

"But I didn't, Patrick. Instead I prayed for mercy and silence and a few years later Colin Murphy appeared in our lives. John met the old man at a local pub one night. He came across the ocean alone and sick with tuberculosis, struggling just to get to the pub for the drink. John became his 'go to' man. John, go to the pharmacy and get medicine. John, go to the pub and get whisky. John convinced the old man that moving west would be better for his health, and he, Mary and I, could be his personal escorts."

I casually took another cookie.

"While John was off being the 'go to' man, Mary and I had some time alone," Bill winked, "for some quiet talking. Well, Patrick, that quiet didn't last long for nine months later a wee screechy baby who Mary named Angela came into our lives. Why she chose the name Angela was a mystery to me because there was no angel in that baby for the first few months. I appreciated those long hours working on the docks even more. Once Angela was three years old, we packed up and headed west with John and Mr. Murphy to a place called Chicago."

Bill sauntered to the stove to refill his cup with coffee while I took the opportunity to devour another cookie.

"It was just meant to be a small respite for the dear sick Colin Murphy but we stayed for three years. Angela became a sweet angel, John stayed busy with Mr. Murphy, and Mary and I….well Mary and I did more quiet talking." Bill shook his head. "And nine months later Oliver was born." He smiled reminiscently.

"We packed our wagon, left Chicago when he was still a baby, and headed to St. Louis, Missouri. By the time we arrived, Mr. Murphy was near death, or so we thought. The old man lived another five years! On his deathbed, John listened to his last wishes. He had a fine bottle of whisky under his bed, and wanted to be buried and have the whisky poured over his grave so it would seep into his bones. My brother, John, was very accommodating considering the man intended on leaving him a great sum of money once he died; so I was very surprised when John asked if he could filter the whisky through his kidneys before he…before he poured it over his grave."

Bill's brows furrowed in disapproval while I held a confused gaze. "Have another cookie."

As I reached for my fourth…maybe fifth cookie, Bill continued.

"Once Mr. Murphy was buried, John shook the money from its pouch and it filled his palm, surpassing anything we'd ever imagined. We were eager to leave the rebel fighting taking place in Missouri, so we opted to take a steamboat from St. Louis to Fort Benton, Montana. We took everything on that ferry boat: wagon, horses, food, a piano, blankets, John, two children. The paddle boat moved so slowly, I felt I should be out pushing it some days; the water so low I probably could have pushed it some days. Two months later, we arrived at the Montana trading post."

When Bill sipped his coffee, my willful eyes took in the last remaining temptations, but my hands were too slow before his watchful eyes were on me again.

"After we departed the ferry and filled our wagon with food at Fort Benton, we travelled through Blackfoot Indian Territory, eager for a piece of our own land. South of Sun River, we settled here."

While Bill glared at his hands, my own little hand couldn't resist taking another cookie.

"John and I spent months building the cabin and stable. Mary ploughed the fields and planted," he spoke with admiration. "Eventually we found mustangs and the United States Calvary moved into Fort Benton. One bitterly cold night, John never returned from the town. He was last seen alive with Sergeant Earl Jones discussing the purchase of fifty or so tamed mustangs. The next day, I found John ten miles north of the ranch, slumped over in the wagon, smile frozen on his face."

Bill seemed weary as he returned the picture to the iron nail in the wall.

"It was the biggest want for mustangs we'd ever had," he said solemnly. "To this day, I do not allow drinking on my ranch except for St. Patrick's Day and the day after we make our delivery of horses to the Cavalry."

Staring intently into my eyes, his sigh was heavy.

"My brother had a dream. I made it my dream. Gave me a purpose and has served me well all these years."

Without hesitating, he placed a gentle hand on my shoulder. "Find your purpose on this earth, Patrick, and it will serve you well, too."

Bill's smile was brief as he recalled the pasture full of mustangs needing to be tamed. Before he stood, his eyes took in the plate of crumbs.

"And judging by the number of cookies you've just eaten, you better come and burn off all of that sugar or you won't be wanting your supper."

I grinned. I couldn't help it. It was a long story, but worth it if I could eat an entire plate of cookies while doing it. I nodded to Bill's request and followed him to the corral.

That night, I opened the desk drawer and saw my father's letter atop two books. The thin paper book had Lincoln's picture on it. He had honest, sad eyes; and I wondered if that was how my eyes looked. I searched the room for a mirror, but none could be found. I picked up the other book written by Washington Irving called 'Legend of Sleepy Hollow'. The letter got shoved to the bottom of the drawer under Lincoln's face book before I lay on my bed, reading. However, I didn't get very far before my lids got heavy and closed over tired eyes.

Chapter 4

Two calendar months had passed since I was found by Bill and his ranch hands. I kept my vow of silence but it was getting harder and harder to do. The mustangs were coming into the corral with silly names like Paddy, Whisky, Rover, and Clover. I looked at each horse and chose a name based off what I saw in its nature or its appearance. I had a name for every one of those mustangs. I just never spoke them out loud.

Inside the stable, the big excitement was that Ginger was due with her foal any day now. Bill told me to keep away from the agitated mare as she pounded her rump against the walls of the stall whipping her tail wildly. Her belly looked like it was about to burst!

When morning came and Bill rushed into my room, I hastily dressed, still pulling suspenders over my small shoulders while scurrying out the front door to the stable.

I watched Ginger deliver that foal in amazement. How he came out, long bony legs first, and didn't get stuck or hurt was incredible.

Bill tore open the sack and the gangly colt emerged. Ginger let out a low whinny and nuzzled her baby for the first time. Bill asked me to kneel beside him. He said that touch was very important. With his hand over my shaky one, I touched the colt's sticky body, my fingers running the ripples of his jutting ribs.

After he shook the last bit of daze from his small chestnut brown head, the white brush stroke that ran from his forelocks to mouth came into focus. As he wobbled to his feet, Bill said I could name him if I wanted to. The colt had honest eyes that seemed to peer into my soul.

I smiled and the name just slipped out, "Lincoln."

Bill was so surprised that name had popped out of my mouth he had to say it himself. "Lincoln, it is."

I smiled shyly.

He smiled back, nodding.

I was a boy of few words. Naming horses were some of those few words I spoke and it kept me busy….so busy that sad thoughts had little time to enter my mind while I was awake.

Except for this one particular day when I was at the corral watching Bill break a dark brown mare. The memory came slowly seeping in, but it was a happy one even though……it was my birthday and Momma had made a deep dark chocolate buttermilk cake. I'd never seen anything like it before. She was so proud. It came out looking pretty decent even though the centre had dipped in a little.

When she cut into it, it was warm and gooey inside. It was like nothing I'd ever tasted. I asked for another piece of that brown gooey cake. Two pieces later, and I was in sheer delight. That's what this horse was like with Bill. She put up a small fuss but was easily calmed. She was lean and strong, had grace and pride.

I could tell Bill was impressed with her. He called me into the corral and told me to pet her, show her love and gratitude. Then he put me in the saddle and took me for a walk, never leaving my side.

"Well, do you have a name for her?" he called out.

I smiled, shouting, "Browney!"

That horse was pure delight….pure delight.

Bill watched me as I sat atop that horse. He seemed happy that I was happy. I giggled, forgetting about the boy who suffered for so long if only for a few moments before I remembered why I was here.

That night, when Mary and Bill were in bed, he spoke of hearing me laugh for the first time while riding Browney.

"I think those horses have a lot to do with Patrick's healing and well-being," he whispered.

"I think you've a lot to do with his healing and well-being," Mary replied.

"He watches everything I do very intently and is a hard worker. I worry though, Mary, for his spirit is still troubled. It's as if the weight of the world still sits on his small shoulders. He never speaks of his mother or his past. His eyes tell a painful tale if you look deeply at them."

Bill held Mary tighter.

"We must have faith that in time he will feel comfortable to confide in us or in God. He just needs more time."

****

While Bill was busy breaking mustangs, I continued getting used to riding Legend. I practiced staying relaxed, giving simple commands, and learning how to turn right and left with my reins and the pressure of my legs.

I also spent a lot of time with little Lincoln, getting him used to my touch, my voice, his name, and other sounds that he would encounter in his life.

Bill took time getting Lincoln used to wearing a halter and yielding to pressure from a rope while being led around the corral. I was Bill's shadow, watching and learning everything he did.

When Bill felt comfortable, I began leading Lincoln around that corral. He became my best friend. I taught him some commands like 'WALK' and 'WHOA' but mostly I taught him all about me. Lincoln knew more about me than Bill did. If that horse could talk, he could answer a lot of questions that still plagued Bill.

By late summer, the mustangs were tamed and ready to go to Fort Benton though a small group would remain and be set free to range the foothills of the mountains. I was invited to go to town and make delivery alongside the men. Bill took me in the wagon because it was a long trip.

I had only been to a town three times in my life. The time I broke my arm and couldn't get the cast, the time I got the cast, and the time the ragged dirty thing came off.

This town appeared busier. For one thing, Fort Benton was the final stop for the massive steamboat that slowly paddled along the Missouri River. Bill said it was loaded with more than two hundred tons of cargo. How it stayed afloat was a mystery to me. Its shrill whistle indicated it was ready to depart, and I wished I could have been one of its three hundred anxious passengers.

The men were going into the saloon for a drink while I was given two bits to take to the mercantile. I was so eager to get to that sugar rush that I nearly got run over by two fiercely fast horses pulling a seemingly agitated man and his wagon.

Bill grabbed me by the shoulders and pulled me back onto the wooden boardwalk.

"Look both ways, Patrick!" he shouted as I coughed, rubbing gritty eyes of dust and dirt that billowed in the air.

Bill shook his head as I unwaveringly walked through the lingering brown clouds determined to get to that store.

I was given a huge brown bag that I happily filled with candy. I stuffed it with chewing gum, peppermint sticks, rock candy and my favourite, taffy, which was brown, chewy, and stuck to the roof of my mouth. I loved candy. I loved Fort Benton.

As I approached the saloon, I could hear music before I reached the swinging doors. I peaked in to see Bill having a whisky with his friends, but it was the music coming from the piano that grabbed my attention. It was very lively. Grown men were singing to it and pounding their glasses against the hard tabletops. I thought I'd like to learn that kind of music. I called it 'happy people' music. It would be Mary who would teach me that they were 'drinking music' songs.

****

Winter came and it got quieter on the ranch. I still did my chores in the barn and stable, but I had more free time in the afternoon; so Bill thought it wise I learned how to clean out the stalls.

His philosophy was that an idle child would make a lazy child, so the busier I was, the more active I would stay. I would gladly do stable chores all day and give up barn chores. I hated going into that chicken coup. There was this one hen that always nipped at me when I took her eggs.

When nobody was around, I threatened that hen. "I'll have you for supper tomorrow if you don't cut that out!" My threats didn't work. That cantankerous hen still nipped at me.

Bill and Mary said quite often how helpful I was and that made me feel good. I worked hard and that made me feel better.

But I still woke up from bad dreams and haunting memories. One particular night, Grandpa grabbed me by the ear and dragged me out of the Sullivan ranch. Bill and Mary couldn't do a thing. I was his grandson.

I awoke in such a sweat I put my coat on and went outside to cool off.

The dry, frigid air felt so suffocating that I coughed heading to the stable. Aside from my annoying hacking, there was such a stillness and peaceful silence. I moved speedily through the snow for I decided against wearing my thumping boots through a quiet kitchen. The stars shone brightly in the black and cloudless sky adding a shimmer to the snow covered ground.

Once in the stable, I immediately went to Ginger.

"I don't understand why Grandpa was so mean to me. I didn't do anything to him. When I think of him, I'm very sad and angry."

Ginger looked at me with sensitive, brown eyes. I imagined her saying *you're safe now. He can't hurt you anymore.*

"I hope not. I hope he never finds me."

Resting my head on her warm body, I instantly felt comfort and safety.

As I came out of the stable, a tiny light flickered in the cows' pasture. My curiosity stopped me dead in my tracks. I watched as the tiny light grew and a silhouette began illuminating.

When Trey's face became clearer, it was too late. His eyes found mine, and I found my feet literally frozen to the ground.

"What you doin' out here, kid?"

Trey had a rifle slung over his right shoulder. As he walked, his unbuttoned coat flapped open revealing a pistol holstered to his ammunition belt, the tips of the bullets twinkling around his slender waist. He was carrying more metal than a travelling peddler.

"I….I heard a horse whinnying," I stuttered.

"Same horse you heard last night and the night before that?"

"Yep," I swallowed.

"You in your bare feet."

"Yep."

"Best you wipe those feet in the snow real good. Don't want the sheets to smell like shit. Mary don't wash those sheets often."

I nodded, "Yep."

"Don't say much, do you?"

"Yep….I mean no."

Wolves howled just beyond the dirt passageway.

"Git your ass back to bed, and don't let me hear that stable door tomorrow night or I'll feed you to the wolves!"

"Yep," I said, ripping my feet away and dashing to the house. So much for feeling safe and comfortable; my incessant shivering from the icy snow and Trey's icy words lasted for hours.

****

The next morning, I came into the kitchen, yawning.

Mary glared at me. "Do you know what time it is, Patrick?"

I shook my head sleepily.

"It's ten o'clock."

I was in shock. I never slept in that much.

She approached and patted my head. "Do it now because come the spring, it'll be back to six o'clock mornings."

Mary was right. Spring came and six o'clock mornings came, as well. Bill eyed me across the breakfast table, yawning, feeling very tired and weary. He looked like he was trying to understand why I was so sluggish. I should have confessed that I had unhappy dreams.

I began eating my porridge when he turned to Mary. "Do you know what day it is today?"

"No, but I'll get my calendar."

"April fifteenth, Mary," he divulged, "ninth anniversary of Lincoln's death."

When my spoon clanked noisily against my bowl, Bill shot me a perplexed look.

I swallowed as my chest began to tighten.

"Patrick?" he asked with concern.

I tried to speak but couldn't. Thoughts were swirling in my head….my momma, my birthday, my cousins. I bolted out of the house, tears wetting my cheeks, and headed for the only place that gave me comfort.

Bill found me tucked in the corner of Lincoln's stall, weeping uncontrollably, head buried in my knees.

Kneeling, he put a gentle hand on my quivering back.

"You can only fight those memories for so long. I just want you to know that you're not alone. I'll help you every step of the way."

I slowly peered up. "You can't help me bring my momma back."

"No, I can't," he spoke solemnly. "I can only love you like a father would and Mary like a mother would. I know it's not the same, but it's the best that we can do."

"It's my birthday, today. I'm nine years old," I confessed sadly.

"Happy Birthday, Patrick." Glancing about the stable, it looked as if he was searching for something. "How do you like your birthday gift," he said, eyeing Lincoln. "You won't be able to ride him for a while, but you could take good care of him and help me teach him to be a good horse. Until such time, your riding would continue with Legend."

A somber smile formed as I peered at Lincoln. "Thank you."

"Well I know you'll take good care of him," Bill affirmed. "Finish your breakfast, then we'll go fishing."

I got a few steps when his voice rang out, "Oh and Patrick, you will need to change. You've sat in mucky straw, which will happen if you choose to sit in a horse's stall. Give your dirty clothes to Mary. I'm sure she'll be happy to get them."

I nodded with a quick grin.

When I entered the kitchen, Mary looked so worried.

I assured her I was fine but that it was my birthday.

She held me tightly but released me hastily when she sniffed, then saw, the dirty straw stuck to my trousers. I was promptly told to change and give her my soiled clothes.

I liked Mary.

Though she wasn't my momma, she showed me kindness and I felt better.

Thoughts of going fishing with Bill improved my spirits. After rushing to put on fresh clothes and wolfing down my breakfast, a fast and elated voice told Mary about our fishing plans; and she was overjoyed even though she was gawking at my shirt. As her fingers put my buttons in the correct holes, she mentioned how proud she was of Bill, and how happy she was to have him and me in her life.

That night, when I saw the cake she baked, I gave her the same sweet, bashful smile that Bill had witnessed when Lincoln was born. They didn't know that my smile revealed more than just dimples in my cheeks. It revealed a smile my father shared with my momma many years ago.

****

Sean Thomas didn't smile very often. His face revealed a weariness of being hunted for years and years. He couldn't stay long in one place so he couldn't keep a steady job and henceforth, always ran shy on money.

When he entered Fort Benton, a lady in red caught his eye, fanning the unpleasantness of gritty dirt and horse dung away from her senses. He soon found out that Katherine was nothing like her cousin, Amelia Boudreau. While Ms. Amelia appeared matronly and sophisticatedly dressed in black, Ms. Katherine, pro-prietor of the Wayward Hotel, wore brightly coloured dresses that clung so tightly, her beautifully full bosom scantly stayed covered. She flirted with a passion.

"Why Sean Thomas, my cousin has spoken highly of you."

She caressed his arm, doting on every word he spoke while exuding sexuality and playfulness. She said she would have entertained him herself if she wasn't so busy. Instead, she brought forward Ophelia.

Ophelia had deep, dark brown eyes. Her flawless porcelain skin, minus a small mole atop full scarlet lips, beautifully contrasted raven black, curly hair. When her sensual mouth curled into an alluring smile, one of Sean's bald eagle coins was enticed to spring from his pocket.

Like a wildflower waving in the breeze, she swayed so naturally in a violet sleeveless bustle dress. Her hair was drawn up with a pearl comb, apart from a few spiral wisps that delicately brushed pink cheeks. He imagined kissing the nape of her slender neck before he was even in her bed.

Moving to a secluded room at the back, she motioned him inside with a long and delicate arm, palm outstretched.

With coin paid, she wasted no time in small talk. Her velvety smooth fingers removed his hat and ran along dark stringy hair to the bristly whiskers of his rigid jaw, her lips just inches from his. While easing off a worn dusty jacket, she peered into hazel eyes, seeing either deep anguish, or seething anger, or sexual frustration. She always got those three emotions mixed up.

"Well, Sean Thomas, you just going to stare at me or are you going to do something about it?"

He needed no further encouragement, tossing her onto the bed with strong arms. His mouth found the part of her neck he so desired as his hands tore away at her dress and undergarments. She ripped his vest and shirt open, sliding the sleeves from chiseled arms while eyeing the taut hairless chest that would be pulled to warm breasts. Unbuttoning his pants, she slid them from lean thighs.

When she got hold of what she wanted, she hurriedly inspected at it, firm and healthy, before bringing it to her.

His fierce thrusts were a welcome change. Lately, she had a string of men who took so long she started counting the pine planks of the ceiling.

Sean didn't take very long at all. He moaned, he shuddered, and was breathless when he rolled over. She casually peered at him; however, he now seemed fixated on that plank ceiling.

A few minutes later, he stood, pulled up and buttoned his pants, grabbed his jacket and hat, and walked out the door.

Ophelia thought, *I hope to see you again, Sean Thomas.*

As he walked along the hallway, he felt the release he needed. His thoughts of Mandy had vanished and been replaced by those of staying alive by killing every vigilante in his path.

With his hat hung low, he only got a few steps beyond the brothel when five lawmen headed his way. Instantly, he recognized the man in the middle as Frank O'Flaherty, pain in the ass brother number three.

Feeling outnumbered, with an empty pistol to boot, Sean's vengeful mind soon changed; so he changed course for an alley and waited for the men to pass.

At the nearest Mercantile, Sean procured bullets and food with the last of his coin, and rode out of that town as quickly as he entered it.

Moving north, he crossed the border into the Dominion of Canada to discover how lucrative smuggling whisky from Montana could be. It was a very profitable proposition; however, he would have to go back to Fort Benton to get the whisky, and that was a ridiculous proposition while O'Flaherty and his men pounded the town's dusty streets. He would have to find another way of making money in this wild Canadian land or learn to live among the creatures of the many forests and rivers the virtually uninhabited terrain offered.

When it became too cold to survive without warm shelter, he cautiously moved south to Fort Benton and his favourite whore, Ophelia. She never disappointed him, being just what he needed: a passionate lay with no conversation and no broken promises.

He gambled at the poker tables and was a good bluffer. Too good! Scooping up his winnings one night, he became too recognizable, and was forced to flee from the gambling hall, keeping his life, but leaving his winnings.

He also made acquaintances with the Roberts gang. They were a rough foursome who enjoyed robbing banks. Gary Roberts, eldest of the gang, convinced Sean to rob a small bank on the outskirts of town. Sean flat out refused; said it wasn't his thing. Gary thought it might be his thing after the whisky flowed out of a never-ending bottle.

Sure enough, Sean was eager when he was intoxicated. He was so liquored up he could barely stand let alone look the teller in the eyes.

The teller got the idea that Sean was three sheets to the wind, so he slowly went for a pistol. Sean would have been riddled with bullets had Gary not hoisted his pistol in the air, firing off three rounds, warning the teller and any others who wanted to be hero, it was not a good day to die.

Sean had to get out of town again so he fled south. But not before catching a glimpse of his reflection in the mirror hanging from a boarding house room. He didn't see Sean Thomas anymore. The man in the mirror had a slovenly appearance with cold eyes amidst a face marred by weather and scowl.

He journeyed to Butte, Montana where silver was just discovered. By then, it had been nine long years since Eddie O"Flaherty was killed and six years since his brother Michael had met the same fate. He hoped he could keep the mining job for a while.

****

Ethan's saw mill was more than a day's ride from Butte. Sean thought about getting back in the saddle again to see his friend. He shook off that thought when his saddle sores and aching hip screamed out in pain. That pain was soon forgotten one night with a bottle of what he called 'tornado juice' on account of the way his head felt tossed around the next morning.

He woke up to find himself by a small stream under a giant cottonwood tree thirty miles outside of Virginia City. The pain in his backside returned with a vengeance completely surpassing the pain in his head. Medicine could be procured in Virginia City, and there was that boneheaded bartender he was itching to reunite with. Killing two birds with one stone seemed like a good idea.

He busily groomed and fed his tired horse. But when it came time to put the blanket and saddle on, the four-legged animal trotted off. Sean followed the unruly steed, bulky saddle in hands, for a quarter mile until he pulled his pistol and threatened to put a bullet in its haunches. The horse smartly returned to his owner as Sean glanced around the grove of cottonwood trees that lined the bubbling brook.

At the Beaverhead mill, Ethan was going over financial papers when there was a knock on the door. It was Mr. Holden's assistant, Jane Anderson.

"Mr. Holden, there's a gentleman here to see you; says he's Sean Thomas."

Ethan looked up from his work in sheer astonishment. Swallowing, he said hoarsely, "Please send him in."

Sean walked in, now middle-aged with long hair, but still lean. It was his face though that openly expressed a painful scorn and bitterness.

"Ethan," he said in a low and vacant voice.

Ethan came around the desk and shook his hand, pressing the other into Sean's shoulder. "I thought you were dead," he said contritely.

"I came close a couple times," he replied with anguished eyes turning away. "Looks like business is good."

"That's thanks to the silver find in Butte. It's the next big town," he said with a small grin. "Take a seat."

There was a short pause before both men began speaking at the same time.

Ethan spoke faster. "Mandy went looking for you over a year ago. I assume that she never found you."

Sean was perplexed. "She never married?"

Ethan hesitated with a wag of his gloomy head. "No Sean, she waited patiently for you until she......she decided it time to find you."

It seemed fitting that he would find this out now. The words hit like bullets to his chest, both agonizing and painful. Then he remembered the child.

"She left with your son, Henry," Ethan imparted, "north to Fort Benton. We didn't hear from them after that. I went to the town a couple of times; even hired a detective. He turned up nothing. It's as if they vanished."

Sean was clearly stupefied.

Ethan was too consumed by his own thoughts to notice the growing ire in his friend.

Silence consumed the small office while both men pondered Mandy and Henry's disappearance.

Sean finally stood and widely swung open the door with a pent up rage that had to be released.

As he stomped away, Ethan hastily stood up. "Sean, write to me! Let me know where you are!" he bellowed. "I still have hope that Mandy is out there, and if she ever contacts me, I will contact you. Please, Sean!"

Ethan's hollering continued as Sean stepped off the boardwalk with regretful thoughts.

How foolish; how many years I wasted when I had a woman clinging to my promise and a son who's never known his father. He felt such hatred, such guilt, for the choices he made.

Mounting his horse, he set a course for Fort Benton. If she was there, he would find her and make it right.

When he took a deep seat in the saddle, he soon remembered his painful woes.

It reminded him of a time long ago in a place far from him. The day began as ordinary as others. His sister was tending to the garden while he chopped wood in the back yard. Emily was pulling carrots from the moist ground when she squinted into the blinding sun.

To her surprise, a man stood aside a tall horse, his features shaded in darkness.

Robert Thomas was rendered speechless when he saw his daughter had grown into a woman, hair radiant in golden tones, gingham dress framing her slender figure.

She moved toward him while he tried to summon his voice. When her child-like smile warmed his heart, he took quick strides to embrace her.

Sean came around the corner with two armloads of wood, walking blindly, figuring it was more efficient than having to make two trips. He miscalculated the rotting woody stump in his path and lost all but one of the logs.

His confounded attitude was short-lived when he saw the tall man standing with a wide-mouthed grin beside a beautifully poised chestnut Morgan. He was distinguished with a tailored suit; however, it was the belt cinching his waist, the buckle resembling a shiny plate of gold, that held Sean's fascination. The man looked at him curiously.

His father would later comment that Sean looked as stringy as a bean pole.

The door creaked and Lydia appeared, nervously holding her breath.

Sean watched as the tears flowed from Robert's eyes and all he wanted to do was tell his father that she was better, though still pale and delicate, she was better.

As his mouth formed words, Arnold Blethem came storming over, axe in one hand, flailing chicken in the other. He had the bird by its wiry legs, white wings flapping against gravity's pull, yellow eyes bulging toward hard ground.

"Is this your son!" he charged.

"Yes," Robert replied, dumbfounded.

"He's been pilfering my chickens for years!"

"Is this true?" Robert asked as the breeze dried his cheeks.

"That old coot hasn't fixed the latch on his dirty coop," Sean sneered. "Them chickens were liberated. Came pecking on our ground, free to do as they pleased, so I was free to do as I pleased with them."

"I'll pay for the chickens," Robert offered, reaching for his satchel.

"Is that how you handle things west of the Mississippi?" Blethem spat out.

Robert glared at his son. "You knew you were stealing?"

Sean took a minute to contemplate his answer. He knew he could get hanged for stealing, but just a slap on the wrist for lying, so he lied. "No!"

Sean contemplated wrong. The belt he had admired minutes earlier snapped into pliable condition after a protracted workout on his hide. The pain lingered for days though he adjusted to it better than his father did.

Robert's eyes stayed heavy with sorrow and pity after Lydia enlightened him on life without her steady paying job; life with just one paltry meal a day; life with a neighbour who had more chickens than he could count; and life without a father.

Robert would never lay an angry hand on Sean again.

The reins tugged the direction of Virginia City. Sean needed a drug store and a drink, and he knew the perfect saloon to get one.

By mid-afternoon, he made it to the quiet town while the golden sun still warmed the western sky. Ambling along the dirt road, his hat sat atop shifty deep-set eyes. Much had changed since his last visit. Some businesses had closed. For those that remained, some had new names. The Donevan Hotel was now the Andover Hotel.

Virginia City was much quieter without the lure of gold. Most of the miners had flocked to Helena or Butte, attracting the business owners to those locations, as well.

To Sean's surprise, the Golden Nugget Saloon was still open, and he only hoped that his old friend was still bartending. He could barely hide his contempt as his spurs clicked toward the bar.

"What can I get you?" Ned asked.

Sean slowly peered up. "Hello, Ned." Lunging at him, he grabbed fistfuls of shirt before hoisting the lanky man over the high counter and onto the worn whisky-stained floor. With his pitiless boot over Ned's throat, Sean stretched as far as he could.

"Thought maybe I'd get an apology out of you but see you're having trouble breathing."

Ned's arms flailed as he gasped for air through a crushed gullet. Thankfully, the saloon was sparsely filled with patrons, although one bravely approached. Sean drew his Colt single-action, cocked and ready to fire if the patron became a threat.

"I just wanna drink and if you kill that bartender, how am I gonna get it?"

"It's self serve and get me one, too!" Sean snarled while glowering at Ned, who was turning blue. "Next time you fire a shotgun at someone, you may want to get a little closer!"

Sean downed the shot of whisky that was nervously given by the patron, and walked away feeling much better that his pent up feelings were released on Ned's neck. Eager not to be a Virginia City target anymore, he spurred his horse into a gallop. The only thing he would leave behind were clouds of dust he hoped Ned would choke on.

Chapter 5

It was a frigidly cold start to autumn at the Sullivan ranch when I loped Legend. Bill was the most patient and experienced teacher I would ever know. He could command Legend to do anything with the sound of his voice. He could command me to do anything with the sound of his voice, too.

"Don't grip with your knees! Don't lean too far forward! Don't hold on to the reins too tightly! And, oh…..relax!" he commanded.

I learned that balance, body language and rhythm were very important. I could control the direction Legend turned, slow him down, or make him go faster if I did it properly. Bill taught me early in my riding with Legend about being fair and consistent, respectful, polite, and never forceful. I felt these qualities could be used not only with horses, but with people, too.

As I was putting Legend back in the stall after one such lesson, I turned around and there was an Indian staring at me. I must have jumped three feet. The Indian stood calmly with his arms crossed as if he knew me. Bill walked in to see the anxious fear on my face.

"Patrick, this is Kevin Strong Bull. He's a friend."

I glanced at Bill in surprise, then the Indian, whose firm, rather grim face remained unchanged. The Indian comfortably extended his hand to me, though I took my time extending my shaky hand to him.

"I'm going hunting with Strong Bull, tomorrow. "Would you bring in the rest of the horses and wash up for supper?"

I nodded, watching Bill and Strong Bull leave the stall together.

During supper, I kept gawking at the Indian. He was dressed in a white top and black vest, his pants made of deerskin. When he removed his wide brimmed hat from his head of braided hair, his russet face had high cheekbones, critical eyes, and broad lips that never smiled. I wanted to know more about him, but Bill kept talking and talking, while the Indian kept nodding and nodding.

Finally I blurted out, "Bill, can I go hunting with you tomorrow?"

It was obvious he didn't care for my rudeness while Mary just shook her head.

"You're too young. I think it best you stay with Mary," Bill advised. "Why don't I teach you how to use a rifle and you can go with us the next time."

My eyes went sad faster than I could swallow my cubed potato.

"Does it have to be a rifle?" I whined.

That made Bill very curious. "If not a rifle, what would you suggest?"

Peering at the Indian, I shrugged my shoulders before solemnly eyeing my supper plate.

The men returned from hunting with two bucks. I entered the back field with a pail of water to find them cutting into one of the large carcasses hanging from a cottonwood tree. The animal's insides had been taken out where it was killed and there was very little blood dripping onto the ground; however, I was still happy I hadn't just finished a meal.

They were working quickly on the animal.

At one point, Bill offered the knife to me, but I said, "Another time."

It was really gross, but Bill said killing an animal and preparing it so it could be eaten safely in the future was an important lesson in survival.

I asked Strong Bull what his Indian name was as he held the antlers and cut away at its neck.

He peered up with the severed head staring back at me. "Tatanka Watanka."

I knew I'd never forget his name or that scene, briskly walking away, sucking in big gulps of fresh air to settle my uneasy stomach.

Bill pickled his meat in brine while Strong Bull dried his so that he could make pemmican. After the meat was dried, it would be mixed with dried berries and marrow, making it last a long time and be easily transportable.

At supper, I tried the pemmican and the buck's braised tongue; but it was the baked ribs smothered in tomato preserves and pot roasted rump that tasted so delicious despite I was so tired I could barely chew it.

My restless nights, which occurred more often than not, were shortening the length of time I could stay awake. Dark shadows always lurked under my eyes.

Bill motioned that I could go to my room and when I did, I discovered a bow and arrows in a buckskin sheath on my bed. With newfound energy, a huge smile came across my face. I would dream of being Sitting Bull hunting the great buffalo that charged the Plains.

Bill appeared while I was lying on the bed, fingering the lines like lightening rods that ran down the shaft and flicking the bone tip.

"That arrowpoint can do a lot of damage," he said, "even at a hundred yards."

I turned, propping myself on my arm. "How did you meet Strong Bull?"

"We met him in Fort Benton. Before the Cavalry moved in, Fort Benton was a trading post. Strong Bull was trading horses and furs, and that is how we got our first mustangs. John managed to convey that we wanted more mustangs and Strong Bull liked what we had to trade. Eventually, he became a guide and helped us search out places together. Of course, he was not Kevin Strong Bull at that time. "

I pleaded to hear more and Bill relented rather easily.

"We were travelling southeast to the High Plains when the skies opened up, teeming us with buckets of water that flooded the road. The wagon wheel got stuck and no matter how hard we tried, we couldn't get it out. Strong Bull grabbed the wheel with both hands, and miraculously pushed it out of the muddy hole."

Bill paused as I yawned wider than my bed.

"At the campfire, we saw that Strong Bull had cuts on his hands from pulling the wheel from the deep rut. John asked for some whisky and I thought nothing of it as he often drank whether there was a campfire or not. John knew a lot about alcohol. He knew how it made his mouth sores better, numbing the pain after some shock. He claimed he always had mouth sores so he always drank. John poured whisky on Strong Bull's hands and he was none too happy. No sooner were those hands around John's neck as he choked out 'it's for ye own good! It'll ward off infection!' Strong Bull calmed down after he licked his hands and discovered it was just whisky."

I rubbed my eyes but didn't think Bill noticed.

He continued, "I thought that we should give him a Christian name, and John piped in that Kevin would be a wise choice. He told me about the time when Paddy McGee's horse fell over, crushing his leg. Well good strong Kevin McCourt came right over and lifted that horse off of Paddy's leg. Didn't do Paddy any good; died anyway. But that Kevin, he was Strong like Bull, too." Bill smiled fondly, wagging his head.

Bill went on to say that they found those wild ponies and it was a good thing that they had Kevin Strong Bull with them. The horses were on land claimed by the Sioux, and Kevin Strong Bull was able to talk with them peacefully. Bill remarked about how he always offered something in exchange for being on their land.

Sounds of my slow and peaceful breaths filled the room after thick lashes covered the dark circles under my eyes. Bill placed the bow and arrows on the floor and gingerly pulled up the blankets.

"I pray for your restful sleep," he whispered with much emotion.

As I slept, his kiss to my head of brown, silky hair was bittersweet. I didn't realize how much I reminded him of someone else. How would I ever have known that his love was not just for me? That it was also for one that he lost too soon.

In the morning, I rushed through breakfast eager to attack unfriendly trees. My aim with those arrows was less than perfect. And when I did hit a tree, the arrow bounced off the mighty trunk, its arms of leaves shaking with laughter. Despite that, I continued my tree hunting into the afternoon when I saw Mary picking wildflowers along the eastern edge of the fenced property.

I followed her, pretending I was still an Indian quietly pursuing my foe as she moved towards a massive cotton-wood tree with long and gnarly branches.

Mary looked up as she knelt on the ground placing flowers against a grey stone.

"Why, Patrick, I didn't hear you," she said, surprised.

My attention was lost on five headstones, all etched with names, except for one.

She stood up. "It's John's birthday today so I thought I'd bring some flowers."

My curious gaze went from the stones to her soft smile. "The farthest graves are two stillborn babies, followed by John's, and my son's, his name was Oliver. Patrick, this last grave….this last grave is your mother's."

Mary approached, holding out her small hand, but I just turned and walked away, plainly shaking my head.

I spoke no words at supper, still unable to believe Momma was this close all the time and I never knew, never felt anything.

That night, I had the worst dream. I struggled against Grandpa's indomitable weight as he dragged me to the dining room. His strong and callused hand crushed the muscles of my neck while the other mercilessly yanked my arm, forcing me to look at Momma on the long table.

"Look what you did to your mother!" he barked. "Look at her!"

I was struggling to get away, screaming and kicking, when I heard Bill calling my name, hovering over me.

Pushing him away, I scurried to the corner of the room curling up as tightly as I could; however, the image of her, pale and lifeless, wouldn't fade.

Bill tried to touch me, but I pushed him away, wailing, "No…no…no!"

My mind screamed, *can't you see what I've done? How I killed my momma? I don't deserve you. I don't deserve to be loved. I don't deserve your help!*

"Fine, I'm going," Bill cried hesitantly.

He slowly backed away as my body quivered into the walls, head buried in my knees.

"Did anything happen today?" Bill asked Mary when he entered the kitchen nonplussed.

"He's found his mother's grave. What do we do?" she spoke with anguish. "How do we stop him from crying so?"

"Stay by his room, but leave him be. He may not even be awake, and if he is, he should tire soon of this; it's taking all of his breath."

Bill stormed out of the house with questions lingering heavily in his mind.

When the house was finally still and everyone was safely in their beds, Bill tossed and turned until Mary gazed at him with most curious eyes.

"I didn't know I was keeping you awake," he smiled.

"It should have been a most peaceful night without that thunderous snoring, but you keep taking all the sheets with your moving this way and that way. My legs are quite cold," she spoke matter-of-factly.

"I can't stop thinking about Patrick's reaction to my help. How he pulled away; didn't want to be consoled or held, which doesn't make much sense unless…unless he feels he doesn't deserve it."

"Why would he feel he doesn't deserve it? It's not as if he hurt the poor woman."

The wheels started spinning in Bill's brain. "I think I understand what Patrick is feeling and hope I can help him. He's somehow shut out his mother's death, but could no longer do that, and as her tragic end became real, his actions became real."

Mary was so weary, she pleaded, "Will you be helping him tomorrow, Bill? Because if so, maybe we could get some sleep now?"

Bill floated the quilt and sheets over his sweet Mary and held her in his warm and brawny arms.

****

Bill watched as I sauntered into the kitchen, rubbing narrow, sleepy eyes.

I went mechanically to my bowl of porridge already on the table, glancing briefly at Bill, who was drinking his coffee and reading the Bible.

"Patrick, it's Sunday," he declared. "After breakfast, get dressed and bring out your Bible."

He observed me scratching the back of my neck. It was some kind of nervous habit I never knew I had.

"Are you sure?" My face was full of uncertainty. "I thought it was Friday?"

Bill calmly shook his head while reading the Bible.

Despite that I was out of sorts this morning, Mary wasn't in the kitchen so it must have been Sunday.

When I returned, Bill said he wanted to tell me a story first. I hoped it wasn't a long one because I was surely tired this morning and there were no sugary cookies sitting on the table to keep me awake.

Bill spoke about when he was a little boy, playing hide and seek with his brother. He wanted a good hiding place and saw the well behind his home. Figuring John would never find him there, he grabbed the notched rope, pulled it into the well and slowly climbing down.

He was right.

John finally gave up and walked away.

Bill waited a few more minutes before he slowly climbed the rope.

Suddenly it came loose, plunging him into water. Darkness fell around him as icy wetness seeped through his clothes and shocked his body. The only relief he felt was in knowing that he was at the bottom of his well and couldn't fall any farther. It took his father and John twenty minutes to find him and pull him up.

Bill looked at me somberly. "I believe you're at the bottom of your well and it's time to bring you up."

I nodded even though I was very confused.

"Please turn to Psalms thirty-two and read aloud verse one, three, four and five."

I began to read the first passage slowly.....

"Blessed is he whose transgression is forgiven,
Whose sin is covered.
When I declared not my sin,
My body wasted away through my groaning all day long.
For day and night thy hand was heavy upon me;
My strength was dried up as by the heat of summer.
I will confess my transgressions to the Lord,
Then thou didst forgive the guilt of my sin."

"Patrick, do you believe in God?" Bill asked with direct eyes.

I nodded without hesitation.

"And do you understand what you've read?"

"Yes," my voice a nervous whisper.

"If you confess any sins you feel you have, God forgives you and you're forgiven. Let's pray together, let's pray."

I wound my arms around Bill, hugging him tightly. Then I prayed in his arms, confessing my sins and asking for forgiveness, in a quivering voice, but my voice.

Bill's arms embraced me as he prayed for God to give me comfort, to lift my heavy burden, to restore joy in my young heart, and to help me accept love.

Mary interrupted our prayers when she walked into the house. "There you are, Bill. What are you doing reading the Bible on a Friday?"

"Oh, it's Friday?" Bill seemed surprised. "I tell you, Patrick, the mind plays tricks when you're my age. Well, I guess we best go feed those horses."

"Not before you be speaking with the cattle rustler waiting on the porch," Mary informed.

His supportive arms were still around me as he watched and waited, waited until I nodded, nodded with an appreciative smile. He seemed to understand me even more than I understood myself. The fear I faced faded, along with the guilt and shame that tormented my soul; and the dark, ominous shadow that followed me finally disappeared.

Bill grabbed his hat, with me set to follow, when Mary held me back.

"Wait for Bill to be finished his business."

When the door closed, Mary and I watched through the window as the cattle rustler turned and held his hand out to Bill.

"If Bill knew it was Nelson Story waiting for him, he'd not be so keen on leaving the house. He's not fond of the man, but it's because of him, we have longhorns grazing our fields."

I watched as Bill shook the man's hand rather reluctantly. Gazing over the field of Longhorn cattle, their voices were just a garble when Bill began shuffling his boots against the floorboards rather stiffly.

"It was Indian country Story had to cross," Mary said lightly. "It was a Sioux camp Story had to…to stomp through. If he didn't, we'd be eating a lot more pig."

'Or,' I said silently, 'searching for someone like….like my grandpa.'

****

The days of autumn ticked away. Every morning, we awoke to a frosty ground; and every night, darkness fell on the Sullivan ranch earlier. On one of those chilly mornings, Mary announced that their daughter, Angela, and her husband were coming for a visit after their fall crops were harvested. They would be making their way from a place called Oregon.

"I can't wait for you to meet Angela. She's a wonderful woman," Mary beamed.

She hadn't seen her daughter since they headed west two years ago. Mary secretly hoped that Angela was pregnant and coming home to share the good news.

"Well, Patrick, this house is going to get a lot busier," Bill said with trepidation.

I nodded, taking a big bite of my crunchy bread smothered in homemade currant jam.

"You and 1 can always break free to the river if it gets too noisy," he winked.

I had to admit that I was a little nervous about meeting new people, but if they were related to Bill and Mary they should be good and kind people.

Angela and her husband, Edward, arrived on a Saturday morning. Mary was in tears as she held out loving arms to her daughter.

Edward shook Bill's hand and seemed very proper.

Angela was pretty with big blue eyes, red hair, and a sweet smile just like her mother. She came right over and gave me a warm hug.

Then she introduced me to her husband, who inspected me from head to toe like I was a plump pig for the supper table. It was easy to say that I didn't get a warm feeling from the slightly overweight, average looking man. But he was affectionate towards Angela because he had his arm around her all of the time.

I went to the stable while everybody else went into the house. As I was cleaning out Ginger's stall, Edward touched my shoulder. After nearly plunging the shovel's handle into his chest, my heart thunderously pounded against ribs as he smiled grimly.

"So Patrick, where you from?" he questioned rather coldly.

No one had ever asked me that. I was rendered completely speechless.

He waited, his eyes on me, glaring like I was utterly slow for taking so long to answer.

"I'm not sure," I mumbled, wishing I could just run away, but he blocked my path.

"I'd imagine your family's worried sick about you."

He eagerly awaited my next response like the horses eagerly awaiting their afternoon oats.

"My momma's dead. She's not worried any more," I said sadly, and with that, continued shoveling the straw and manure out of Ginger's stall.

His meddlesome body got so close I could see a loose button on its last thread. "Your momma the only family you had?"

Just then, Bill walked in. "Edward, Angela is looking for you."

Edward gave me a frosty glare that raised every hair along my shivering skin. Bill waited patiently until the stable was empty before he walked over to my jittery body.

"Edward can be a little forward. I'd like to think he's just protective of this family."

"He asked me where I was from. Do you ever wonder where I'm from?"

"When we found you, you were pretty downhearted, and I didn't want to put you through any more pain. It's unnatural to see someone so young in such a deep melancholy. I figured maybe too selfishly that this was the best place for you until you were better."

"I don't want to leave," I said in desperation as tears of panic welled in my eyes.

"You never have to. This is your home for as long as you want it to be," he said, reassuringly putting arms around me.

When it was time for supper, I pretended I was sick. Didn't feel like talking, so I told Mary I was going to lie down. She kindly offered to bring food to my room.

While atop the bed, hands behind my head, voices wafted straight to my ears, so I couldn't ignore them.

Angela and Edward were talking about their farm and the troubles they had with their crops. They struggled with a rainy spring and a dry summer which gave them low yields, and in turn, made them less money. Angela was hopeful that next year would be better.

Bill offered them money, but Edward flatly refused. He boasted he was going to make it on his own.

Mary recommended they stay and Edward could do the round-up with Bill.

I silently cried 'no, please no.'

Edward said he wanted to try farming for another year which put my mind at ease. That is, until he generously offered to lend a hand should Bill need any help at all.

I vowed to myself that I would be the only help Bill would ever need.

Then Mary and Bill talked about what a blessing I was to both of them.

Bill said I was a natural with the horses, so gentle and attentive.

Mary complimented me on my intelligence and willingness to learn. She talked of me so lovingly, I almost bawled. Instead, I grinned at the thought of Edward's face during all of this glorifying of me.

Edward asked where I was found, ruining my pleasure.

"Sounds like the boy fell from the sky and landed in your lap," he said unbelievably loudly.

Bill glared at him, soberly. "Patrick was found south of Helena….only survivor in his party. We took him in as any good Christians would. I searched the town for any signs of family, reading newspapers when I could get my hands on them, but there was nothing. Patrick is welcome in our home for as long as he wants, and there's nothing more to discuss."

And there were no further discussions about me.

During the next week, I stayed close to Bill or kept busy in the stable. Edward didn't seem too fond of the mustangs. I think he was secretly afraid of them. Once, I heard him call them wild creatures. I surely wasn't gonna tell him that the ones in the stable were tamed and mostly thoroughbreds. It made me curious, though, about what other kind of horse lived in this stable because if there were differences, I surely couldn't make them out.

Edward found me one last time in the barn with Iris.

I kept my eyes on filling the pail with milk.

Leering over me, arms folded, he sneered, "Take you for a Virginia City boy."

I felt like saying Virginia City bastard but held my tongue.

"Maybe I take a ride down there. See if I can find any more of your kind," he threatened. "Boy should be with his own kind no matter who they are."

His presence was heavy over my shoulders, but I just kept at my work.

"You like it here, don't you boy? I don't know how you're gonna like it when I come back for good. Maybe by then I'll have found your family and we can all live happy." He left with a fiendish smirk on his face.

I hoped I'd never see Edward again. Iris mooed and kicked up her rear hoof as I squeezed her udders too tightly. I apologized to Iris and promised I would be much gentler if she'd just fill the pail a little faster.

Chapter 6

The sun was fading behind a craggy mountain ridge as Sean winded north along Trunk Road. Crossing the border, his wagon was loaded with whisky barrels destined for a fortified trading post nestled between the St. Mary and Oldman rivers.

He was all too aware that the liquor in his barrels was completely adulterated, so much so that the Native Indians could die or go into shock from the 'firewater'.

Despite the dangers, demand for the toxic drink was so high, men would offer their wives and daughters when they ran out of furs to exchange. Sean continued supplying the market long since banned by the Hudson's Bay Company; however, his days were numbered when the Canadian Government dispatched a mounted police force from the East, tasked to put an end to it.

Upon arrival at Fort Whoop Up, the only light came from a gibbous moon which appeared then disappeared through quick moving clouds. When the wide oaken gates were opened, the town within the fortified walls came to life. Despite the blackness and small soothing patches of light hanging over porches or coming from the windows of barracks, the men weren't lulled into sleep. They clamoured about, slurring threats or feats, sloshing alcohol from their swaggering bottles, and making steamy puddles in dark corners.

Sean's whisky barrels were carried into a dimly lit cabin. As soon as his wagon was emptied, he would move to another cabin brimming with buffalo robes and other fur-bearing hides.

While anxiously waiting for the wagon to be loaded high, he tried to breathe heat and strength into cold and stiff hands, but gave up and headed to the noise of the shanty drinking barracks. Moving through the haze of smoke and clusters of men swirling about in drunken stupor, he arrived at the bar and ordered two whiskies.

"Cuthbert!" a man belted out. "Cuthbert!"

Sean twisted his neck to watch a thin man bark out the name again before fixating a stare oddly on him. He shook his head believing the man to be delusional.

"Cuthbert!" the fool beckoned, slapping Sean's back with the palm of his gangly hand.

Sean's hand was no sooner on his pistol when the man laughed heartily.

"It's me, Curly Johnston! Come now, don't remember the man you saved from a frozen death?"

Sean reached for his shot glass when Curly snatched it and tossed its contents over his shoulder.

"Don't wanna be drinking that poison! Come with me. I have something worthy of a saviour."

Curiosity killed Sean's prudence so he followed the fellow, who was brash and brazen, despite that his face was a pink patchwork amid blisters and flaking skin, to a table with a small man blanketed in stripes hunched over his amber drink.

"Cuthbert, I'd like you to meet Angus McNulty. Angus, this is Dilbert Cuthbert; man who saved my cantankerous life and opened my eyes to the whisky trade."

Angus tipped his hat and smiled subtly.

Curly clamped his teeth around the cork of the bottle and settled its contents into Sean's empty shot glass.

"Try this. One hundred and eighty proof mixed with a little water…guaranteed to put hairs on your chest and elsewhere. Ain't that right, Angus?"

Curly slapped his knee, roaring heavily until he doubled over, wincing horribly.

"It may also be burning a hole in my liver but that's 'side the point. My piss 'ill never freeze long as it's got this rum in it."

Sean slammed back the shot. It did not go down smooth, but the blood returned in his hands and feet almost instantaneously.

"Don't remember me, Gilbert, do you?" Curly inquired.

Sean eyed the wiry man with intensity but couldn't for the life of him remember any acquaintances with a mop of curly black hair, pestilent skin, and scantily fair eyebrows and beard.

"Let me freshen your memory," Curly said, pouring more liquid into Sean's glass before dribbling it across his hand, the table, the floor.

"I was coming up Trunk Road mightily fast and a white flash of snow swooped across. I didn't see the gopher hole but my horse found it, snapping his leg plum in two. Went down fast with my foot caught in the stirrup but managed to wriggle free. Foot was busted though; horse was done in, too. I thought I was a goner until you came along and went right past me until I fired two shots with my Remington revolver. You stopped right quickly, showed me what you was packing, but in the end offered to take me into Fort Whoop-up; and I was much obliged."

Sean nodded at the recollection despite that the face had marred Curly's identity.

Curly scratched at his forehead, finding a flap of skin he just had to peel off, roll between his fingers and pop in his mouth like it was a candy bean.

"I've had my fill of myself ever since Angus showed me how he can breathe fire. I didn't believe it at first, calling him a liar…that is until he filled his cheeks with rum, struck a match, and lit my face aglow. Singed my brows and whiskers; made my skin so hot I could fry an egg on it!"

There was a peculiar expression donning Angus's face. If he thought Sean was going to call him a liar, he was dead wrong.

"Shall we have another, gentlemen," Angus offered.

Sean covered the rim of his glass with his hand.

Angus challenged, "Had enough, have we? Americans have such little tolerance."

Sean lifted his hand and slid the glass his way. It would be the last thing he could recall in his mind hours later.

His sense of smell awoke before anything else. Flanked in utter darkness, he figured he was lying in a barn stall with the horse dung permeating his nose and the uncomfortable ground lining his back. He shifted his head into a hard, rigged object and lifted his hand to find a boot brushing up against his cheek. His fingers found his flask rising and falling with the breath of his lungs.

As he struggled to sit up, his arms felt pinioned to his chest.

Blinking profusely, a shadow of a man emerged lying opposite him. It was Curly Johnston sleeping as soundly as a dead man.

Sean stood and fought the tightness surrounding his limbs and chest while the cold night air cut through.

When the white fabric came into focus, he soon discovered it was Angus's blanket. Sniffing it, he soon realized it reeked of sweat, smoke, and feculence.

"Son of a bitch," Sean muttered. With anger welling up, his fingers filled with Curly's coat until the man moaned before Sean could hurl one fist.

"Cuthwaite?" he croaked. "My eyes is shot!"

"Where's my tailored coat!" Sean bellowed.

"Oh…oh, not so loud," Curly grimaced, rubbing throbbing temples. "Well, when the heat came, you dripped sweat and stripped it off. Angus tied his pointed blanket to you and dragged you here insisting he not sully yours in muck and dirt. He must a forgot he was wearing your frock."

"Where is he?"

"Gone to be with his kind. He's Metis you know. Wouldn't know it with the hair ripe as yellow corn and freckled complexion. He's long gone, but you have his capote. It's a fair trade."

Sean fitfully yanked the tie away and squeezed into the frayed fabric, too narrow for his shoulders. He stuffed the flask into the waist of his pants while his arms remained pinned back to keep the fibres from splitting in two. Moving to the doorway, Curly moaned again.

"Filbert," he whispered. "You're a good man. You're a good man, Filbert."

Sean paused, his tongue poised for fuming reproach, but in the end just shook a weary, muddled mind and stomped away.

Moving quickly to his wagon, the gibbous moon had yet to fade into dawn. Minutes after leaving the protection of the fort and its solid heavy gates, the chains began rattling against the tailpipe.

Eager not to wake every Blackfoot from their warm lodge, he tugged on the reins and pulled the emergency break.

While he was shifting the furs toward the centre of the Prairie Schooner, a twig snapped in the forest of looming evergreens, and he squinted at what appeared like the silhouette of a man. He shook his pounding head, figuring it was just swaying trees tricking his mind. He lifted the tailgate, secured the chains, and turned only to be blocked by a young Indian.

"Son of a bitch," he muttered under his breath.

The man's moist, broad lips shook and shimmered in the moon's light.

"Whisky," he stuttered.

"Go line up at the wicket and get your whisky!" Sean said gruffly while pulling the ill-fitted robe around his gleaming flask.

"Whisky," the Blackfoot stammered again, his trembling hand pointed at Sean's chest.

"I see English isn't your strong point! I don't have any whisky!" Sean spoke as he would to a man with lost hearing.

He took two long strides when the Indian knifed at air. Sean raised his pistol, barrel poised at the young man's chest.

"You don't want to do this, kid. I'll put a bullet through you!"

The Blackfoot's body just shook. His knife sparkled as it lunged at Sean, who reacted swiftly, firing one slug into the crazed man, his shirt puffing like a canvassed wagon on a windy day.

The knife fell, the Indian wobbled, until both, weapon and man hit the ground hard.

Sean tested the tailgate, wiggling it one final time before he passed the man, whose chest no longer heaved or sank. With a November chill in the air, it would be no time until he was stone cold dead.

"That was a crazy thing to do, kid!" He glanced at the knife that would easily have shorn the hair from his head before impatiently climbing the wagon and slapping the reins against the horses' haunches. Clucking his tongue, he made a speedy exit from the Blackfoot camp that loomed nearby.

Two days later, he arrived into the sleeping town of Fort Benton, the glow of his lamp lighting the way through the black of night. He went directly to the saloon and gave the bartender furs in exchange for five dollars a piece. With money in hand, a glass and bottle of whisky in the other, he found a spot with his eye on the door.

"This isn't any of that bug juice that's in those barrels?" Sean asked the bartender, Harry Mills.

"No, you deserve the real thing," he replied.

Sean was poised to pour when he turned to Harry with a heavy head. "Would you brew me a cup of coffee?"

Normally, Harry would rib a man who had a hankering for coffee in his saloon; but the wind-chaffed face with black sunken eyes glazed for sobering up melted his mocking tone.

"Sure thing…sure thing."

As Sean stared at the bottom of the empty glass breathing a heavy sigh of relief, trouble by the name of Carl Healy walked in. Sean lowered his hat and let out a sigh of angst, hoping to be unrecognized.

Carl trundled over and invited himself to a chair across from Sean. "Where's the rest of your tribe, Chief," he snickered.

Sean glanced up with icy disdain. "Hello, Carl," he grumbled. "What brings you to my neck of the woods?"

"I needed a change of scenery," he replied, warily scanning the room. "Say, you still carrying that Navy Colt?"

"No, I'm carrying a forty-five now."

"A peacemaker. Guess we ain't sharing ammunition now. Shame since I'm fresh out."

The breeze in the room changed direction and Carl leaned back in his chair.

"Jesus, you're one ripe son of a bitch!"

Sean's heated scowl didn't alter Carl's soured face.

"Did you run out of stores to rob in Helena?"

"Ran into a little more trouble than I bargained for."

Sean knew exactly the kind of trouble Carl was getting into and didn't want to be part of it. His eyes shifted to the creaky saloon doors and a man with an unfamiliar face, who sauntered to the bar.

"How much you take in robbing mercantiles, ten, twenty dollars?"

"Last hold-up, oh about four," he paused, "about four thousand," Carl boasted.

"Four thousand?" Sean asked skeptically.

"Shopkeeper didn't trust banks. Kept the cash in the cellar. It was supposed to be an easy job except…the wife had to get in the way. Said I could take the cash over her dead body so that's what I did. Hey, what's it take to get a drink around here?" Carl bellowed, waving his empty pistol.

"You killed a woman?" Sean stiffened. "What's your reward set at now?"

"I'm at five thousand thanks to that woman. You know, there was a time when I'd wave my gun and people'd cower. Now they question me like I wouldn't use it."

"You didn't have to kill her!"

"She had a big mouth! Just had to shut it up! That's probably why her husband didn't hear me…deaf as a post. She couldn't keep her hands off other men either," Carl insulted with disgust. "She was doing Jack Wilder! That loose-lipped Kate was a whore and I couldn't trust her. Sure wish you was carrying that Navy Colt."

"You have that kind of money filling your pockets and you're out of cartridges," Sean sneered. "Should add them to your shopping list!"

"Well, that's the funny part. Only thing lining my pockets is lint. I climbed over that heap of soiled flesh, and all I found was two mouldy onions and a limp carrot. You see the meaning in that? Seems Kate's husband was too aware she couldn't keep her legs together so he stashed the cash in the bank."

Sean got distracted as a ghastly rotund man in an oversized black coat entered the saloon looking his direction.

"You've been followed. Tommy Sells just graced us with his presence," Sean muttered through clenched teeth.

"Two ton Tommy? Are you sure? Isn't he like the size of a whale? Shouldn't the floorboards be moving?"

"Oh, he's still as big as a whale. My vision's not what it used to be, especially after drinking firewater; but he's one large sight," Sean observed, cocking the hammer spur of his pistol under the table.

"Are we gonna take him like we did scar face?"

"O'Flaherty," Sean answered.

"Right, O'Flaherty. Seems I shot him in the leg, slow him down some," Carl bragged.

Sean shook a lugubrious head. "There are things I can't condone and killing a woman's one of them."

"Why you….."

"Put it down, Carl!" Tommy Sells bellowed.

"Ah hell," Carl muttered as Sean smirked at the wide-waisted man.

"You too, Thomas!" Sells drawled, snatching Carl's gun. "There's a gun pointed at your head, too. My new partner, Wade Curtis, would like nothing better than to put a bullet in your skull!"

Sean lifted his gun by the handle and Wade quickly seized it.

"I can't believe my luck," Tommy smirked. "Two outlaws sitting in the same saloon!"

"Looks like you haven't skipped many suppers!" Carl snorted.

Tommy whacked Carl in the temple with the butt of his own gun. "We have to get you back to Helena! People in that town want you hanged yesterday!"

"What do we do with Thomas?" Wade asked.

Harry quickly hoisted his shotgun, aimed to fill Wade's body full of holes.

"You shoot my partner and you'll hang with Thomas and Healy!" Sells warned the bartender.

Harry kept his gun raised. "You're mistaken. That's not Sean Thomas and seeing as you ain't lawmen, I'll just say it was a robbery gone bad."

"Looks like you have a friend," Tommy uttered, knowing he needed Wade's help in getting Carl and himself safely back to Helena. "It's your lucky day!"

Wade emptied the chambers of Sean's Colt forty-five, its bullets thundering the hollow wooden floor.

Sean eyed his empty gun, then Carl's grimacing face.

"Better watch your back, 'cause I aim to put several bullets in it!" he threatened.

"Healy, get up off your ass!" Tommy barked. "Poster says dead or alive. If you don't move fast enough, I'll take you dead!"

Carl kicked out his chair, hands reaching for Sean's jugular, until Sells used a strong arm, catapulting him out of the saloon.

When the doors stopped swinging, Sean quickly reloaded his gun and thanked Harry.

"We'll see you next Tuesday?" he spoke optimistically, hoping that by keeping Sean alive, his profitable venture would stay very much alive.

Sean nodded out a grunt but wanted to rant 'not likely', his glance firm on the sawed-off shotgun still lying atop the bar counter.

He would never smuggle whisky again. He never had the chance again. The North West Mounted Police appeared in the fall of 1874 throughout the barren western Canadian land, shutting down the whisky trading posts and abruptly halting the illegal trade with Native Indians.

Sean lingered a few minutes in the saloon, eager to be distanced from Tommy and Carl. When the coast was clear, he took the back entrance into the brothel and bumped into Katherine in the narrow hallway.

"Why Sean Thomas, it's a pleasure to see you so soon," she lied, delicately placing a slender finger to her nose.

"Do you have any news regarding my search?"

"Come to the front room. I'll lock the door."

Sean wearily eyed the settee but stayed standing.

Katherine was relieved but easily saw how uptight and rigid he was. She sensed a visit with Ophelia was eminently needed.

"Unfortunately I don't have any news regarding the missing woman and child you mentioned. I took the liberty of speaking to Ophelia who swore to be discreet. She may have some information for you. Please follow me," she smiled.

She knocked on Ophelia's door, which was hurriedly opened as soon as Sean's name was spoken. Grasping his hand, she ushered him into the room.

"You're a sight for sore eyes," she swallowed with a contrived smile while undressing.

Grabbing her hands, he muttered, "Ophelia I'm not here for that. I merely want to know…"

Relief flashed across her face for a brief moment while innately quelling her sense of smell.

"I know what you're feeling, she began. "I was married and had a son once. He was just three years old when he died, followed by my husband shortly after. I promised myself I'd never live that life again, and I won't."

She smiled sadly. "I haven't been able to locate your son or his mother but won't stop looking for them. I have a friend who has a farm. She takes in orphans and they help to manage the place. Although she doesn't have any boys his age, if that should change, I will let you know."

Her hands ran through his tousled and heavy hair.

His breathing slowed and shoulders relaxed. It wouldn't be long before other parts of his body relaxed, too.

"We do what we have to… to get through the night," she implied by sliding her indigo ruffled dress from slim shoulders, whispering, "I have what you need if you have what I want."

"I have money," he answered, his somnolent eyes never leaving her pleasing face.

With lips curling into an alluring smile, she removed the rest of her undergarments.

Sean couldn't resist her no matter how mired in exhaustion he was. She relieved his tension and made him forget if only briefly why he kept coming back to Fort Benton.

When she stood naked, he wrapped his arms around her, rubbing his stubbly cheek against a round belly. Her wanton body ignited a hunger in him that had to be satisfied. Responding quickly, he pushed her onto the bed.

She yanked and tossed his clothing as far away as she could, frankly hoping the stench would abate from an unclean body.

While kissing her white supple breasts, his calloused hand gently moved along the silky softness to the centre of her being.

Ophelia shuddered.

As he moved atop her, she felt his thrusts as slow teasing rhythms.

Even though his desire was strong, he was struggling to perform, his body weakening.

She gripped him and flipped him, making faster and deeper waves of rawness and heat until he shook in blissful release.

"Opheila, you're worth every penny," he moaned, breathless.

Don't I know it, she thought. "Word gets round, I may just raise my rates."

Sean grinned devilishly. "I'll keep it to myself."

He started to rise, but Ophelia easily pushed him down. "You've paid more than enough money to stay the night, besides you look like hell."

She rose from the bed, snatched her clothes, then snatched his. "These clothes need to be laundered otherwise Vigilantes will smell you coming!"

She closed the door and the room went silent.

He reached for a small mirror from the bedside table.

"Oh God," he cringed.

Though his face wasn't as fried as Curly's, his brows and beard resembled worn horsehair brushes.

A few minutes on the feather stuffed pillow, and the lure of sleep easily won over. During Sean's slumber, he dreamt of meeting Carl Healy in a poker game in Helena.

Carl and others had lost a lot of money to Sean, who was leaving on a high note, pockets thick and jingling. The young lanky man, who was just inches taller than Sean, followed him out.

"You leaving so soon?" Carl asked.

"Yep, don't stay long in one place," Sean replied with a hand on his Colt. "Just have to get some supplies and I'm out of here."

He had to procure more ammunition. There were five in the cylinder and no more. He hoped he didn't have to put any into Carl. The last man who followed him out after a card game wound up with a ball in his head.

As they walked on, Frank O'Flaherty and two cohorts were heading towards them.

Sean turned into a dark corner. "Son of a bitch."

"You got trouble coming your way?" Carl asked.

"No, I like lurking in dark corners!" he snarled.

"Well let's get the hell out of here."

"Got to hit the mercantile. I'm out of ammunition."

"I've got cartridges. You carrying a navy colt?"

"I travel alone, Carl!"

"Not tonight if you want to stay alive. Besides, I don't mind dying with my boots on," he stated, brushing back dirty blond hair from a crooked grin on his unwrinkled face.

"How old are you, kid?"

"Old enough to save your hide from a sure hanging."

Sean figured far be if for him to change a mind. Besides, his back was against a wall.

"Fine," he grumbled. "Stay close to me, though."

"Like butter on bread."

"Not that close!" Sean sneered, set to tell Carl to vamoose when O'Flaherty appeared.

Despite that the clouds shrouded the moon, spurring heavy darkness over the town, O'Flaherty recognized Sean and a pursuit began. After a short run on foot, horses were swiftly mounted while gun flashes ignited the black night like fireflies in both directions.

Sean's pistol was soon rendered useless so he sped through a thick grove of pine trees, the branches and pine needles whipping at his face.

A cabin yards from the shimmering river came into view. He bolted inside the empty room frantically searching his pockets for bullets.

The door flew open and Sean stood face-to-face with Frank O'Flaherty, pistols aimed at each other's heads.

"If I counted correctly," Sean asserted. "You're out of bullets, but math was never my strong suit."

Suddenly, both men dropped to the ground as shots pummeled the cabin, shattering its small windows and breaking the mud slats that sealed the log walls.

"There a lawman in here, you idiots!" Frank bellowed once the gunfire ceased.

When the moon's light brightened the cabin, he grasped his knife and lunged at Sean.

As it pierced flesh, Sean desperately struggled for the shiny barrel of his pistol.

Stretching fingers, the muscles of his shoulder started to tear, until finally, Sean felt metal and slammed it against O'Flaherty's temple. While thrusting the knife away, its tip sliced Frank's left cheek.

Sean straddled the inert man, forced his chin up and placed Frank's blade on the soft skin just above his adam's apple. One swift slash and it would be all over. All over until his reward got bigger, sending more men chasing after him.

The cabin went into darkness again. All Sean could see was a faint mist from his heavy breathing as he loomed over the cataleptic man.

More gunfire erupted but went across the quiet forest.

"Sean, you in there…you alive!" Carl shouted. "If so, get the hell out of there, now!"

Sean ran from the cabin and mounted his horse.

A box of cartridges got tossed his way, and he hastily stuffed the chambers. Slamming the cylinder shut, a shot whizzed past his head causing his horse to buck. As Sean struggled not to fall, Carl returned fire. His gun blast forced a numb ringing sound to pound Sean's ear.

O'Flaherty clutched his bleeding leg, stumbling from an already unsteady balance.

More lead whizzed past ears like mosquitoes hungrily searching for blood. Sean and Carl galloped through shadows of lofty pines while returning a wave of firepower.

As Sean tried to shake the ringing that droned in his ear, one thought ran through his mind: he who hesitates is lost; and he almost lost his life. He would never question whether to kill O'Flaherty again.

As they reached Fort Benton, Sean decided it best to part with Carl. As Carl hesitantly moved into the town, Sean continued north. He rode another hour before a farm came into sight.

Stealthily, he entered the barn, found an empty stall, and with weary hands removed the bridle, saddle and blanket from his horse. Then he climbed the ladder to a loft meaning to sleep a mere hour or two. But when he awoke, light was streaming through the cracks of the worn wooden planks as footsteps approached. Ramming five cartridges in the cylinder, he aimed for the ladder.

A curious boy peered at the shaft of the gun and the darkly clothed man that held it so tightly. His grey eyes widened, awaiting his fate.

"I'm not gonna hurt you, boy. Just wanna get out of this barn."

The boy fretfully nodded as he slowly descended the ladder. He watched, frozen in fear as Sean climbed down and walked toward his horse.

"I groomed and fed him," he rambled nervously.

Sean nodded in appreciation as he bridled and saddled his horse.

The boy stood in curious immobility as Sean walked past him.

"Thank you," he said, flipping a coin the kid's direction.

When Sean was taking steps away from the farm, a man called out, "Welcome to breakfast, if you like!"

He turned to see a burly, middle-aged man standing alongside his son twenty yards away. Sean paused before strangely accepting the man's hospitality. He didn't know when he'd eaten last and the journey to Canada would take hours.

As he sat at the breakfast table, his eyes focused on the pale freckle-faced boy, who was busy stuffing hot cakes into his little mouth.

"Thank you," Sean said, sipping his coffee.

"Buchanan….Jared Buchanan," the red-haired man with the short, thick beard grinned. "You looked in need of a meal."

"How old's your son?"

"Luke's nine," Jerod replied as the boy glanced up in admiration. "You can leave the table and tend to your chores."

"He's a fine-natured boy," Sean observed.

"Much like his mother was, good spirited and kind hearted."

"Could get him hurt."

"Might. I pray it doesn't, though I wouldn't change him even if I could. The world needs more of his kind," he said, taking his napkin and dampening it with water. "You headed far, Mister?"

"Thomas….name's Thomas," Sean spoke wearily. "I'm headed north into Canada for a while."

Jared handed Sean the cloth and pointed to his throat.

"Beautiful country. A man could get lost up there if he wanted to."

Sean wiped the dried blood from his neck. "That's what I intend to do. Must be leaving, but I do thank you for your kindness; it's much appreciated."

As Sean left the farm, he caught sight of Luke aimlessly shooting at bottles with his rifle. He could have given him a few lessons if he wasn't so eager to leave

Montana. He must have been forty yards away when he aimed his pistol at the elusive glass bottle.

It shattered.

Luke turned in astonishment to the quiet gunman. It was a small piece of satisfaction; just something to keep Sean moving forward on his journey into the wild northern land.

****

O'Flaherty limped his way into the Golden Nugget Saloon. Every time he straddled a bar stool, he thought of jabbing his knife along Thomas's jugular, forever wiping the smug smile off his ugly mug.

"Hey, Frankie," Ned leaned in close as he deftly poured whisky to the rim of two glasses. "Henry Wilkes is at the end of the bar. Been coming here since the Occidental closed down. Most times alone, but the odd time he takes a table with Marsden's wife late at night. She must tuck the old geezer in before tiptoeing out the backdoor. Sips back booze like water and still keeps her head above the table," he said with incredulity.

Frank eased off the stool, drinks in hand, and sauntered over to Henry, hunched over an empty glass with eyes intent on his sturdy hands.

"Mind if I join you, Henry?" Frank inquired with a gentle slide of his offering.

Henry glanced over, "Do I know you?"

"It's Frank, Frank O'Flaherty. Sorry, I haven't been around much."

"Keep busy," Henry muttered. "Hands must keep busy."

"That's right, Henry. But maybe I come by the ranch, tomorrow. Bring your pretty daughter some flowers."

"Away," he mumbled incoherently.

"Pardon," Frank persisted.

"She's away," he said, aimlessly staring across the bar. "She'll be back soon, though; as soon as she realizes she's chasing a ghost. She is chasing a ghost, ain't she?"

Henry turned tired, bloodshot eyes Frank's direction. "You mean to tell me he's still breathes!"

"How long's it been since his last letter? Unless you're keeping something from me, it's been years. The man's gone...cold in his grave," Frank lied through clenched teeth.

Henry reached into his pocket and scattered coin across the counter. "Then bring her home! Hope that more than meets your travel expenses!"

"Ned!" Frank stammered. "Pour us another round and leave the bottle."

Henry slammed back the whisky, its shot glass remaining stoutly inconspicuous in brutish hands.

Thirty minutes later, Frank walked out with the loose coin pressed tightly into his palms. He never thought Amanda Wilkes would chase after Sean Thomas.

Once Frank had provisions, he'd set a trail for Fort Benton. He only hoped he wasn't too late for the happy reunion. He had a gift for the wayward father.

Chapter 7

It was a busy breezy morning when the Sullivan ranch welcomed another horse into the stable. The grasses were bending to the mighty earth when Maggie had her foal. I touched the light brown filly, still sticky in parts. My first instinct was to call her Taffy. She looked like it, felt like it, sticky and brown.

I didn't linger long with Maggie and her filly. We were going to Fort Benton: The journey to and from the old trading post would take three days.

As the horses trotted the wagon away from the ranch, I waved to Mary until she was the size of my fingertip.

My teeth rattled and my bones shook as we travelled along the bumpy trail over fallen branches, exposed tree roots, and into deep ruts that threatened to take the wheel right off of its axel. Bill was just happy the skies were clear and our trail was dry.

We stopped after thirty miles on the winding road that would lead us to the town. Our temporary home was erected among the shade of the cottonwood and pine trees. While Bill made a fire, I cooled the horses in the river, watching schools of fish swim just past my hand's grasp. It didn't take long for us to catch two of the brown trout that measured the length of my arm when they were no longer gasping for air.

As the soothing sound of the flowing river filled our ears, our eyes were entertained with the sight of shooting stars in the black sky. I loved being with Bill and wished upon one of those stars that he would always be in my life. My prayers that night were that he would stay safe from harm, and that I was bountifully grateful to God for bringing the man who towered in strength and kindness into my life.

In the morning, the twisting and bouncy journey continued. We stopped once for food despite that my appetite was less than eager for nourishment. I stumbled out of the wagon and took in the area called Great Falls.

Bill said there were a number of canyons and steep cliffs waiting to be explored when we weren't so rushed to get to our destination.

We walked to the Missouri River where he introduced me to a waterfall. I imagined jumping and screaming from the watery ledge into the cool bubbling waters below. I vowed I would return to this place when I was older and didn't live by the sound of a ticking clock.

After Bill tucked the watch into the pocket of his vest he veered the wagon for the United States Cavalry to discuss rounding up horses for its troops.

When we arrived, the town was bustling with people, especially Military men, looking honourable and duty bound in their uniforms. Bill was meeting Sergeant Earl Jones at the saloon so I went to the mercantile in search of candy.

I took no time grabbing handfuls of chewy candy, particularly black licorice, candy beans and taffy. As I continued to fill that paper bag, two men behind me were talking loudly about the outlaw Bill Hickok.

"He ain't the only outlaw in town. Sean Thomas has been seen too," one of the men divulged.

"Well, maybe they run into each other....have a good ole shoot-out right here on the street," the other man suggested.

"If I run into Wild Bill, I tell him to look for Thomas in the brothel across the road. He's always in there."

"How would you know, Clancy?"

"Cause Dhalila's got a big mouth. She's always saying 'why can't you be more like Sean Thomas' and I don't know what that means. She says 'Ophelia has it easy with that stud.' None of them care to tell the Vigilantes just how often Thomas frequents their brothel. Dhalila says the lawmen come in there and stiff 'em all the time."

Both men broke out laughing.

"Hey kid, you gonna pay for that candy?" the storekeeper said so loudly both men went quiet and shot glaring eyes my way.

I slowly took my hand out of the candy jar, nodding erratically.

The storekeeper nodded back at me erratically, holding out his hand.

I nervously tossed two bits into the storekeeper's hand and ran out the front door.

My face felt a deep shade of crimson as I crossed the dry, dusty road. Just as I stuffed a huge piece of taffy in my mouth, a woman approached me.

Her dress was so tight I thought her...well that some things might start popping out. If it wasn't for the taffy gluing my mouth shut, it would have been wide open.

She asked me where my father was.

I gave her a look of terror.

Quickening my pace towards the saloon, I accidently ran into a cranky old man who told me to watch where I was going. Suddenly, I wanted to escape Fort Benton.

Before reaching the swinging doors, a fast tune on the piano was filling the air of the boardwalk.

Peaking in, I looked desperately for Bill, who was at the far end of the room talking to a uniformed officer. He glanced over and waved me in.

My attention was quickly diverted to a man playing lively on the black and white keys. If Momma had taught me such tunes, I wouldn't have fussed so much with piano lessons.

"Patrick, this is Sergeant Earl Jones."

With mouth still preoccupied chewing candy, I nodded and shook his outstretched hand. My hand was so sticky, it got stuck to his palm so much that I thought I'd be going home with Sergeant Jones.

The Sergeant's lips disappeared beneath a thick dark moustache when he smiled, "Pleasure to meet you, son. I see you're enjoying your candy."

With my teeth finally unstuck, I said, "Yes, sir."

"You'll want to watch his teeth, Bill. Dentists are not friendly people," he said, speaking from his most recent experience with tooth extraction.

"Patrick, I have a little more talking to do. Would you like to sit down or wait outside?"

My face went pale. I just wanted to go home, looking anxiously around the saloon.

"Are you feeling sickly?" Bill asked, concerned.

"Maybe he's had too much candy," Sergeant Jones commented.

"I'm fine," I muttered. "I'll just sit there." I pointed to a chair tucked against the wall.

"So, we have an arrangement for next spring?" the Sergeant asked.

"I think that's fine, Lord willing. I'll speak to my men." Bill shook Earl's sticky hand.

"I must tell you that this will be the last time you'll be seeing me," Earl said, wiping his hand clean against dark trousers. "My regiment is transferring to the Seventh Cavalry stationed in the Black Hills."

"Black Hills?" Bill questioned. "Sioux Territory. Why's the Cavalry in Sioux Territory?"

"Gold's just been discovered. We've been ordered to turn out the miners."

Bill sighed deeply, his face turning horribly grim as he sat back in the spindle chair.

"What does the Military plan to do with the Sioux who have a treaty giving them part of South Dakota Territory that includes the Black Hills?"

"I'm not sure," Earl spoke with hesitation.

Bill's head shook in frustrated disbelief. "I wish you luck Sergeant because I believe you'll need it."

I gazed at the Sergeant's dull countenance while the buttons on his navy coat gleamed.

As we walked out of the saloon, I asked Bill if he wanted a piece of taffy. He looked pretty angry so I thought the sweet might cheer him up. He took one and said he'd never try it again. No matter how hard he tried, he couldn't get the stuff out of the deep ridges of his teeth.

Once we were in the wagon amongst tall ancient trees, I peered at Bill who seemed quite distracted and unhappy.

"Patrick, in my life if a man goes against his word, he isn't worth a grain of salt. If a Government goes against its own written word, then all faith in its fairness and honesty is shattered. The Sioux couldn't even read that treaty when it was signed. They will be pushed out again, because the land has something of value that the United States Government greedily wants; and that makes my skin boil. They prey on the few; order them to do things that will inevitably break their spirit and crush them. The Sioux will no longer be a threat, but they'll also become virtually non-existent."

The wagon creaked along while the horses' hooves pounded the hard ground at a walking pace. Bill's mouth took a lengthy pause until I could no longer hold the question that had been nagging me since I left the mercantile.

"Bill, what's a brothel?"

There was another pause as he tried to answer without providing too much detail.

"It's a place where men go and pay for a woman's affections."

"Like quiet talking?" I asked in a confused manner.

"No Patrick, this affection is very noisy and…and unclean. It's lust of the flesh and it's no place for a good Christian man."

I was so disappointed upon hearing that my father was seeking another woman's affections. Maybe if he hadn't been spending so much time in there, he could have found me and Momma. I had already wasted too much of my life hoping he would come home to us. I didn't want him as a father. I prayed that he'd never know me as his son. I was feeling such sickness in my stomach that I thought I might throw up my candy.

Bill was about to move the horses into a trot when he saw my pale and sickly face.

"Patrick," he paused.

I felt another story coming on and at this pace he would have plenty of time to tell it.

"The Sergeant called you son back there."

I nodded, still queasy and uneasy.

"When a child is without parents he can be adopted and his adopted parents would be his mother and father. An adopted father would call that child his son."

He stared ahead, though he now looked uneasy.

"You would be my father, and I would be your son?" I asked, barely audibly. "For how long?"

"If you let me, I'll always be your father," Bill spoke confidently. "Always."

I wanted to hug him but gazed away when my eyes watered and went blurry. "I want to be your son."

We rode on a little farther until I had the courage to ask, "Since you're going to call me your son, can I call you something other than Bill?"

As my timid eyes peered up, his smile assured me.

"I'd agree to anything except old man," he said comically.

"I'd like to call you, Pa," I said with joy.

"Well, then, Pa it is!" Bill announced proudly.

"I'd like to call Mary…..Ma if you think that'd be fine," my voice trembled.

I felt Momma would be fine with that since she was never coming back.

"I think she'd really like that….she would really like that," he replied, gazing away.

Suddenly the evergreens appeared more vibrant a-gainst the pale sky, the sun warmer on my skin, and the bumps along the winding trail less noticeable, sitting beside my Pa.

****

That fall, Mary caught me playing the piano. She was in the garden when I entered the house to change out of my dirt stained clothes. I picked up that soft red flannel shirt again, and the smell of Momma's soap filled my nose as I brushed it against my face. Her image appeared and she hugged me. It was one of the few peaceful memories I had of her since she was gone. I didn't mind memories like that rushing in.

She was still on my mind when I saw the piano.

'Play me a song….play me a song,' her voice whispered.

Momma managed to teach me one classical piece called 'Moonlight Sonata'. Why she forced me to continuously practice that one particular song was beyond my childish grasp. She would just smile as I played it and I loved to see her smile.

Whispering again, she pleaded, 'Play it…..play Moonlight Sonata one more time for me.'

I doubted I could do it without music sheets. After I brushed my fingers over the ivory keys, hitting the wrong notes a few times, I played the somber tune. It felt like Momma was beside me, her long slender fingers guiding mine.

At some point, Mary came in and nearly dropped her basket of vegetables. When I was finished, she squealed in astonishment, "Patrick!"

I almost jumped off of the piano seat.

She rushed over, hugged me, and said what I played was the most beautiful song she'd ever heard.

"Why didn't you tell me you could play the piano?"

Mary proceeded to the rollaway desk and there in her hands were Momma's beloved music sheets.

"The men found what they could," she said, passing them to me. "They were scattered everywhere when they found you."

I smiled sadly, touching the lines of notes Momma would have studied, memorized, practiced, until her fingers played them perfectly.

Mary put her small hand to my face.

"Whenever you're ready, Patrick, I will play her music with you, teach you more songs, and maybe you can teach me the piece you just played."

"Ma," I hesitated. "Could you teach me some lively Irish songs?"

"Lively Irish?" she asked, confused.

"Like you hear in the saloon."

"You mean lively Irish drinking songs." Her laughter filled the room. "I'll try, but we may need your pa for some help," she said, squeezing me. "Patrick, you are such a blessing, my Patrick."

Happily, she kissed my forehead and that made me so happy.

****

Throughout the winter months, Ma and I would play the piano most evenings. She liked to sing the songs. She had a beautiful voice.

Most nights, Pa would read, though the odd time I caught him peering up from the pages of his book or newspaper, eyes smiling, twinkling.

My mornings would be spent in the stable or barn, and my afternoons consumed with reading, writing, and ever despised math. While math was my least favourite subject, my least favourite chore would always be the daily trip to the hen house and that nasty nippy hen I aptly called Feathers. She made such a fuss over me stealing her eggs that her feathers just flew off, floating gracefully to the ground.

One day, I asked if I could pick the chicken for supper with a devilish grin.

Bill said, "Feathers is too old and she's one our best laying hens."

It was true. She popped out eggs faster than I could count them.

That winter brought some frigidly cold days, and on one such day I went with the men to where the river opened wide. Pa needed to refill his small ice house so I watched the men cut large slabs and load it onto the wagon.

Jimmy was his usual jovial self and decided to tell a joke. We all laughed, including me, and as I turned, a sudden gust of bitter prairie wind stole my breath. I coughed and coughed while trying to shake it off, smiling nervously.

When the coughing wouldn't go away and the breathing got a little harder to do, I walked away, my cheeks already rosy from the chilliness, thankfully hiding my embarrassment. I stumbled to the lake figuring a sip of water would end the ceaseless hacking.

I could hear Pa frantically calling me, but I was solely focused on getting to that lake, hastening my wobbling pace as my breaths became shorter and more difficult.

I never got to that lake.

In the blink of an eye, I was in front of a roaring fire surrounded by blankets with Ma handing me warm cider.

"I've never seen sickness come on so fast," his tone expressed great concern.

As the cough subsided, Pa watched me intently.

"You hear that, Mary?"

She listened to my chest. "It's like you have a creak in your ribs, Patrick!"

"I'll go for the doctor," Bill decided.

"I'm fine," I cried frantically. "The wind just took my breath, but I'm fine now."

Bill was dourly shaking his head with determined steps out the front door.

The doctor came out of my bedroom and was given a cup of black coffee as Bill and Mary nervously awaited the diagnosis.

"Patrick's fine…he has asthma and the cold, dry weather can aggravate that condition," he informed. "The wheezing you hear will subside once the inflammation subsides. He must stay indoors, though, on frigid days like these."

"Should he avoid anything else?" Bill asked warily.

"It's hard to say. If this is the first time you've heard it, then it's a good sign. Just keep an eye on him and if he's short of breath or starts coughing, keep him calm and upright."

The doctor's face turned grave. "There is the chance that his breathing can become so rapid that he can't get enough oxygen to his lungs and because of that, I recommend a few things. Mary, give me a pen and paper. These things can be procured from the drug store in Helena."

As the doctor was leaving, I heard him tell Pa that I was one very worried, quiet boy throughout the examination. Though it was true, I thought I was hiding my emotions very well. I'd have to try harder next time.

Pa immediately came to my room. I was lying in my favourite position, staring at the spiderless wall.

"Patrick, come out and stay close to the fire, son," he suggested calmly.

Hesitantly, I did as told with my head hung low to the floor.

Pa sat across from me and said that there was nothing to worry about. He told me exactly what the doctor had diagnosed and more importantly, that I was always to come for help if it ever happened again. The worst part was telling me that I was to stay indoors during days like these, which I felt happened all of the time in the winter.

"What am I supposed to do?" I asked, feeling useless and thought that Bill would find me useless, as well, and not want me anymore.

Pa must have picked up on my panic and despair. Touching my shoulder, he said, "There is much you can do in this house. You can help Mary. You can play that piano. You can read. Come with me, Patrick."

I followed him to the keeping room and the cabinet of books.

"How many books do you see?"

"Twenty?"

"Much more like thirty. These books will teach you things about the world you live in, take you places you've never been, and give you the chance to go on big adventures. Imagining you're some place else may help you deal with some of the fear this asthma brings on."

"What about the horses?" I cried.

"The horses aren't going anywhere. As soon as the weather warms up, I'll have you in that stable cleaning up stalls and feeding them. You have my word. Rest assured, Patrick, you're important to this family, to this ranch."

His smile and quick embrace reassured me.

"Why don't you choose a book and read it in front of the fire. Look to the top shelves for adventure books."

I chose to read a book called 'Last of the Mohicans'. As I walked to the fire, my worry and fear faded away.

"Pa?" I called out.

"Yes, Patrick."

"Can you tell the joke? I couldn't hear how it ended."

We sat together by the fire.

As the flames danced and whirled, Pa spoke lightly. "Jimmy and Mike were sent out to saw ice with a cross-cut saw. They had never sawed ice before. They looked at the ice and then looked at the saw until Jimmy took a penny out of his pocket, and he says 'Now Mike, be fair, heads or tails, who goes below'?"

We laughed together until the aggravating cough returned, bringing a concerned look over Pa's face. That look of concern over me, that look of love over me, made me feel so special, so important, I felt eternally blessed that he took me into his life.

That night, Mary and Bill held each other closely.

"Are you upset about Patrick's ailment?" she asked.

"If I worry, he'll sense it and it'll be a hindrance."

"Will he tame horses?"

Bill nodded confidently. "When the time comes. He has a gentle spirit and a natural way with those horses. I'll teach him to tame horses the way my father taught me. I'll teach Patrick to break horses in a way that they don't break Patrick. I have no doubt that he'll tame any horse that enters his corral."

Mary smiled lovingly and desire filled Bill's heart.

"Are you up for some quiet talking, Mary?"

She gazed into his eyes. "Aye…..I'll always be up for your quiet talking."

Suddenly, coughing filled the silence of the house.

Mary and Bill exchanged worried faces before they were out of their warm bed.

In the morning, thick ice covered my window despite that I was now in the room with the wood stove. I knew it would be the first of many days stuck in the rustic home. Though I never could truly say I had a slow day during that winter.

I taught myself more of Momma's piano music. She would have been truly proud.

I helped Ma in the warm kitchen. There were the monotonous chores like churning butter, peeling vegetables, making candles and soap, and then there were the 'sweet' chores. I eagerly learned to make desserts and more eagerly got to eat samples of my experiments.

Though baking, I found, was less experimental and more of an exact science.

If I used too much flour, the result would be too dry. Too much liquid, and the result would be too mushy. Too much baking powder and the cakes would grow and surpass the edges of the pan. It also made my pancakes rise to unearthly heights. Pa commented that I got the 'cake' part right.

We laughed and ate them anyway with a big splash of molasses. If I didn't use baking powder, my cake was so dense I could hurl it in the air and it wouldn't break when it met the stone wall.

We ate everything I made regardless of how awful it tasted. It just took some creative modifications. I accidentally baked scones with rock salt instead of sugar. They were cut into small pieces, smothered in the sweetest cream, and dotted with currant jam.

Then I made an apple pie and left the peel on the apples. Ma chopped and mashed up that pie and made a spice pudding.

My biscuits could take an eye out. Bill would have had a harder time chopping them than any tree in our forest. We managed to dry and grind them into crumbs to spread over soups and stews.

When I was so full from eating these experimental sweets, I sauntered over to the bookshelf where an adventure was waiting to be discovered by my curious indulgent mind.

One day, I found two books written in a foreign language. When Pa walked in to get warm and pour himself a coffee, I asked about my interesting find.

"I had forgotten these books were still in the cabinet," he paused in recollection.

I knew this would be a short story because he was still standing and didn't offer me any cookies. I ruined that from happening when I became baker of the family.

"Well, one day we moved through the Plains and happened upon a Trader, a very distraught Trader. His horse had, well, I believe the expression is kicked the bucket, keeled over…died. I kindly offered him a horse, and he offered me everything but the shirt on his back. He gave me these books, and at the time, I didn't realize they were in French. Would you like to learn French, Patrick?"

"Yes, please," I replied keenly.

Bill placed his mug on the table, grabbed his gloves and walked out of the warm kitchen.

Minutes later, he returned with Andy.

"Bonjour Patrick, asseyez vous," Andy said, holding out a chair.

He told me that many living in Ottawa spoke English and French. His mother was also French speaking.

Over the next few months and the next few winters, I would learn that French language and read the book titled 'Journey to the Centre of the Earth'.

Despite my busyness in the house, I welcomed the Chinooks that broke the bitter wintry days. The warm massive air was a wonderful natural phenomenon.

I would burst out of the house, saddle and bridle Legend, and spur him into the stable pasture at great speed. The snow was usually a mushy wet slush as the tepid weather warmed the ground.

On this particular occasion, I was so eager to move Legend into a lope that I hastily mounted the horse and got a third of the way into that pasture when the saddle shifted. I found myself flat on the ground spitting out slushy snow. Thankfully, the slush was 'pure' white!

Trey darted over and couldn't hide his amusement as I wiped wetness from my face and clothes.

"You forget to tighten the cinch, boy?"

"My name's Patrick," I stammered. "Just thought I'd try eating this snow before it melted, and it's quite tasty."

With a dash of sugar, the white slush could have been another experiment to sample in the kitchen.

"Then why's your saddle under the horse's belly?" he chortled, fixing it before tapping my head.

I frowned, irked that he touched me, called me boy.

He laughed again, ambling away. "Maybe I let you fix your own mistakes next time, Master cranky-pants."

Chapter 8

Spring arrived, and with it, mornings of dull ashen sky. Trees were beginning to sprout their new tiny leaves as slender grasses peaked up from the dewy ground.

I couldn't fit into my old clothes. My soft red shirt got tucked to the bottom of my dresser for good unless I missed Momma's scent.

I discovered that big ugly machine in the corner of the keeping room was a loom. Ma would make a special fabric called linsey-woolsey, which was simply a weave of linen and wool. The clothing she made kept me warm in the winter, was light in the summer, and best of all, not nearly as itchy as the pure wool clothing I wore back in Virginia City.

We went to Helena for my birthday, and Pa let me pick out a cowboy hat. I got another bag of candy that I was not allowed to share. Then we stayed for supper and saw a Shakespearean play. It was the best day of my life: just me and my parents.

It was also the first time I realized we were a family: a family of people who cared for and respected each other. I felt so loved by these two wonderful people. As my parents watched the play, I watched them with happiness. I laughed, despite that the play was not that funny and made very little sense to me; however, the sounds of the words coming together....were like poetry to my ears.

Momma would have loved this play. I swore I felt her smiling down on me from a celestial place.

Two new chores were added to my list: ploughing the fields and planting seeds. While I was covering another row of dried beans with dark soil, I heard the supper bell. But it should have been called the 'get out of bed, Patrick, bell' as I heard it most mornings when the sun was still sleeping.

I came into the kitchen with a bucket of water which would be warmed on the stove for washing up dishes.

"Have you finished planting?" Bill asked.

"Yes, and I put the plough away and Legend back in the stable," I said matter-of-factly.

"Good, and don't forget to…"

"I know, feed the horses and brush Legend," I said crankily, wishing it was winter again.

Bill was shaking his head as Mary passed him a plate of Irish stew. Before taking one bite, he announced he was leaving for a horse round-up in a few weeks.

Desperately wanting to go, I glimpsed Ma already turning her head from side to side as if she knew my mind. While offering a plate of stew, I searched for the right words to do more convincing.

"I bet you could use another hand rounding up those mustangs," I said zealously while shoveling enormous mounds of stew into my small mouth.

Bill's smiled faded when he peered up from his plate.

"Patrick, slow down, chew your food, and never talk with your mouth full!" he spoke rather condescendingly.

My cheeks were rosy as I conjured more persuasive words to spew from an empty mouth.

"I could wash dishes and clean up after the men so their mess wouldn't bother you so much."

"Let me think about it," he said, glancing up to find Ma staring heatedly at him.

Even I could feel the steam coming off of her body, face beet-red, Irish blood boiling.

I began picking at what was left on my plate.

"Patrick Sullivan, if you're finished with your supper you're excused," Mary said curtly. "Go finish your chores in the stable. I'll wash up the dishes."

If Ma thought she was making my miserable attitude any better, she was dead wrong as I put my dish on the wash table and shuffled my feet towards the door.

I took my time tossing hay into the stalls. When I got to Lincoln, I gave him an earful about having parents who cared more about themselves than what was best for me. I was so disappointed and cranky.

Lincoln neighed and tossed his head as I carelessly threw a mound of hay into his stall. Seems he didn't care for my sulky mood either.

Walking back to the house, I observed the fifteen or so horses that the men had rounded up in the foothills of the mountains. I discovered two colts among the herd and moved their direction until loud muffled voices stopped me in my tracks.

I heard Ma cry out, "You're not taking that child with you! He's too young, it's too dangerous and….."

"Mary, he wants to go, and what better time than with me and the men. We'll protect him! You know that," Bill pleaded.

"What if he has an attack? Will you be up all night tending a fire to keep him warm? You can't protect him from everything!"

"One day he'll leave and he needs to know how to fend for himself. I can teach him all he has to know, to make him strong, and give him confidence. Please, Mary, let me do this for him!"

I didn't understand that she felt like Bill was tearing me from her arms and she wasn't ready to let me go. I didn't realize that her sleepless nights hunched over the Bible while the house rattled from plunging temperatures in the negative digits were solely to keep the home fires burning, to keep me warm. I didn't know she had already lost one son and wasn't ready to take that chance again.

I heard her crying, "No…no…no!" Then the voices stopped.

As I lay in bed, I tried to figure out how to change Ma's mind. I would show her that I was ready to go with Pa…that I was strong enough to come back safely. I would work really hard over the next few weeks to change her willful Irish mind.

I did every chore imaginable, even offering to wash my own clothes. She refused that request, but at least I did offer. I washed dishes, ploughed a new field for hay, planted more seeds, helped cook breakfast and supper, and even learned how to hem a torn shirt.

One night, I just came out and said it.

"I want to go with Pa to the Plains and capture wild ponies! Please Ma!"

I gazed at her with beseeching blue eyes.

She glared back with stubborn green eyes.

"Patrick, I can't let you go."

Out of nowhere, anger welled up inside of me. I thundered out of the kitchen to the stable.

Bill turned to Mary. "I know you just want to protect him, but the truth is, harm could come to him here, out there, anywhere. Patrick's a wise boy. I believe this experience would be good for him, for his spirit and development."

He stood and walked out to the stable. Nothing could prepare him for what he saw.

I ripped Pa's tools from the walls. Ropes, bridles and harnesses were strewn everywhere. I tossed bales of hay as far as I could. The horses started whinnying and freting in their stalls, but I didn't care.

"Are you finished, Patrick?" he asked as I held another bale of hay which fell at the sound of his voice.

"Why are you doing this?"

"How could she be so mean….so selfish? Doesn't she care about what I want?" I cried.

"That's not what I asked. Why are you destroying this stable?"

"Because I'm angry! I'm angry, I hate…."

"Whoa, Patrick! Don't say anything you're going to regret. Sit down on that bale of hay you were so eager to toss around."

I started to protest until Pa spoke firmly, "Now!"

He sat down beside me. He didn't tower over me like my grandpa did, and he surely never hit me like my grandpa did.

"Firstly, your ma is anything but mean. She loves and cares for you deeply and doesn't want to see you get hurt."

Pa peaked over my shoulder, amazed at how quickly I messed up the stable.

"Secondly, you spooked the horses with your display of anger. How would you like it if someone came into your house and spooked you?"

Peering at the horses, I regretted my disregard for them.

"Thirdly, and most importantly, you will always have emotions like anger and frustration just as uncontrollable as the winds that sweep the Plains."

He took my hands in his. "You can, however, control your actions to these feelings. Believe me, Patrick, I'm very unhappy with your display, but I'll not lay a hand on you, or shout at you, or curse at you; and I hope that my example sets you with a good example. Anger begets more anger and that's not what we want."

"I just want to go with you, Pa. It's my happy dream and I just want it to come true so badly," I spoke in a disheartened tone.

"Then tell your ma just what you've told me. Tell her how much you're upset that your happy dream my not come true…but not before this stable is completely cleaned up."

I took in the mess I created and was truly afraid because I didn't seem to have any control over what I had done.

Sensing my fear, Pa hugged it away.

"All you have to do is clean it up, speak to your ma, and then go to bed. That's all," he said plainly. "Stop feeling sorry, angry, regretful. Just do…do as I have asked."

When I finally got to bed, that night, I thought about his reaction to my uncontrolled anger. I still couldn't figure out how he could stay so calm and wondered if I would ever have that kind of control over my feelings. If I was anything like my grandpa, I'd be doomed.

****

The next morning, I awoke to a big surprise. Ma had changed her mind. I could go to the High Plains with Pa. She said she wanted my happy dream to come true and it did.

Pa showed me what to pack for such a journey. We could be gone as long as a month.

Our chuck wagon was full: food, blankets, tents, lamps, shovels, cooking pots and utensils, weapons, bandages, lots of rope and clothing. Too much clothing, Pa said as he fought with Ma about bringing all of my chunky sweaters and trousers.

I was so worried she'd start fretting, I layered my clothes: must have worn two undershirts under a flannel shirt tucked under a dark grey sweater and jacket. I was sweating like a horse, but it was worth it to see that she was subdued, her face no longer as red as her stiffly pinned hair.

I brought my bow and quiver of arrows. Pa also brought supplies like coffee, tea, and heavy wool blankets that he would give to the Indians in appreciation for being on their land.

We left on an early morning in early June. As Legend moved away, I gazed at the ranch and waved to Ma as she wept.

We were a party of five men and one boy.

Moving south along the winding Missouri River, we joined the Montana trail and eventually left the town of Helena and the gulches that now ran empty of the 'easy to find gold' in a trail of dust.

I felt very small as our horses clopped through canyons and mountains lined with evergreens for as far as my eyes could see, that is, until we reached a spot where the Missouri river confluences with the Madison, Jefferson and Gallatin rivers.

We would overnight at the mouth of the Madison and Gallatin Rivers before traveling into the morning sun to another river that flowed across the territory called Yellowstone. Beyond it to the south branched the Big Horn River, its mountains, and Indian Territory.

Our first meal away from home was not unlike any other I'd have eaten on the ranch. Ma had packed buttermilk biscuits, dried fruit, hard-boiled eggs and cheese. Jimmy sliced up a smoked ham. I devoured most of the pickled vegetables for the men didn't seem to be too keen on what they called green and red things.

Mike was gumming a biscuit which made his words even harder to understand.

As I was wiping my fingers of beet juice with one of Ma's well-worn napkins, Jimmy interpreted, "He's happy yer with us, Patrick. Ye'll see and learn a lot."

With several miles to travel before nightfall, we ate heartily and hastily.

When the brilliant orange sun grew large and began its descent behind the Rocky Mountains, we stopped to make camp. My blue eyes admired the orange and red sky that created a believable horizon above the jagged rocks until I was loudly summoned by Pa to help Andy build the tents.

Strong Bull, who magically appeared from a thick haze of dirt, joined us and worked with Mike to chop wood and build a roaring fire as Jimmy and Trey prepared supper. Jimmy was making cornbread skillet while Trey made a stew with beans, cured pork, and a hint of beer, discreetly added.

Naturally, I silently called it beer stew. Our first meal around the campfire was one I will never forget. We were already a peculiar bunch with three Irish men, two Americans, a Canadian, and an Indian. Jimmy had a mouth full of jokes and funny stories.

"An Irishman, Canadian and Indian go to te bar. Te Irishman says 'a pint of yer dark ale laddie', te Canadian says 'a mug of beer, please' and te Indian, well te Indian just points to te beer and ten te bar. Te Indian takes a swig of dark beer and spits it out, te Canadian says it's too heavy for his stomach, but te Irishman, te Irishman says tis is his morning ale; has it wit his toast and eggs, every morning."

Mike commented about the story in his usual mumbled fashion.

"Ye see, Patrick, ye drink dark ale in te morning, like Mike has all tese years and ye'll sound like Mike."

Laughter broke out, deafening nature's sounds.

"I've got one," Trey boasted.

"Is it clean?" Bill asked warily.

"Clean enough," Trey replied flatly. "Nellie says to Clancy….Nellie says 'Clancy we've been married a long time. You're good lookin' and I think you've slept with a lot 'o women. I won't be mad but I would like to know how many if any. Clancy says 'my lovely Nellie, you should know I never slept with anyone but you my darling. All the rest I was awake'."

The men chuckled again.

So did I even though it wasn't really funny. I wondered what was so special about a man who was up and did a lot of quiet talking.

I looked at Pa as he swished the coffee in his tin cup. He looked pretty tired.

Andy pulled out a harmonica and played a tune.

"Ye won't be playing God Save te Queen on tat bloody ting, cause I be ramming it down yer troat if ye were, so far it'd never come out!" Jimmy stammered.

Andy stopped abruptly. "I'm very patriotic, Jimmy; miss my homeland."

"Ten maybe ye should go back tere! I give ye a wee push if ye like," he said, rising.

"Jimmy, calm down," Bill spoke evenly. "Andy, play something else."

Andy played a cowboy tune, and Trey started singing to lighten the mood.

> "Oh give me a home where the buffalo roam,
> Where the deer and the antelope play,
> Where seldom is heard a discouraging word
> And the sky is not cloudy all day...."

Trey's singing was interrupted by a sudden coughing fit. He said his throat was too parched to carry on as he glared at Pa, who kept yawning.

"Well, I'll turn in," he said. "Patrick come along."

"Could I stay up just a little longer, Pa, please? I'm not tired just yet."

I was having too much fun listening to the voices that spoke over the yellow crackling flames.

"Fine, but not much longer," Bill urged with eyes directed at me. "Night, men."

Soft farewells popped out of almost every mouth surrounding that blazing fire.

"Night, Bill. Hope you sleep like a log," Trey sighed, mumbling under his breath, "cause we sure won't once that snoring starts."

"Trey, shut yer gob!" Jimmy spat out.

"Actually I've something else I can do with my gob. Just need to see if Patrick's up for it."

Trey eyed me curiously.

"Trey te boy is just a wee ting. Leave him be," Jimmy warned.

"I'm not a wee thing! I'm ten," I said proudly. "And up for anything you got, Trey."

"Well, I see the Irish comin' out of you now," Trey announced.

"I'm not actually Irish. I'm American," I confessed.

"You want to be Irish, Patrick, 'cause you don't have to be from Ireland to be Irish, and you don't have to know Gaelic to be Irish, right Mike?"

Mike nodded. He obviously understood English. Just didn't seem able to speak it.

"It's as easy as following an Irish tradition," Trey informed, slowly pulling out a flask. "You see, Patrick, we like to have a wee drink the first…and maybe the second and third night out on the trail. Quell our nerves before we go rounding up."

"So that's why you think you're Irish?" Andy spoke with cynicism. "Because you carry the Irish brew and follow Irish tradition. Well," he figured, "what the heck! Pass me a cup of the brew."

"Pass me a cup, Mike."

He smiled his toothless grin, handing Trey a tin cup.

"Trey, ye might be tinking twice about tis. He's just a wee lad," Jimmy cautioned.

I was not just a wee lad. I was ready for this so I held out my hand, grabbed the cup half filled with Irish brew and boldly gulped it back like it was water. I coughed because it burned very unlike water.

"We should all toast Patrick on his move to bein' Irish!"

Trey passed his hip flask after taking a big swig.

My unsteady hands clasped the metal bottle while Trey nodded encouragingly. "I just don't like the way it burns."

"That'll go away," he asserted. "Have another taste."

I swallowed boldly, feeling more like a man than a wee lad. "You're right. It doesn't feel so bad now."

All of me tingled and felt comfortably warm in the cool night air.

"I have another joke," Trey began. "An Englishman, a Scott, and an Irishman walked into a saloon. Each ordered a pint of beer. Then a fly landed in each one's beer." Trey belched loudly but quickly resumed. "The Englishman, turning slightly green, pushed his beer away and asked for another one. The Scott took the fly out, shrugged, and drank his beer. The Irishman pinched the fly between fingers and yelled, 'Spit it out! Spit it out'!"

My chuckle snorted loudly, so seeing Jimmy twisting that fly. I was feeling so good, I loved being Irish.

"Could I have one more drink?" I asked. "Think I feel the Irish wearing off."

With that comment, everybody chortled except for Strong Bull. He didn't laugh at any of it. In fact, I forgot he was sitting by the campfire, quietly puffing on his pipe, shifting solemn eyes my way from time to time. I thought he should try being Irish too, offering the brew, but he shook his sober head. So I took another swig before Jimmy ripped it out of my hands.

"Tat's enough, Patrick. I tink yee've had more than enough to drown out yer pa's snoring."

"I don't think I can ever have enough to drown out his snoring! He told me once he had to reinforce the house. His snoring shook the foundation so bad," I giggled, but it was short-lived at the sight of Strong Bull's stoic face. I gave him a new name that night: Stubborn Ox, 'cause of the way he didn't want to partake in our drinking.

"I have a poem," I hiccupped. "I'd like to say before I go to bed."

I smiled hoping I could remember all of the words.

"I'm an Irish cowboy, can't you see," I hiccupped.
"Heading along the trail, feeling free.
Got my hat hung down low,
Holding on to it, so it don't blow," I hiccupped again.
"Got my pa by my side,
Makin' a good stride.
Looking around takin' in all the scenes,
Just don't want Jimmy to have any more beans!"

Waving a hand over my nose, I hiccupped. I'd take Pa's snoring over Jimmy's stinky farts any day.

The men chortled while I caught a small smile on Strong Bull's face before being ushered to bed.

Thankfully Pa's snoring rhythm never changed as I literally crawled over him to get to my little corner.

But I couldn't sleep, for my head spun while Pa sounded like an angry pig. Then a wave came over me, starting in my stomach and moving to my throat. I crawled over Pa but didn't make it out of the tent before I was sick. So much for being Irish!

In the morning, Pa was the first to rise and was gone by the time I sat up and rubbed my muddled head. I saw my beer stew at the edge of the tent and figured I should find him and explain, but he was nowhere to be found.

"Jimmy, have you seen my pa?"

"He went to te river wit a pail. Should be back soon. Ye look like ye need some water, lad."

He took my arm and sat me by the fire.

I watched Pa slowly saunter towards us, his pail brimming with water. He didn't look too happy so I tried to stand, but Jimmy pushed me back down.

Trey was sitting across from me when the water gushed down on him.

Pa squatted face to face with him and said tersely, "Firstly, Patrick is my family and family's the most important thing to me, and you'll never be jeopardizing my family with your shenanigans. Secondly, there is to be no alcohol in my camp, not in your flask, not in our food, not in my wagon. Thirdly, if you can't obey my first and second rules get out of my camp before I take you horse and leave you with the wolves!"

He thrust the pail at Trey's chest saying he'd need it to clean up his tent.

Trey looked furious, turning his anger my direction for mere seconds, even though it felt like several minutes.

I felt badly for letting him down.

Over the next few days, I stayed pretty quiet adjusting to life in the saddle. Though my legs ached and my body tired, I was thrilled when we arrived in the High Plains. My first impression was wide and flat place. A few lonely trees scattered this landscape. Desert flora like the silver sagebrush, yucca, cactus, and prairie grasses, thrived in this arid land. It provided such a contrast to the western Montana landscape, its Rocky Mountains and abundance of tall evergreens.

We passed some buffalo, which looked like shaggy cows with humped backs and short horns. I was amazed at how many were grazing the open pastures. Bill said there were many more, but the trampling of grasses and mass hunting of them for their skins and meat were causing their numbers to dwindle.

Even though it was spring, there was a cool breeze flowing freely across the empty space. The wild grasses appeared as though they were waving at us. Pa said that the summers were sweltering and the winters were bitterly cold so this was the best time to search for wild horses.

When we entered Big Horn, the landscape changed again. It was a combination of juniper woodlands, Douglas firs, Ponderosa pines, and clusters of shrubs. Spring was in full bloom and the ground was carpeted with deep purple and yellow wildflowers.

As we slowed down, an Indian camp came into sight. The area was dotted with triangular shaped tents which I later found out were called tipis. Poles stuck out from the tops of the tipis, as if they were reaching to touch the sky.

I looked through Pa's spyglass to find people: men with their wives and children, dressed in buckskin clothing with colourful embroidered details that sparkled in the sun. We were about half a mile from the tribe when we stopped and waited. The Sioux claimed the land stretching from Big Horn River east to the Tongue and Powder Rivers as their hunting grounds.

Four Lakota galloped towards us. These native men had white feathers in raven black hair, their darkened faces holding austere countenances. Two wore buckskin shirts while the upper bodies of the remaining two were bare, covered by what looked like a plate of thin shiny bones.

A few children darted over and crept around the Indians' ponies with curious eyes. I appreciated being able to watch them because the sight of the men made my heart quicken and my entire body go uncomfortably stiff. While Pa and Strong Bull got off of their horses to join these Native men, I remembered the last time I saw Indians. Even though it was brief, that day would forever be the worst day of my life.

I began gawking at the one who moved his broad lips. He was the palest and had a long beak nose, though his high cheekbones were similar to those of Strong Bull. He appeared decidedly stern as he greeted Pa, reminding me of my grandpa's expression on many occasions.

My attention got captured by a Lakota girl, who started chasing after another until they were just a few feet from me. The taller girl had long black hair that shimmered and flowed in the breeze, her smile fearless when she peered at me. She was pretty in her deerskin dress of dazzling red and blue beads. The shorter girl ran right into her, prompting the older one to push her to the grassy ground. The scene reminded me of my cousins often pushing each other onto the forest floor. I smiled at the familiar sibling banter, feeling more at ease.

The older girl turned and caught me grinning. Her fascinated gaze held until she got called away by one of the Lakota men.

My father proceeded to call me over.

I slowly dismounted and took apprehensive steps to the group of men while Jimmy and Trey began carrying over flour, sugar, coffee, tea, blankets and a number of small boxes.

"Patrick, this is White Bear, leader of this Minnecoujou band," Pa said slowly.

White Bear scanned me from top to bottom with a slight nod of his head.

Warily nodding in return, I tried to keep myself presently minded. Glancing at Pa, he motioned me back to my horse with a light smile.

After he spoke brief words with White Bear in his native tongue, the Indians loped away.

We steered our horses west and made camp in a dry coulee sheltered by steep mountains.

Pa showed me where the corral was, still standing from previous years. Soon enough, he hoped it would be full of mustangs. With a twinkle in his eye, he told me to watch for the ones with special markings.

"The Spanish breeds," he said with admiration, "descendants of Africa…Arabian tribes."

He taught me that these horses could live on little water and poor forage: that they had exceptional hearts and were tough and resilient, which was why it would take every man to maneuver them into the wooden enclosure.

Firstly, we had to find the horses. Pa said if we waited long enough, some would run right past our camp. Otherwise, the search would begin by the streams and rivers.

He took me to a winding ravine where there must have been a band of twelve or so meandering along the water's edge. I turned the opposite direction to find another band of thirsty ponies. They looked peacefully calm, dipping their heads in the soft flowing waters with backs shining in the warm sun.

The mustangs were short and lean: their colours, mostly browns and blacks, which starkly contrasted the few that were white and slate grey. Some were patches of colours distinctly called Pintos. I squinted to find the markings, but the distance was too great.

We went back to the corral where I was ordered to stay well back.

Pa and the men took their lariats and whips to the ravine while I waited and watched, and waited and watched. They would chase after the mustangs, hoping to slow them through the path of trees that would act like a chute to the corral.

I was getting quite impatient all alone staring and waiting. Mosquitoes kept attacking my neck. As I was smacking and flicking away their bloody corpses, the ground shook before I heard or saw anything. Then came the rolling thunder, followed by billowing brown clouds that blurred my sight.

When the dust settled, Andy, Mike, and Pa were on one side while Trey, Strong Bull, and Jimmy were charging up the other. They were all flashing their whips against the hard ground as the horses started to slow. The men made it look easy as the mustangs funneled into the corral. Pa said the search would continue until the wooden rails were heaving with horses.

While he and Jimmy examined the horses eagerly searching out a rare blue one, or the ones with stripes along their backs, or withers, or legs, my eyes kept wandering to Trey and Andy, mustanging. Disappearing past tall trees, they soon re-appeared chasing horses with their slithering lariats.

Andy was the fastest rider I'd ever seen. He roped a chestnut mare on his first try and never lost his balance despite her whirling and rocking on hind hooves. I hoped I'd be able to go mustanging one day.

While the men set up camp and made supper, I went exploring. Moving up and down the uneven terrain, I reached the base of the east mountain, already winded. Filling my chest full of air, I began climbing the ridge that was as steep as a horse's face and got so high I could wave over to the miniature men. The mountain lured me to climb more, but when I reached up, a tiny voice called out to me. It was so difficult to hear over my heavy breathing, it could easily have been ignored. But the vigorous flapping of Pa's arms was undeniable.

Descending to the forest of evergreens, bow and arrow in hand, I searched for rabbits and prairie chickens, which are just squirrels.

I happened upon a jackrabbit just three yards away and held my wheezy breath, silently taking aim. I missed the hopper by mere inches. Momma would have said 'a miss is as good as a mile'.

Someone giggled behind me. I turned to find the taller Lakota girl with the fearless smile. She got very serious when I glanced her way, so I smiled shyly.

She giggled again.

I cautiously approached as she held a basket filled with various roots, pine needles, wild onions, and a type of berry I'd seen before but had never eaten. Pointing to the fattened berry, she spoke about it. I assumed she wanted me to try it so I took one. More foreign words flowed from her sweet mouth but I just nodded plainly, motioning it'd be put in my mouth. She watched intently as I bit into the berry which made my mouth pucker at its bitterness. I forcefully swallowed it and squeezed out a smile of pleasure. She offered a handful, and I hastily stuffed them in a pant pocket.

I pointed at myself, saying, "Patrick."

She pointed to herself. "Nawaji."

An older boy appeared and spoke callously to her.

She grinned softly, waving goodbye.

I arrived at suppertime and was promptly told to wash up. As the beef stew was being ladled out of the cast iron pot, my pa kneeled, his eyes square on mine.

"Patrick, I don't want you going far from this camp, and I don't want to see you on that mountain.

I guess a look of 'why?' escaped without any words from my mouth.

"This land has many dangers. There are poisonous snakes, black bears, and, and possibly Indians that are not so friendly."

The part about the Indians sent a chill down my bony spine; however, I peered at the mountain with longing. Biting my tongue, I gave an obedient nod.

By the time I got a taste of the beef stew, my weary head nearly plunged into it. The fire didn't help, entrancing me into tranquil sleepiness.

Jimmy was laughing heartily as my head bobbed this way and that way.

"Patrick, best ye go to bed now, before yer Pa comes in tere and shakes yer ground," he advised with much amusement in his eyes.

He was right, though. I didn't hear Pa come in, sleeping undisturbed until one in the morning. When I did wake, his mouth thunderously opened and closed, leading me to such desperation, I clasped a pillow over it wondering if he would be muted. Nope. His breathing just became more muffled but still too loud.

Strong Bull was sitting by the campfire, mesmerized by its bright flames until I appeared.

I sat beside him and inhaled the smoke that puffed from his mouth.

"Can't sleep," I whispered. "Pa's too loud,"

Strong Bull nodded.

I felt something sticky in my pocket and stood to find the crushed berries Nawaji had given me earlier. I scraped them out and threw them into the fire. I didn't even want to lick my hand.

A small smile formed on Strong Bull's face. "Pemmican," he said softly.

I nodded, realizing these berries mixed with dried meat formed, "Pemmican," I replied.

"Strong Bull, how do you say peace in Lakota?"

He glanced my way. "Wolakota   tókhel Lakȟótiya ehápi he?"

I thought, wow! That's a lot of words for peace.

He recognized my bewilderment. "How you say in Lakota, peace."

"Oh, how you say in Lakota," I said in thought.

I asked him how you say in Lakota, "Hello," and how you say in Lakota, "How are you?" I kept thinking about the next time I'd see Nawaji and ask her these questions. As my heavy eyes turned to the fire, its hypnotizing flames put me into a drowsy state.

Strong Bull must have sensed my impending sleep. He brought over a pillow and blanket, and I slept far enough away from the incessant snoring that it didn't bother me anymore.

Morning came too soon. Since I was already outside, I was awoken by breakfast preparations. Jimmy had sore spots on his bottom and was trying to find someone to look at it.

Mike glared at me, speaking a slew of consonants, pointing "yr tn t pk."

I eyed him strangely, vigorously shaking my head. There was no way I was looking at Jimmy's bottom…not after the smells that came out of there every night.

After breakfast, Pa and the men travelled east in search of more horses. I stayed with Jimmy where he thought it wise to teach me geography of Ireland while I washed dishes. I escaped his ceaseless talking to go hunting, however, I was really searching for Nawaji.

I returned empty handed, though the men did not. More horses filled our corral.

Strong Bull urged me to go hunting again. I followed his footsteps until he raised his hand. There was a jackrabbit nibbling on greens ten yards ahead of us. He motioned for me to aim, whispering, "Huhi, huhi, slow."

I took my time but missed the rabbit by mere inches, successfully striking a juniper tree instead. Strong Bull was triumphant though: his smooth, quick and quiet motion getting the next two rabbits. He showed me how to prepare them before being passed on to Trey who did not do his usual whisky marinade.

I brought out my candy to share; however, Andy and Trey were the only takers. Every one else passed on my generous offer.

"Just don't give any of yer candy to Mike," Jimmy advised. "He has tree teet…can't lose anymore."

Pa still had taffy in his teeth from the last time. Trey and Andy picked through it though, eating half the bag.

"Want any more of tis rabbit, Patrick?" Jimmy asked. "We need to fatten ye up."

"No, Ímapi yelo," I replied, rubbing my tummy.

"Well," Jimmy proclaimed. "Bill, it looks like he may be more Indian tan Irish.

Trey piped in, "Yeah, we'll have to find the Indian name for skinny like runt."

They looked to Strong Bull for an interpretation but he wasn't taking any part in this fun. He looked at me with lightness in his eyes for the first time.

Chapter 9

After two weeks of searching through the Plains we rounded up close to seventy wild mustangs. Pa felt that was sufficient enough so we headed home.

I returned to the Sullivan Ranch, dirty, elated, and full of fond memories. While Ma made supper, I took a chilly bath in the Missouri River.

When I returned, I chattered non-stop about meeting the Lakota Indians, especially Nawaji, the horse charge to the corral, and the campfire jokes. I never made mention about drinking whisky or Pa's words to Trey, though I fondly remembered him saying that family was most important to him.

I still worried about Trey. He growled at me with cold eyes amidst a grimacing face despite my sympathetic glances.

By the time supper was done, my head bobbed to and fro from sheer exhaustion. I dragged my tuckered body to bed and slept the whole night regardless of Pa's reverberating snoring.

I couldn't wait for the next horse round-up but that probably wouldn't be for another year or two.

Pa wouldn't let me help break the horses. He said quite honestly that I was not ready and not strong enough yet. I had to contend myself with naming the mustangs and resuming my chores.

That winter, a man from the Cavalry came to see Pa. His name was Sergeant Scott Duncan. When he came out of the stable, his hands moved faster than his mouth, motioning that he'd take all of the tamed horses for a hefty price. He was kindly escorted into the kitchen where Ma served him her specialty, bread pudding.

I enjoyed having the Sergeant around because I never got this dessert in the afternoon.

"Why so anxious for more horses, Sergeant Duncan?" Bill probed with furrowed brows. "Our last delivery was just months ago."

I watched as the Sergeant's forkful of pudding stayed hovering in air while he answered Pa.

"We anticipate some Indian conflict within the next few months. The Sioux were ordered to reservations by the end of January. It is now March and some tribes have not complied with the Government's wishes," he said quite succinctly.

"Government's wishes…you mean demands don't you. We must be careful to use the correct wording. We wouldn't want to get confused unlike over that treaty signed by the Sioux granting them land rights over the Western part of South Dakota. The wording on that document must have been pretty confusing to be so totally ignored," Bill said matter-of-factly

"Mr. Sullivan," Sergeant Duncan spoke abruptly, dropping his forkful of pudding to raise hands in defense. "I take orders from the United States Government. I don't make the decisions. I've been ordered to purchase more horses and have come with a great deal of money to make that purchase. Our mounts from the east arrive too sporadically. Besides, your horses are….well they're more suited for our western conflicts."

He pulled out a large envelope filled with paper money. "The United States Cavalry is willing to purchase these horses for one hundred dollars a head!"

Bill sat back, his chair noticeably creaky in the silence of the room. It was a great deal of money, but he looked angered that the Sioux tribes were being forced off their land into reservations.

"I'll have to think about providing horses for 'our' military. You can have some of the horses in my stable, but I'll have to think about taming others for your....the cause."

"I'll leave this money with you. Trust it'll be returned if you change your mind. Mrs. Sullivan, thank you for your hospitality," Sergeant Duncan smiled politely, tipping his hat.

"I'll see you in the stable momentarily," Bill said as he closed the front door.

"Do you think there'll be trouble here with the Sioux?" Mary asked fretfully. "I'll not be wanting the money if it'll cause this family harm."

"The Cavalry will get their horses whether they come from this immigrant's ranch or not. There's a lot of money on that table which would keep this place running smoothly for a while."

"How much money is it, Pa?" I asked curiously.

"That's a good question, Patrick. One you should be able to answer if you're going to run your own ranch one day. The Cavalry want fifty horses and they're willing to pay one hundred dollars a head. When you have the answer, come out and say farewell to Moonlight and the others."

I reached for the Sergeant's untouched pudding.

Without turning from the washstand, Ma warned icily, "Don't you be touching that man's pudding! You'll spoil your supper!"

****

Another birthday came and passed for me. I turned eleven, and Pa gave me a pocket watch. He thought I should know what time I woke up in the middle of the night, and if it was any earlier than six in the morning, I was to go back to bed.

On one such morning, I awoke and everything was dark. Taking my watch to the window, I discovered it was only one-thirty. I headed for the stable as I often did around that time. The air was cool and crisp, the snow brighter than the stars in an opaque sky.

The only light in the stable came from the moon that waxed and waned through heavy clouds, so I squinted to make out Lincoln and Taffy. However, Lincoln was acting strangely, his arched head whinnying and swaying from side to side; so I lit a lamp and placed it safely on the stool outside of his stall. Stretching to stroke and relax him, I glimpsed movement out of the corner of my eye.

It was a young Indian, possibly sixteen or seventeen, slowly rising. His face was filled with surprise and defiance.

Lincoln was between us when the blade of a knife shone in his hand.

He was trembling.

I was trembling.

Not wanting any harm to come to Lincoln, my voice quivered, "Wolakota! Wolakota! Wolakota! Peace, go now!" I motioned for him to leave.

Cautiously tugging on Lincoln's mane, I led him out of the stall while silently praying for God to keep us safe from the Indian's sharp blade. I remained behind my wall of horse as he stepped lightly around us, his dark eyes never leaving mine.

"Wolakota! Wolakota!" I kept repeating even after he shot me a baffled face before fleeing the stable.

Pa was informed about my encounter with the Indian, and though he said I was very brave, I was authoritatively banned from the stable during those early morning hours.

He worried about whether he should leave the ranch for the round-up of mustangs the Cavalry were so willing to pay dearly for.

Regardless of his decision, I was to stay with Ma. Jimmy would remain, as well, in case we had any more Indian threats.

Pa hired three cowboys to make the trip to the High Plains. Strong Bull hadn't been reachable. Pa wished he could have talked to him, for if so, he'd never have left the homestead.

During that second week of June, I watched as the sagebrush men clucked to their horses, chuck wagon following closely behind, clanking pots and tinware.

Ma was incredibly nervous as Pa pulled out of sight. She clung to me so tightly, she made me incredibly nervous. She claimed we all had intuition. Pa called it a feeling in his gut. She wished Bill had listened to hers.

****

During the time that Pa was away, I was busier than a one-armed wallpaper hanger, grooming the remaining horses and mucked out their stalls; continued planting, weeding and mending fences; including the one that sent messy pigs fleeing and screeching through the pasture until I was caked in mud, my clothes sticking like skin to weary bones.

When I came in at noon, sweating, filthy, hands stiffly sore, Jimmy was comfortably chatting with Ma.

He alleged that he was keeping her from being too lonely.

I rudely spat out that she liked being lonely…did it most of the time while Pa and I worked the ranch.

Ma forced me to apologize to him so I grabbed my food, making it 'to go' as I stormed out the door in frustration.

Lincoln was in the corner of the stable pasture shaded by four tall Pine trees.

"Hope Pa gets back soon," I grumbled, "my hands have blisters, and Jimmy keeps nattering on in an effusive way to Ma's lonely ears."

I took the last bite of my ham and cheese sandwich while holding the apple in my left hand. Lincoln boldly grabbed that apple, nearly taking two fingers with it.

Scolding him, I pried half of it out of his mouth before he nervously galloped away. I lazed on the thin blades of grass, hands behind my head, figuring I deserved a rest.

The slight breeze swaying the boughs of the trees made a hypnotic rhythm, obscuring the sun from time to time.

I must have dozed off for Nawaji appeared and offered another chokecherry: the name so apt for a berry that chokes one with its acrid bitterness. I said no politely and she got very sad. She looked beyond me, and I became very curious. Turning, I found Momma watching us. When I peered back to Nawaji, she was gone.

Something was wetting my lips. My eyelids fluttered open to see Lincoln nuzzling my face. I pushed him away rather harshly.

He jumped.

I bolted out of the way.

Now fully awake, I was ready to resume my chores when horses approached the ranch.

I ran the quarter mile in lightening speed as Pa and his men came through the front gate. When I reached him, he squeezed me tightly until he saw how out of breath I was.

"Let's go see, Mary," he said, his arm tightly around me until we were in the house.

Pa sat me in a chair while he embraced Ma.

Jimmy stood up with much disappointment on his less than joyful face. Eyeing his coffee, I figured I'd drink it all up and add more disappointment to it.

His garrulous nature went strangely quiet as I put the empty cup down, smiling devilishly. I also realized something more important than upsetting him. The coffee settled my breathing quicker than anything else I'd ever tried.

At supper, Pa spoke of his travels to Big Horn and his quick retreat from Big Horn. By the time he was back, the most famous battle of all Indian battles would be over.

I would learn from Pa's newspaper that the Battle of Little Bighorn was the last battle Custer and the Seventh Cavalry would ever fight in. He, along with two hundred and fifty soldiers, including Sergeant Jones, were killed.

I would learn from the men in the bunkhouse the grizzly details about their deaths. It happened after I offered to bring over a warm dried peach pie.

I made it just like Mable taught me. It was probably the last good memory to come from the Wilkes ranch: her protective arms around me, dark fingers scattering light flour across the table, and strong but gentle hands kneading and rolling the dough to make a fine shell. She reiterated how she made the flakiest crusts of all the cooking slaves in Pulaski County!

When I saw the peaches on a dusty shelf in a Helena mercantile, I smiled. Mable would be proud. Her recipe was now mine.

How I wished my grandpa felt me worthy enough to teach me to hammer in a nail, to saw the wood, to build a good memory of him.

Even so, any recollections of those years were few and far between. Who could blame me for having a wandering mind while I was there, dreaming of brighter pastures, listening to my pet rocks speak with voices louder than the shouting ones in nearby rooms, or for imagining being on distant mountain tops too far from angry hands to reach me. My memories, if I could hang them on a wall, wouldn't cover half my bedroom.

As I carried that pie, garbled voices echoed across the spring fields but came in clear as a bell when I approached the door.

"It was two shots that killed him," Andy announced, speaking of Custer.

"I wonder if they mutilated his body like they did the others," Trey spoke with irritation.

"Where ye be hearing tis from?" Jimmy inquired.

"Straight from the horse's mouth in Fort Benton."

"Thought you were just visiting whores," Andy said.

"Yah, and havin' the odd drink every now and then at Callahan's saloon," Trey divulged. "These boys were all fired up. One of 'em, said he was part of Gibbon's column, survived a club attack, head all bandaged up. When he returned to the field to bury the soldiers, the dead Indians were all gone, but the soldiers….stripped, mutilated, scalped."

I must have pressed my head against the door for it creaked, and the next thing I knew, swung open. I came tumbling into the room, peach pie wobbling out my hands and onto the floor.

"Patrick," Trey growled.

"Just…just dropping off a pie," I stammered.

"You got the drop part right, now scoot," he sneered. "Before I box your ears!"

Chapter 10

In my twelfth year, we were making plans to leave the Sullivan ranch for another round-up; so I was too busy to notice I had another growth spurt until Ma pointed it out.

"Patrick Sullivan," she said crisply. "You'll not be leaving the house with those pants on."

I was already at the front door, hand twisting the knob, when I glanced at my suspendered pants, hanging well above the ankles. "I don't think the horses will care, Ma."

She looked at me hotly. Her look could melt the wick of a candle without any flame.

"You'll not be leaving this house with those pants on. Go to the keeping room and take them off. Away with you, now!"

I stomped to the keeping room and stripped the pants off. She turned over the pant leg and there was no hem: just frayed fabric.

"Augh!" she sighed as she took the tape measure and got too close to my inseam.

"Patrick Sullivan, I want to get the proper fit!"

"You gonna make 'em right now, Ma? I have work to do and I won't be doing it in my drawers!"

"Go and find yourself a pair of pants with a hem I can let down. Go away with you now!" she said, deeply frustrated.

I tore through my dresser leaving a pile of clothes strewn on the floor until I found a hemmed pair and angrily stomped to the keeping room.

"Sit down, Patrick Sullivan, and don't you be scratching the back of your neck or stomping your foot in my house!"

I wondered why she never yelled at Pa like that. I thought it was very unfair.

"Ma?"

"Yes," she answered, busily cutting at the hem's thread.

"Pa said there were lots of men coming across the Ocean on the boat but very few women. Why did you choose Pa?"

Ma looked up from her cutting, perplexed. "Why did I choose him? Oh, Patrick, it could have been because your father wasn't throwing up. Nothing worse than a grown man throwing up. It could also have been his smile. He has a wonderful smile."

She grinned warmly and stopped cutting away at the hem.

I was starting to regret my curiosity.

"It also could have been........his strong arms. I knew those strong arms could be put to good use building a home, tending to a field, and holding me when I was shivering. I shivered a lot on that big boat."

Standing to take the pants, I could see why, towering over Ma's short, slender frame by at least five inches. I felt I'd be considered very tall for twelve, though anybody would feel that way beside Ma.

Despite her small size, her strong Irish blood and unbelievable strength put me to shame everyday. She was always the first to rise, last to bed, and some nights never reached the bed at all. There was never a chore too hard for her to complete, and I was in utter awe of her.

Pa told me to watch out for the powerful gale in her tiny package or I could get blown to shreds.

"But they would be lies, Patrick," she stated, interrupting my thoughts, "for I didn't choose Bill. He chose me," she spoke matter-of-factly. "Why do you think he came to America?"

"To capture wild horses in the plains of Montana," I answered hesitantly.

"How would Bill know there were wild horses in Montana?"

My mouth opened, but no sound came out for I truly didn't know how he would know.

"Bill didn't tell you he came to America chasing after a girl, a poorly catholic Irish boy chasing after a protestant girl?"

I didn't know how to answer, but her harsh face made me very nervous and very scared for Pa.

"It could have been a girl," I said most fervently.

"How did he say we got the money to get here?"

"Uh…there was this man who made John the 'go to' man," I said, trying to remember his name. "He was quite sickly."

"The who?"

Her small frame got larger as my head and shoulders shrank, wishing they were invisible. It looked like she was chewing on a chokecherry.

"Patrick, Bill came here to find gold," she divulged. "He first saw wild horses from the ferry as it travelled through the northern plains of Montana. And as for the 'go to' man, well that was my father."

I couldn't hide my disappointment in finding out Bill's dream was like so many others. Ma must have noticed for her face softened.

"When did Bill tell you these stories?"

"Just after he found me. He told me it was his dream to find wild horses."

"Oh Patrick, dreams change. I suppose it was more appealing than hearing about a catholic boy chasing after a protestant girl he should never have loved. Protestants and Catholics mix as well as oil and water, but your father converted and has probably read that Bible more than I have."

I nodded but sensed a lingering discontent in her demeanor. "Ma...."

"I'll have some new pants made be the morrow. Get your old pants on and see to your chores."

I took the pants and dressed quickly. "Thanks, Ma."

Her green, Irish eyes smiled at me.

"Oh, and Patrick, find your father and have him come to the house with a bucket of water."

****

When my birthday arrived, I was full of anticipation. We would be going to Helena, now a tradition I hoped would never change as I aged. I got a new Stetson hat, Wellington boots, and tan leather gloves.

That May was particularly cold so Pa splurged on a coat he hoped I would wear for more than a season. I went for my usual candy but had to be rigorous about cleaning my teeth afterwards, finding out too painfully what it was like to have a cavity and a pulled tooth.

We had to go back to Helena, my face less than blissful this time though, to see a Dentist named Leander Fray. Dr. Fray and his wife also came to Montana seeking gold. And like so many others, he turned up nothing but dirt and rock in Virginia City. Once the gold played out, he came to Helena empty handed to resume his profession in Dentistry.

In 1874, a fire ravaged the town. It started in the gulch and funneled its way through the busy street destroying practically every building including Dr. Fray's. Pa said Dr. Fray needed to pull a lot of teeth to recover from that fire.

I figured I had so many he could pull the one that was giving me pain for a considerable length of time. Pa also said it would end the ceaseless moaning in my sleep and the redness in my skin from the constant rubbing of my jaw.

"Patrick, sit in the chair," the kind, bulky-sized, balding man said in his crisp white apron.

Pa whispered a few words in his ear.

The dentist nodded grimly before turning to me and offering a sniff of chloroform to make it less painful and more relaxing.

I shook my head, unsure how that would make me feel, opting to take it like a man.

Pa smiled and looked proudly at me.

"Fine, son. Just don't bite, punch or kick me."

Dr. Fray already had a soft bruise on his right cheek.

"You're gonna have to open that mouth wide and keep it open. Remember no biting!" he warned gently.

Clasping his teeth forceps, the metal reflected a small bouncy shadow on the far wall. When he got close to my face, I could smell his warm breath through wide nostrils and it reeked of whisky. I guess he needed something to relax himself. I don't know why he didn't offer whisky.

"Open up wide, Patrick!"

I found that reflection on the wall, watching its erratic movements intently as the forceps grabbed my aching tooth.

Dr. Fray was a rotund man, and as he moved closer, his body pushed into mine. It got so bad that I started pushing back. My heart began thumping when my hands got lost in his flabby chest.

"Not long now," he stammered while I inhaled the sweetness of his liquored panting.

He finally pulled the tooth, his weight releasing so hastily, I impelled him into a protruding table.

He yelped.

I instinctively muffled, "Sorry." And a pocket full of blood sprayed over his apron and my blue plaid shirt. I looked at the deep red splatter against the bright white cloth in horror waiting for his response.

"It's fine, son. Blood washes out."

I sighed in relief, still unsure of what to do with the rest of the blood swishing around my tongue and finally swallowed it like a man would.

"Here, spit the rest of the blood in this cup."

I shook my head.

"Oh, that's fine, too. Just might make you feel queasy."

"You can say that again!" I replied, glancing at my ghastly pale complexion through his wall hung mirror.

Pa wagged his head, grinning.

Dr. Fray told me to mix some baking soda and water together to make a paste, rub it against my teeth, and rinse with cold water. He said it should prevent any further doings with the forceps.

Once we were finally out of the small office, moving toward the horses, I began rubbing my jaw.

"Does it hurt much, son?"

"No, I'm fine," I said bravely.

"Let me take a look," he said, turning and peeling back my lower lip.

"It's a little swollen. When we get home, I'll give you a dram of whisky. Thank goodness for your pouty lower lip. It'll hide the hole in your teeth.

I smiled.

"Do we need anything else before we leave Helena?"

"I guess candy's out of the question?" I asked delicately.

He laughed, saying I was a tough lad.

I was a tough lad…but some images I never forgot. I never would forget the image of the blood on that crisp, white apron. Some images just stayed ingrained in a person's mind. It was a constant reminder for me to clean my teeth everyday.

****

Before we set off for the Plains, I had something weighing heavy on my mind. As I gave Taffy a handful of oats, Pa came into the stable calling me for supper.

When I gave him a confounded look, he motioned me to a bale of hay.

"What's troubling you?" he asked.

Scratching the back of my neck, I stammered, "It's about the Indians…the Lakota Indians. I can't be rightly sure, but I think they were…they were there that day…that day my momma…."

I was struggling with the words so Pa helped me.

"What do you remember about that day?"

"There was this fog heavy in my mind so my recollection's quite hazy. I heard gunshots…. and then a man's voice screaming, 'No!' It became very quiet until I heard my momma's screams…."

I began tossing my head because the next thought was always so painful to remember.

"What do you feel in your heart towards these Indians?"

"I feel confused. Should I hate them, treat them scornfully, Pa?"

"If you fill your heart with hate, there will be little room for love. If you fill your heart with anger, there will be little room for peace. Patrick, just as God can forgive you, you can forgive, as well. You can forgive anyone who speaks unfavourably of you, commits a crime against you, harms you. You have that power."

While I contemplated his words, my heart was also filled with fear. "Pa," my voice trembled. "Do Indians scalp only those they kill?"

"I'm not sure, Patrick."

"Would they ever," I implored, my eyes searching his, "would they ever scalp a woman or a child?"

"No, Patrick, I don't believe….no, Patrick, no."

I nodded in relief.

"Patrick, you're a kind, intelligent, faithful person; and I've no doubt that you will love, give and serve in life, and be a strong example to others in their time of need. If you're ever unsure, pray for guidance. Listen to God's voice, listen to your voice, and you'll find the right answer."

We sat, gazing at the horses settling for the night.

****

It was a brisk day in May when we headed away from the ranch. In some places, snow was still covering the ground and bending the boughs of the pine trees. Small masses of ice were floating with the current along the Missouri River.

That first night at the campfire was full of funny jokes, singing, and of course, Jimmy's smelly farts, which weren't getting better with age. We didn't partake in any Irish traditions, at least I didn't anyway.

When the men were in their tents, I stayed up to learn more Lakota words from Strong Bull, eager to speak them to Nawaji. I couldn't hide my disappointment when Strong Bull believed the camp would no longer be there.

"Strong Bull?" I asked as the fire raged between us and the smoke blurred my eyes.

He nodded solemnly.

"How did you get those teeth?" I asked, watching them dangle whitely against his russet neck.

"These bear teeth. I not wise as Sitting Bull," he murmured, untying the beaded choker and handing it to me.

"Why not?" I asked curiously while moving my finger against the smooth sharpness of the teeth.

"Sitting Bull sleep under tree when he heard bird," he motioned, closing his fist, moving it several times.

"Knocking," I said.

"He heard bird knocking….no move no move. Sitting Bull open eye, see bear over him. Sitting Bull no move and bear smell him, touch him, walk away. Bear think Sitting Bull dead. I not so smart. I jump when how you say big bear?"

"Grizzly," I said.

"Grizzly bear come." Strong Bull raised his hands, gnarling fingers like claws. "I grab rifle and shoot."

"How many bullets does it take to kill a grizzly?" I asked, my eyes wide open, alert.

"One to heart, but I not so lucky so I shoot many."

I handed the necklace back, yawning.

"Night, Strong Bull."

"Sleep well, Patrick."

There was a damp coolness in the air as we followed a different trail to our coulee in the Mountains. I was thankful for my coat and gloves. My thankfulness wore off when I wandered off, my feet trudging up small hills and leaping down small canyons, until amongst the pines, I found myself at the base of the east mountain that I was forbidden to climb.

Stripping the superfluous layers from my sweaty body, I glanced to my left, then to my right, checking for snakes, bears, and Indians. Packing my lungs with air, I made fast and limber movements up the steep ridge raring to gaze at the land that was Custer's last stand with his formidable foes.

As I climbed, a tiny voice sounding much like Pa's filled my head with doubt. And to make matters worse, the air was getting harder and harder to find. My palms got sweatier, slipperier. But it wasn't until my vision went fuzzy and I clutched at nothing, that I slipped, my leg slamming into hardness, my face scrapping a rock smooth.

That's when I peered around to find I had passed the tops of tiny trees to see a blur of vast sky.

I was shaking, very afraid, empty of breath, and alone. "Please God!" I cried. "Help me please and I'll never disobey Pa again!"

"Slow breaths," a voice whispered through the winds. "Slow breaths, small steps."

And that's what I did. Two slow breaths, one step down, two slow breaths, one step down....

When I neared the ground, Strong Bull snatched me from the rock, cloaked me in my warm coat, and led me to a wooden stump.

"Slow breaths, Patrick. Slow breaths," he said, lifting up my pant leg.

Removing a satchel from his shoulder, he madly searched its contents. "Stay," he commanded, pointing.

A wiped the water pooling my eyes, forced my heart to stop rapping against ribs, and the wheezing subsided.

By the time Strong Bull returned carrying pine limbs, my eyelids were fluttering to stay open.

With deft fingers, he closed my open gash and smothered sap on it.

I looked up and squeezed the stump, rocking the pain away.

"I can't do it," I said sadly as he wrapped my leg in cotton and tied it tightly. "I'll never climb that mountain."

"Come," he spoke quickly.

I followed him to a deep cave. In the darkness of its ceiling were shimmery bats. It was the most fascinating place I'd ever seen.

"This sacred, Patrick. No white man here. I take you places white man never be. Take you places you no climb."

"I wanted to see the battlefield," I confessed, "to see where Custer was killed."

"Battle on Little Big Horn River, Patrick. This," he pointed east, "Big Horn River."

"Oh," I said, feeling foolishly naïve.

We watched as the bats took flight into a dusky sky before returning to the camp.

My pa glanced up, worried, eyes on my bruised face, until Strong Bull patted my shoulder.

"Your supper's getting cold," he spoke with great forbearance. "Sit down."

And that's all he said to me. If he knew I'd been hanging off of a cliff, he showed little indication of it.

Little did I know that I would get the chance to see 'Little' Big Horn River and cross the battlefield clean and clear of any remnants of war except for the white stones that poked out from tall grasses. But that wouldn't come until we found more mustangs.

Mumbled discussions about that topic ran well into the night. I was so curious about what Pa was saying that I snuck out of the tent and crept closer, my ear stretching as far is it could.

He was worried that if we went east we might encounter a battle between the Sioux and the Cavalry.

My eyes widened at the thought.

Strong Bull believed that most of the Sioux had fled this land and were now in Queen's country. He knew horses could be found along Tongue River.

During the many battles that started with Red's Cloud's War, the Shoshone were scouts for the Cavalry. They witnessed thousands of Sioux ponies being captured and eventually set free in military camps near the Tongue River.

Strong Bull spoke of the old and unused trail named after a man called Bozeman. The trail was meant to get miners safely across Indian Territory. Forts were built to protect its travelers; however, the Indians continually attacked anyone using it, anyone protecting it, because it cut into their prime hunting grounds.

My Pa reiterated that many lives on both sides of the battle had been lost over that trail, the remains of the forts burnt out, and still visible.

"We will go through the mountains of Big Horn," Pa asserted, and ominously added, "with rifles loaded."

"Patrick!" he bellowed.

I jumped.

"Go back to bed!"

Out from the Big Horn Mountains to the south flowed the Tongue River and its mountainous canyon of limestone. I felt safety in these walls of solid, ancient rock until some skittered away from a high top bluff.

Pa hurriedly pressed his hand into my chest while the other reached for his rifle.

When all of our horses' hooves no longer crunched along the floor of rocks, we could hear the faintest of voices, dreadful sorrowful voices.

"Pa...." I tried to say.

"Shh!" he replied.

Our eyes scanned the bluffs of the canyon until something flashed brilliantly. Strong Bull pulled out a mirror and flashed back.

We headed north until a small Indian camp came into sight.

As we got closer, the stillness and hushed cries of the camp felt deathly eerie. I glimpsed something shiny and reflective coming from one of the lodges. Strong Bull firmly told us to stop.

Two Indians approached on horseback. As they spoke to Strong Bull, their voices were fast and troubling, their faces filled with undeniable panic and grief.

Strong Bull faced my pa and said that the tribe was sick...dying...dead, and that we best move far away.

While the Lakota spoke through Strong Bull, I continued toward the camp feeling like I was being pulled by something beyond my control.

When I was just yards from the first tipi, Pa began yelling for me to turn around. Horses were forthcoming so I spurred Legend into a gallop until I was well within the band's confines. Nothing could prepare me for what I saw. I wore a bandana around my neck which hastily covered my nose as the smell was powerful, almost overwhelming.

Some Lakota moved in a frenzied way, carrying water to tipis, or removing buckets of sickness and dirty cloths. Some were just wandering, shaking their heads, bewildered in a sort of wild feverish haze.

I didn't see Nawaji until a row of small dead bodies came into view, their tiny faces grey and sunken. It appeared that the children were most vulnerable with the outbreak of this illness. The smell was acrid, the sight horrid, and just as I thought of turning around, I saw her.

She was alive but leaning over someone small. I left my horse and walked to her, my eyes taking in her face full of tears, trembling…trembling over her lifeless sister. I knelt, my arms wrapping around her shaking shoulders.

Pa's terse, booming voice interrupted my saddened and sympathetic thoughts.

Slowly, I peered up in anguish, weeping, but it didn't melt any of the fury he expressed towards me. I knew I had to let her go. Averting my eyes, I mounted Legend and left the camp. I knew what I had to do and he wouldn't like it.

With lucid vision, I moved to the wagon, grabbed a shovel, and climbed my horse. I could hear Pa yelling again. Every fibre of his patient being would be tested as I rode to a place of high pines and started digging.

"Patrick, you're not staying here. Get on your horse now!" he commanded.

"I'm not leaving," I said, continuing to dig. "Those bodies have to be buried. They smell and carry disease."

"And that's why you have to leave! These people will die whether you do this or not!"

"More people will die if I don't do this. I'm not stopping! I have to do this!" I shouted back as my shovel plunged into hard soil, my body shaking with uncertainty. While I admit to disobeying him from time to time, I had never defied him.

He grabbed me and I waited, waited for him to hit me.

"Please Pa, I'll just dig. But please don't stop me from doing this! I have to do this! I just can't walk away." My eyes stung as I searched for approval.

When that didn't come, I pulled away from his tight grip and proceeded to dig. Strong Bull remained with me and began shoveling away dirt as Pa and the rest of the men went further up the Tongue River.

I don't know why I had to do it. I just had to and couldn't stop it even if I wanted to. It was a forward momentum that came from somewhere deep inside and was chipping away at my wavering feelings toward the Lakota.

As I charged at the earth, sweat began dripping from every pore in my body. I finally tore off the gloves and pealed away my wet shirt. Every now and then, Strong Bull shoved a canteen of water my way.

Day turned to night; however, I maintained a vigorous pace until I couldn't see a foot in front of me in the dark hole. There was no moonlight to aid me tonight as my shovel struggled to find soil. I couldn't see any more; I couldn't move any more. Didn't know how wide the hole was, but it was at least four feet deep. As I attempted to scramble out, I fell back.

I lay there, hoping a few moments rest would give me the energy to climb out. The cool wetness of the ground was soothing against my sore muscles. I became quite still until…until I heard a familiar, eerie sound. The last time I'd heard that sound, I was in an apple tree.

I couldn't see where it was but knew it was near me in my hole.

"Shuck!" I mumbled, frozen in exhausted fear, praying it would just slither away. I didn't have the strength to fight it even if I could find it. Closing my eyes, I heard a 'wsh' sound. Metal flashed, and I blinked to find a shovel thrust into the snake, the snake no longer slithering, the snake no longer a threat.

Strong Bull was standing at the edge of the hole, holding a lamp. When he painfully squeezed my blistered hand, he emphatically said, "Go!"

With finger pointed to a campfire several yards away, clearly his patience had worn out, too.

As I walked over, the chilly night air cut through my bare skin. Shivering violently, I was ready to jump into the welcoming flames to stop my teeth from chattering so loudly. It was the appearance of Nawaji that made me forget about the coldness until Strong Bull threw my shirt at me. As soon as he saw Nawaji, he spoke harshly to her, insisting she leave.

She snarled at him, and this fiery banter continued until I pleaded for them to stop.

"She make you sick! You sick, you die!"

Nawaji spoke again, in a pleading voice, pointing to a bucket of water and cloth.

He shook his head, glaring angrily at her.

I took her by the arm and led her to the fire, blatantly disregarding Strong Bull's blazing stare.

She carefully washed and soothed my hands, peering up from time to time with such caring eyes. The smile that formed from her red lips was soft, delicate, and acted like a salve for my aching body. She began to speak, and I just watched her beautiful mouth move as the Indian words flowed foreign to my mind.

Strong Bull finally began translating from the far side of the campfire. "She say she care for sister after mother die. Only sister she has. Now dead. She very sad but happy to see you. She has name, gift for you."

I nodded while my eyes remained transfixed on her sweet face.

She gave me a strange object that could only be described as a spider's web held by a large ring before speaking again.

Strong Bull translated, "She say make bad dreams from come. She say sorry for your mo…"

Strong Bull stopped curtly.

Her fearful face frightened me. While a hand searched a deerskin pouch, she stood with an apprehensive glance to Strong Bull. After she placed it in my swollen hand, she ran away.

I sat heavily on a rotting tree limb holding Momma's necklace with the heart locket, never letting my eyes stray until I could no longer keep them open.

I awoke alone and uncomfortably twisted in a heavy blanket. The sun was peaking through the tall, thick evergreens as I stiffly walked through the forest. I could see dirt being flown over the sides of my hole by four Lakota.

Pa appeared and put a hand to my shoulder, saying it was time to go. As we turned to leave, the band's leader,

White Bear, acknowledged me with a nod from his solemn, grief-stricken face.

We soon met up with the rest of our party, ready to leave Tongue River. Our journey continued north and the landscape opened to prairie canyon and grazing mustangs. Without a wooden enclosure to trap them, the men ran the mustangs for hours until they tired. It would be two full weeks before our feet touched home.

During that time, I brooded over thoughts of Nawaji, the loss of her sister, and the closeness of sickness and death. I hoped she had someone like Bill and Mary to comfort and love her, and also prayed she would survive the disease that was devastating her camp.

Though my hands healed quickly, the image of her caring for them lasted several weeks.

Naturally, Pa commented on my unruly behaviour. He told me that I was very brave and fearless, but also very careless and disobedient. I jeopardized not only my life but the life of the men in our camp.

He said, "Some choices have to be made for the greater good, though good judgment comes in time and experience."

****

After a few restful days, I was given the chance to break a horse. But not before Lincoln's stall was mucked out. I was doing a poorly hastened job of it when Pa appeared.

He said matter-of-factly, "You're making more of a mess than you are cleaning it up."

My heavy shovelfuls kept falling back on the stable floor. I had a flash of the past when I got smacked by my grandpa for doing the same kind of shoddy work.

"Patrick, I know this may seem like an unimportant job, but you've got to focus your attention to it so that when you're in the corral, you'll have it practiced enough to tame that horse. Horses can be very unpredictable, and if you're not focused, you can get hurt and you can hurt the horse. I want this stall completely cleaned before you go into that corral. Focus on the task at hand."

After I stayed steadfastly focused on cleaning the stable properly, I was ready to pick out my first mustang when Pa held me by the shoulders. He already had one picked out. Andy was bringing it into the corral.

I was hugely disappointed to see what I thought was a chestnut yearling staring back at me.

"This is a filly," I whined. "She's so small! Why'd you bring her back from the Plains?"

"Well, when there's seventy or so mustangs corralled together, sometimes the small ones stay hidden. Besides, she's four years old, stands at twelve hands. I want you to look at the horse and tell me what you see."

I carefully watched the horse.......pony for a few moments.

"She's quivering like she's cold. Her tail's swishing and her ears are perked up."

As I walked towards her, she looked directly at me with alert eyes before scurrying away.

"She's scared."

"Very good. How do you think you should approach this horse? Should you rope her?"

"Anything come flying at her will just scare her," I said fittingly. "She needs to know I mean her no harm.....by speaking gently and touching her softly."

Bill nodded silently.

"I'll bring her food…try to feed her by hand," I said, turning to Pa for agreement.

"Very good. Once you tame this horse, you'll be able to tame virtually any horse. It will take much patience and kindness, but I think you're quite capable."

I started bringing in oats by the handfuls, though this half-pint wouldn't take anything by hand; so I left piles on the ground. It took days until finally she came to my outstretched hand and nibbled, her soft velvety nose and short firm whiskers tickling my palm. My gentle touch moved up her white brush stroke to stringy forelocks, then under her tangled mane, until she shook and darted away.

Once she was used to my touch, I got her used to the feel of the rope along her gleaming body. I also introduced her to noises: whistling, jumping up and down, and shouting. I used one of Ma's sheets which carelessly flapped in the breeze as I moved it over her head and along her narrow barrel to slender legs, uniquely striped. Roping her was the easiest part after weeks of getting her used to my touch and sounds.

Pa was always close by.

One day, he was leaning against the top rail of the corral when Trey approached him. Watching out of the corner of my eye, Trey's mouth went a mile a minute while Pa's body stiffened. I strained my ears to listen but their words were just incoherent murmurs.

"Bill, we don't have time for this! Cavalry's expecting these horses and Patrick's spending too much time in the corral!"

"It's just a half-hour, twice a day. Gives you time to do chores and the opportunity to break your horses even faster," Bill replied with eyes never leaving the corral.

"Cavalry won't even want that horse. She's too frail and afraid."

"Not after Patrick gets finished with her," he said confidently. "Patrick, time to bring the horse into the pasture!"

"Why you care so much about this kid!" Trey remarked too loudly.

Bill eyed him with a hurtful glare. "I cared about you the same way not so long ago."

When Pa approached sullenly, I cheerfully blurted out the pony's name. This half-pint mare's 'Whitestreak' went from the tips of her forelocks to the tip of her mouth.

For the next few days, all I did was work that horse loose with my lariat and voice. When we got finished, she was groomed from head to haunches. By the end of the week, she was ready to be saddled.

Mounting Whitestreak for the first time, I tilted her head in with the reins so she wouldn't buck. Once I was saddled and balanced, I stroked her while she got used to my weight. Within the safety of the high rails, I spurred her into a trot.

She started to fuss, lowering her head, indicating she was gonna buck. Tightening the reins, I kept my leg on, took that deep seat, and went for the ride.

When I finally pushed her into a lope, a huge grin lit up my face.

Breaking in horses was a lesson in patience. I would continue to practice that lesson for the rest of my life, on and off a horse.

The men each gave me their own lessons that summer, and I'd never forget them.

Jimmy taught me how to shoe a horse and shave its teeth. I never forgot his teachings because he always showed me examples of the pain one would endure if those chores were done improperly. He said that 'when shoeing a horse, it was important to stay as close to the hoof as possible' because if you were too far away like Jimmy was, getting kicked in the head or foot was much more painful.

As Jimmy hobbled to the horse's mouth, he showed me that when putting a hand in its mouth, it could only be done safely in the space between the jaw and the teeth at the side of its mouth where the tongue was eventually pulled, as well. Failure to do any of these moves properly resulted in some severe biting and bleeding as Jimmy shook his hand in the air.

I think he just got hurt so he could see Ma for some nursing and a shot of whisky, which she warmly offered to ease the pain.

Jimmy was also free from having to shoe another horse or rasp its teeth for the rest of the day.

Trey showed me how to lasso the longhorns in the cow pasture until I had all of our bovines angrily stomping the grasses, which made Pa none to pleased.

Andy taught me the best lesson of all. He taught me how to fly! We would gallop along the outer fence of the horse pasture, around the pines between the ranch and the Missouri, and back to the main Sullivan gate.

Some days, we would just race across the cow pasture to the edge of the eastern fence when Pa wasn't looking.

"Hey Patrick, we got a clear strip of cow pasture to the fence. Loser finishes cleaning the stalls!"

I didn't need any more encouragement than that as I cautiously saddled Legend. I cinched him, and cinched him again, because eating grass wasn't in the cards for me today. Scanning the fields, Pa was nowhere to be seen.

"Just to the stump before the fence, Patrick," Andy said warily.

I agreed, and he counted down, "Three, two, one!"

As we neared the stump, Andy pulled back on the reins, but I kept going, leaning into Legend for a jump over the three foot wooden fence.

When I glimpsed the pasture, exhilarated with a smile from ear to ear, I saw Andy shaking his head and several yards away, a tiny figure that I hoped wasn't Pa.

The smile was promptly wiped from my face when I squinted to see that moving shape dash to the passageway. Moving Legend around the pasture slowly, my hope waned as the small figure grew taller, clearer, and had his arms crossed.

A sudden breeze ran through the air. It must have come from the heavy breathing he was surely doing as I gingerly approached him.

Meeting me partway, I was coolly asked to get off the horse.

"Patrick, these horses were not meant for jumping! What you did was careless and dangerous to you and this horse. Get back to your chores and leave the horses untouched until I feel you're responsible enough to ride them again! Are your ears open to my words?"

I contemplated how to answer. This wasn't the first time I jumped Legend over a fence or fallen tree limbs, and Legend was quite capable of jumping. Instead of explaining, I opted for an obedient, "Yes sir."

I was banned from riding horses for three days, which seemed like an utter eternity. When my term of punishment finally ended, I was jumping off the walls when I found out another lesson that summer would be to break Lincoln after he was gelded.

That event would come after the Calvary got their horses with the exception of Whitestreak and another horse I called Breeze, on account of the way her light golden mane swayed in the breeze. Breeze would be our third broodmare. I was wholly surprised considering Breeze was a mustang. Pa subtly grinned as he led me to Maggie's stall.

"Maggie's father is Goliath," he stated, "however her mother is a mustang. It's what happens when your thoroughbred stallion gets loose in a pasture full of wild mares."

"That means Taffy's part mustang. I guess that explains the black stripe running down her back."

"Yes Patrick. Murphy, Midnight, and Moonlight, are also part mustang. I would've given Taffy an 'M' name, as well, if you weren't so eager for Taffy."

"You want me to rename Breeze?" I asked curiously.

"Patrick, when the range horses are rounded up and brought back to the ranch, there are more half-bred horses than thoroughbreds. Breeze can keep her name."

Pa wanted to focus more on breeding rather than rounding up wild horses. Mixing the breeds seemed the way to do it. It made sense….that Pa wanted to focus on breeding. He was getting older; his pace seemed slower. He often fell asleep reading a book in the keeping room, his snoring abruptly halting any pleasant sounding piece of music Ma and I were playing.

****

I couldn't sleep the night before Lincoln was to be gelded, so I went to him and gave that stud the best night of his life before the change. I cleaned his stall, groomed him from head to tail, and offered a handful of oats.

In the morning, when I propped myself against the rail of the fence, Lincoln was already in the corral.

Jimmy appeared with a knife wrapped in a clean, white sheet. I hoped this lesson wouldn't end for Jimmy in another trip to see Ma.

Andy joined me, followed by Trey, who rather uncomfortably placed his hand on the back of my neck.

"Lincoln will be much easier for you to break after he's gelded," he said derisively.

I felt like telling him *if you don't get your hand off my neck I'm gonna geld you, you shucking son of a....*

My bitter thoughts were interrupted when Bill whirled his rope and slithered it along the ground, snagging Lincoln's forelegs until he hit the ground hard.

Mike held his head down while Pa tied his hind legs together. The quick movement of Jimmy's knife and the ensuing blood that followed left a lasting memory.

When Lincoln was untied, he moved around the corral in a slow state of shock.

Pa's glanced at me.

Lowering my eyes, I turned away. With long strides to the far fence of the cow pasture, I snatched a few wildflowers before continuing to the five grey stones. The breeze fluttered the leaves of the cottonwood tree as I knelt at momma's grave with the blossoms of blue, white, and yellow. Her name was now etched into the thin slab.

"Happy Birthday, Momma," I whispered softly. "I see your wonderful smile at dawn's first light, feel your touch like a warm summer's breeze and your sweet voice, it echoes across these pastures in the stillness of twilight. I feel your spirit everywhere and it will never fully fade."

With eyes watering, I struggled to say the next words. "However, I'm now Patrick Sullivan and my parents are Bill and Mary. I will always live as Patrick Sullivan, and when that time comes, die as Patrick Sullivan."

After scratching a hole in the dirt, I pulled out Momma's embroidered handkerchief. Unfolding it, coiled around the heart locket, was the gold necklace.

"Whatever love that man felt for you is dead…is dead just like you," I said sadly.

I released the necklace but couldn't let the soft white square go. I remember her concentrated eyes pulling pink thread through it….remember her at the kitchen table wiping tears with it….remember her by the creek trying to wipe my nose with it, me laughing, and her out of breath.

"I remember," my voice trembled with emotion.

Glancing at the stone, I released a deep, pensive sigh. I hated to leave her but had to….I had to let her go. I willed the wind to carry the memory of her away and it did.

Chapter 11

That autumn, just before the first snowfall over the Sullivan homestead, I broke Lincoln. I roped him, walked him, bridled and saddled him. Pa offered a firm supportive voice, but now stayed behind the fenced corral.

By the time the ground was covered in white flakes, Lincoln would respond to anything I did, whether it be from the sound of my voice, the touch of my leg, the way I sat in the saddle, or moved the reins. Lincoln only tried to buck me off once. After that, we had a mutual respect and understanding.

"What's Patrick doing?" Mary asked Bill as she stepped onto the porch, pulling her shawl tighter around small shoulders.

Lincoln was making small circles with hooves tossing up dirt and snow, until he was pressured into thundering across the quiet pasture.

Bill watched in amazement at the control over the horse. "He's just working that gelding without a saddle or bridle, or he's trying to make us feel very sick, Mary. Patrick's thirst for learning should be quenched, so I think we'll take him hunting."

That early morning, I was using a whetstone to sharpen the arrow tips in preparation for my first hunt.

Pa walked into the bedroom, eying me. "Are you weapons ready to do battle?"

Grinning, I peered up. "The metal tips have been dulled hitting every tree this side of the Missouri."

"Well, maybe today we try your aim at a moving target. We best be on our way."

I hastily stuffed my buckskin sheath with the sharpened sticks and followed Pa out to the stable where Strong Bull was waiting.

We went west under a dull November sky and soon were cloaked in a forest of evergreens just below the ridge of the Rocky Mountains. The boughs of the pines were heaving from the weight of slushy snow.

A cold dampness in the air sent shivers down my back despite the layers of clothing Ma forced on me before I could leave the ranch.

Pa said we would probably be seeped in puddles by tomorrow from this sudden, warm air that swept through western Montana. Despite the deep mud holes and bone chilling wetness, I loved Chinooks. They brought a welcome change to the bitter and dry coldness that always stole my breath.

As we walked silently through the forest, Strong Bull taught me how to track the elusive and easily spooked whitetail deer. The first sign to indicate we were on a deer path was the markings to the trees. The buck's antlers rubbed a branch or stem until the thick and scaly bark was removed.

The second sign was scrapings the buck made to the ground with his strong hooves that he then filled with urine.

In both instances, the buck was leaving powerful signs to attract female deer and hungry hunters.

It wasn't long before Strong Bull caught my arm, pointing to a buck drinking from a small stream. We were fifty yards away when my first arrow plunged just behind its shoulder. Strong Bull told me to wait a few minutes until he bled out. We listened for his heavy body to hit the ground.

The buck was still alive when we reached it. Strong Bull placed my hand on its slowing heartbeat. I never felt anything like it before. It slowed my heartbeat too, bringing a peace over my entire body. That peace would end when he showed me how to prepare the animal for transport. It was not for the faint of heart. Every organ and entrails had to be removed before we took it home.

Of all of the jobs I learned, this one I would give up to a butcher any day. It took days to get the smell out of my nose and off my hands.

Pa said it would serve me well in the future, even keep me from starving to death one day. I'd like to think civilization would advance enough that I wouldn't have to hunt for my own meat when the time came.

It was all worthwhile when we had fresh meat for supper, though. Whenever an animal was slaughtered, whether it be a buck or one of our cows or pigs, very little went to waste. We had too many hungry men to feed, whose appetites never waned.

The haunches and saddles of the venison would be used for roasts, the neck and shoulder in braises and mixed vegetable dishes. Trimmings from steaks and roasts were ground to make a tasty Shepherd's pie. Organs like the heart and liver were also ground into the cleaned intestines of the animal to make sausages, or were braised, or fried with onions.

On this night, Ma made a venison roast with potatoes, carrots, and parsnips. We also devoured fried liver and onions. I dribbled her thick and rich gravy over everything, including the stewed yellow pumpkin and pickled green beans.

Strong Bull and Pa spoke about John while I soaked up the leftover gravy with a chunk of warm Irish soda bread.

I waited for the right time to interrupt the men when Pa finally took a lengthy pause to chew his meat.

"Strong Bull, did you fight in the battle at Little Big Horn?"

He glanced at Pa, who was sipping his sweet tea.

"Strong Bull was not born Lakota Sioux," Bill began. "He was taken as a baby while his tribe was being raided by the Lakota. They raised him, taught him to hunt buffalo; however, Strong Bull knew he was not Lakota. When he was about your age, he decided to return to his tribe, the Shoshone. While the Lakota were hunting near Tongue River, Strong Bull fled the camp."

I couldn't deny seeing a grim weariness on his darkened face.

"As I move through Plains, I find trap," Strong Bull spoke slowly. "Five white men take me from trap, tie me to tree," he swallowed. "Four white men use whips and ropes, one white man watch."

"Strong Bull was beaten so badly he couldn't move," Bill said.

"Why would they do that?" I asked in astonishment.

"Maybe fear….fear that Strong Bull meant them harm," Pa offered bleakly. "Patrick, cruelty exists everywhere."

I had a frightened look of disbelief.

Strong Bull stared keenly at me while resuming his story. "Quiet white man return; maybe to bury but I still breathe. He take me to cabin, heal me. Broken bones take long time to heal. He teach me English. I teach him hunt Buffalo."

My expression softened.

"I want return to Shoshone, leave white man. Journey long," he paused in sad reflection. "My tribe smaller, sick, hungry. I trade for them. We trade horses. Shoshone have horses before others….claim all Montana to Queen's country," he remarked, making wide circles with his strong hands. "Until Blackfoot get guns, kill, steal horses."

"Where do you live?" I asked.

"I go south to my people when sun is strong, bring horses, supplies. When winter comes, my bones pain. I return to white man's cabin."

I nodded, still trying to comprehend his battered past.

"How do you know when we do the round-up?"

He eyed my Pa, who took his time wiping his broad bottom lip with a linen napkin.

"Well Patrick, this is what I do," Pa said plainly. "I take one of our horses and ride over to the mountains. Then I climb a short crag, wait for the wind to change southward and howl," he inhaled deeply. "Strong Bull, we do roundup June fourth, two weeks from Monday!"

"Does that work?" I asked quite naively.

Strong Bull and Pa exchanged quick glances.

I couldn't read their faces.

It was Ma who giggled like a little girl and that's when I knew it wasn't true.

"Your Pa write letter. I get in Virginia City," Strong Bull confessed.

I chuckled, feeling a little foolish, which soon disappeared when Ma brought out her warm apple pie with thick cream. I managed to stuff in two slices when Ma asked me to take over a pie to the men in the bunkhouse.

As I walked the sweetly spiced dessert gingerly to the bunkhouse, an unpleasant memory of long ago in

Grandpa's barn tried to make its way in, but I shut it out as I opened the door.

The pleasant smell of baked apples and spice was obliterated by a pungent mix of sweat, manure…and boiled meat. There wasn't a speck of wooden floor showing: just clothes strewn everywhere like there'd been a giant wind storm. My grandpa would've curled his whip around all of these grown men. Thankfully, they didn't notice my appalled face.

I was warmly greeted as they looked up from their card game to see, or somehow smell, what I had to offer.

Jimmy squealed, "One of yer pies, how delightful!"

He snatched it right out of my hands.

"Not this time," I replied haughtily. "Been hunting all day!"

"You couldn't kill anything with those sticks," Trey taunted.

"As a matter of fact I did," I boasted. "Got me my first buck and he was the tastiest meal I ever had."

"That a boy, Patrick," Andy mumbled through a mouthful of food. "Next time kill one for us, too."

"What are you playing?" I asked.

"Poker," Trey muttered, dealing out the cards.

"Mind if I watch?"

"Sit," Jimmy said. "Would ye like a piece of pie?"

"Why not?" I replied, grinning. I was sure there was room somewhere in my bottomless stomach for more pie. I squeaked a chair in beside Trey.

He coldly scoffed at me.

I didn't care for his demeanor, though I cared a little more when I saw the gun holstered to his belt smothered in silver bullets around his slender waist.

I whispered, "You always bring a gun and all that ammunition to a card game?"

"Yep, but don't worry, kid. Only have three bullets in the cylinder. I wear it 'cause it bring me good luck. All I have to do is lift it and these three cowards be changing their pants."

Andy was forever gnawing on something brown and chunky from his bowl, until he caught me staring too long.

"Patrick," he mumbled. "Want Trey's some bitch stew?"

"It's son of a bitch and I doubt Patrick'd have the stomach for it," Trey sneered.

"Nonsense," Andy replied, moseying for a bowl. "Probably won't taste like your buck but what the heck."

He handed it to me and it felt like half the cow was chopped up in it.

"What ya think?" Andy asked.

"It's a bit chewy."

"Well, we know it ain't the testicles," Trey spat out. "Your ma done scoop up that swinging beef as soon as they was lopped off."

"Maybe it's the stomach," Andy interjected as bits of stew came flying out of his mouth.

"You could always add onion to it," I suggested.

"Why'd I want to waste a good onion?" Trey snarled.

I clamped my lips around that stew, chewing and watching, as the men threw coins into the centre of the table, calling out words like call, fold, and raise.

Jimmy had nothing, so he folded.

Trey had aces and queens...two pair, a good hand, but not as good as Andy, who had a full house.

Mike had a straight, but Andy's flush beat it out so he won the round.

"Can I play?" I blurted out while my tongue appreciated the sweetness of the pie over the taste of that drab stew.

"You got to have money," Trey responded dryly.

"How much?"

"Well buy in is five cents a pop 'cause Jimmy's so cheap. Then you need money to raise. We're lucky if we have a dollar in the centre of that table each round," he grumbled, glowering at Jimmy.

"Ye know I be sending te dole to me sister, Kate…" Jimmy stammered.

"I know, ye sister Kate, who's married to the drunk and lazy Eddie Monahan, who can't keep a job to save his life," Trey mimicked in a strong Irish lilt.

"I have gold," I said, and that seemed to shut everybody up.

Trey gave me a hard stare. "Patrick, were you born under a rock?"

I gave him my best confounded look.

"You don't go spreading word that you got gold to a bunch of rough and rowdy cowboys." He leaned in to me, whispering, "Andy over there's a foreigner. He'd no sooner slit your throat, snatch your gold, and hightail it over the border. I doubt we'd ever find that gold again."

I peered at Andy, devouring his stew, smiling innocently enough.

Leaning into my uncomfortable chair, I swallowed a forkful of pie making it appear like I hadn't eaten in days.

"Mind you," Trey said with an unusually contemplative air. "Maybe we'd enlist a man tracker to find him. One came by the stable today looking for another horse."

"That so?" Andy inquired. How'd you know he was a man tracker?"

"He's on the hunt for an outlaw, name's Thompson, I believe. Killed two men in Virginia City, though he doesn't have an outlaw name like Wild Bill or Billy the Kid. Doesn't show his face much. Some say he's a mountain man, now."

"I think they called him Montana Kid," Andy divulged. "But that was a while ago. He ain't a kid now!"

"Tey be Irish lads he killed!" Jimmy hollered. "Tose lucky bastards struck gold, ten lost teir lives to te marauding heathen! Depopulating te territory of te Irish, he was!"

"There's no chance of that!" Trey scowled. "Your kind outnumber ours two to one! Besides, the two he killed in Fort Benton didn't have a lick of Irish blood in 'em. They was bounty hunters! Come at him guns a blazin'! He launched them into eternity fast and hard!"

"But ten he went after another Irish bloke in te mountains! Maimed him for life!"

"The cheap son of a bitch still has his life! I wonder if he saves his coffee grinds like you do, squeezing the water out of 'em and drying 'em so he can make muddy water again!"

"Anybody want another piece of pie," I offered, grabbing the knife from Trey's reach.

"Doesn't matter much!" Trey bellowed as his face shed its crimson hue. "Man tracker will find him. My pa knew him during the war. Lots of men got squeamish after their first battle and ran for the hills. Tiberius Grant would track 'em down, and turn 'em in to the grey coats to be hanged or shot. Must have captured twenty," he contemplated, "hell, thirty yellow-bellies by the time we left in sixty-three."

I shifted my nervous eyes to the cards fanned out in Trey and Mike's hands, but quickly got confused over how Trey kept tossing in nickels even though Mike had a full house.

"Now," I spoke loudly. "Why would someone keep raising the pot if all he had was a lousy pair of eights?"

The men chuckled except for Trey.

"Patrick," he mumbled through clenched teeth. "Its way past your bed time! Now go and…give me that pie!"

He ripped that plate right out of my hands.

My cheeks went blood-red as I slowly left the card table.

"I'm amazed he's survived this long!" Trey exclaimed callously. "Somebody should have pulled him out from that rock, sooner. If so maybe his momma'd still be alive!"

My heart felt a stab of pain upon hearing his words. I slowly sauntered back to the house with my head dangling to the ground.

"Oh hell, you know what I have!" Trey hollered, tossing his cards and leaving the table.

"Patrick!" he called into the night with footsteps speedily catching up.

Hastily yanking free of his grip, my eyes raged.

"I didn't mean to…I know what its like," he stammered, "lost my own parents when I was nine."

"Have an odd way of showing it!" I hissed, stomping away.

I was no more that three feet from him when the night air must have cooled his compassionate heart.

"Least I'm not whimpering about it anymore!"

****

Twenty miles southwest of the ranch, Frank O'Flaherty was sitting at a saloon in Helena waiting for a pint from a frisky bar wench offering more than just a lift to his spirits. Glaring at his Da's gold watch, he found himself a tad bit early. He smiled at this oddity considering he appeared late for everything else in his life.

Three days previous, he was in Virginia City, climbing the steps of his house to find his wife, Pauline, sitting fingers crossed, on a rocker. Her carpetbag was stuffed, resting at her feet, while she stared desolately at the wild roses that crept through the spindles of the wrap-around porch.

"I'm leaving you," her voice spoke dispassionately.

Frank gazed at his feet, willing them to keep walking.

"Have you nothing to say?" she asked incredulously. "I've washed your clothes, warmed your bed, cooked your meals, for fifteen years, and you've nothing to say."

"I have to find him, for Michael's sake, for Ruth and Ian's sake."

"Ruth has moved on! Been married five years! Has a new baby on her hip! I sit here in an empty home with empty rooms while you keep the company of whores and watch a woman north of the gulch tend to her farm! Why do you not see me?" she cried, but refused to let tears stain her pale cheeks. "I've prayed for you to forgive him and come back, come back to me! Time for praying is over! I'm going to Salt Lake City. Keep an eye on your mail. Divorce papers will be sent forthwith!"

She grabbed her carpetbag with a stern hand and stiffly passed by Frank as if he was a mere stranger.

Frank was feeling much like a mere stranger at Sam Greer's saloon until the doors flapped open and Tiberius Grant swaggered in.

Tye's steely eyes scanned the room until he spotted Frank, who gave a simple nod, before a curly haired brunette leaned into him.

Frank brushed her aside, but grabbed his beer and motioned for Tye to sit.

The bar maiden didn't skip a beat, turning, smiling coyly, her bosoms heaving from a corset dress.

"Anything I can get you?" she cajoled.

The myriad of tattoos covering her breasts, shoulders, and arms always held his fascination for a few moments.

"You can get me a beer, too," he answered in a no nonsense way.

"Must be a carnival in town," Frank sneered.

"Annie's had a rough life. She's just coping the best way she can," he said justifiably.

"How long you been tracking along the foothills of the mountains?" Frank asked the white-bearded, straight-faced man.

"I've been in the ramblings of the mountains going on ten years now. Tracked just about everything from Colorado to the Canadian border. Sam here's hired me to do some interior decorating," he said, pointing. "That bald eagle behind the bar and the black bear perched on the far wall, well over five hundred pounds, just about damn near killed me! Won't have any trouble finding your man. What makes you think he's in these mountains?"

"He won't leave Montana. At first, I thought it was because of the gold. Found him at a mining camp in Diamond City about forty miles east of here. Son of a bitch blended in with the rest of the pan diggers, gaunt, bearded, and haggard. Chased him into the mountains and he hopped through thickets of bush like a jack rabbit. Coward doesn't rear his ugly head often."

"If he's in the mountains, I'll find him and bring you his ugly mug."

"You don't have to bring it. I'm going with you," Frank said in his surefire way. "Bringing two Vigilante lawmen with me. We've come north from Virginia City through Dry Gulch around Ten Mile Creek, up to Last Chance Gulch. I want us to move north toward Fort Benton, then west into the mountains."

"That's a lot of miles and steep terrain," Tye advised.

Frank's cold stare and rigid posture remained unchanged, indicating an implacable manhunt that would see his prey relegated to dust.

The following day, the four men took the freight route through Prickly Pear Canyon. Tye's eyes shifted along the high ridges of ancient seabed shale as the horses' hooves echoed throughout the winding trail. Just a few hours into the journey and rain fell in torrents. Weather would not be on their side.

Cooking that night was rendered impossible, and thus began a feast of dried biscuits and beef jerky. No one complained when the whisky was poured in more than a dram ounces to keep the chills at bay. They coiled up in blankets, grumbling their way to sleep, with a canvas stretched over their sleeping bodies.

The next day, their trail was washed clean, and so were their clothes, still damp and cold.

Tye tracked the best he could under such wet circumstances. He examined broken branches, poked horse dung, listened with perked ears while perched on his horse. His constant stopping and stooping, measuring and sniffing, were wearing on Frank's patience.

Frank couldn't understand how a man could pick up small animal bones and curled tree shavings, and ponder them like they were rare finds in forests where big animals ate small animals and stripped trees bare.

That afternoon, with the rain coming down sure and steady, they came upon a meadow and a small cabin, grey smoke billowing from its chimney.

Frank and Tye approached the cabin while Arthur and George kept watch. A middle-aged woman answered and, upon hearing that they were Vigilantes searching for a dangerous outlaw, offered a reprieve from the infernal downpour and a steaming cup of coffee.

When Tye was comfortably seated, he surveyed the small one room cabin to find seven children scattered on beds or by the fire on a bear rug. The youngest sat on Mrs. Jurgen's lap, gurgling and chewing on her mother's apron string.

Frank began asking the gangly woman simple questions while Tye examined their simple surroundings.

A little girl approached and rattled a carved horse along the table until it reached his arm.

He smiled lightly at the child with vibrant big brown eyes, tiny cleft in her chin, and curly blonde hair.

She smiled sheepishly. "He gave it to me," her voice whispered while holding up the wooden toy.

Tye whispered, "Who gave it to you?"

"The fisherman. He calls me Emily even though my name is Mattie."

"Mattie!" her mother barked. "Go back to your bed!"

The alarm in Mrs. Jurgen's voice sparked suspicion in Tye's mind.

"Ma'am, in our need to catch this unsavoury reprobate, it would be most prudent to search your barn," he said in an assertive tone.

While Tye searched the two stalls for clues, Frank took an interrogative tone to the widowed woman, who proved to be as tough as iron nails.

With her children safely tucked in the cabin, she curtly asked the men to leave her premises.

All Frank left with was a pounding headache, and Tye, the deduction that if Thomas had been there, his visit was not recent.

By the tenth day, Tye began to wonder whether he should have just headed south to New Mexico where the air wasn't necessarily drier, but was surely warmer. He knew he'd never go east of the Mississippi where the ghosts of men fallen in battles on farmer's fields and in verdant forests, assailed his nightly dreams.

Shaking his dampened head, he knew he'd never give up until he got his prey when something flickered in the corner of his eye. It was the flash of a knife.

Racing towards the light, he found a coulee. Dismounting quickly, he peered into the clear waters to find soap lather and, at the bank of the other side, a muddy boot print. He followed the tracks a few yards and found a tall shadow darting between evergreens.

A fast whistle through his puckered lips and the men were in hot pursuit. They fanned out with hopes of flanking the fleeing outlaw.

Tye was loping as straight as he could around Douglas firs when a branch swung around knocking him off of his horse.

Shaking his head, he sat up. Inches from his forehead, a short barrel loomed. Behind it, stood Sean Thomas, bare-chested, half-shaven, and very irate.

"You a lawman!" he said testily.

"A tracker," Tye swallowed.

"Lose my scent or you'll lose your life!"

With Sean's arm raised, Tye blurted out, "Emily misses you!"

Sean froze while Tye hoped to hear horse hooves approaching.

"That's odd 'cause she's been dead twenty years!"

The branch swung again, cracking against skull, and Tye's light was put out.

Sean mounted the tracker's sorrel thoroughbred and galloped away from the Vigilantes. The horse was found void of his saddle and belongings a few miles away in a gully.

By that point, the posse was a few days ride from the Canadian border. Eager to capture Thomas before his move into Queen's country, Frank cinched his saddle to the red gelding, forcing Arthur to give up his saddle to Frank and ride bareback.

Tye was angry enough to spit hot water, and angry enough to straddle another man's saddle for hours, until he felt like he was being split in two. Frank was considerably taller and larger than Tye.

As the rain poured out from the rim of their hats, Tye's mumbled cussing was washed out. It wouldn't be long before his anger would be replaced by weariness and doubt that the miscreant would ever be found again. He vowed that if his prey made it to the land of the Red Coats, they could have him. The chase would be over for him and a hasty retreat to warmer climate would prevail. Breathing heartily, he veered his horse into the steep landscape of the Selkirk Mountains.

In the morning, his cantankerous demeanor changed when he found a fire, its charred remains still warm, and a couple of pine shavings, untouched by the smoldering heat. He sauntered over to a thatch of weeds and sifted through it meticulously until he crouched on haunches.

George peered over his shoulders, announcing, "It's just some scat."

"Nope, this is excrement," Tye replied after a good snuffle of the fly covered mounds.

George shook his head, saying, "Same thing."

"Human excrement," Tye clarified.

"That's less than I've seen a rabbit pop out," he snickered. "Looks like Thomas needs more oats in his diet!"

Tye was sure his prey was near, until steps away, his shoulders sagged at the sight of fresh horse dung. Before horse hooves drove his prey away, boot prints and Tye's satchel were found hanging from the knotty nub of a pine tree. He peered into his bag and quickly growled. The chokecherries pummeled the forest ground as he mercilessly shook the bag empty. Poking up from the rounded mound was rolled tobacco papers.

Arthur unfurled a paper. "Eat your last meal, then click your heal," he recited, before grasping another piece, "on your horse, set a course," his hand madly digging through the bitter berries, "on a southern slope or you'll be choking on my rope."

George snickered.

"Who's he think he is, Shakespeare?" Arthur jeered.

Frank scowled while Tye's face stayed as straight as a pin. He recollected the prey's smoldering eyes, so unlike the fearful eyes of the few Confederate deserters he hauled to summary execution before his conscience got the better of him. He knew this reprobate would defend his life until the bitter end.

The night remained pleasingly dry, so they feasted on beans and a freshly caught rabbit while the fire took the dampness from their chilled bones.

Arthur pulled out a harmonica while Frank returned with plates and cutlery, dripping clean.

"What kind of small-legged cayuse's hauling your gear, Tye?" he questioned.

"That there's a mustang."

"Indian pony?"

"Yep."

"You break her?"

"Nope. A man named Sullivan and his son did that without using a quirt. Take my hat off to them," Tye said, most complimentary. "That mare's less ornery than my thoroughbred."

Arthur filled the night air with a screeching tune.

When he paused to suck in air, Frank interjected, "Ever track a woman, Tye?"

"Once," he muttered, poking at the fire with a stick.

Arthur belted out one note before Frank interrupted, "Please enlighten us!"

His cold stare sent an icy chill to settle in their bones again.

Tye knew the questions would keep flying out of Frank's mouth as long his eyelids kept fluttering open.

"A wealthy plantation owner wanted me to bring back his fleeing wife. I refused, so he hired Harley Oswald to do the deed. I wouldn't have it that way. Harley was a grisly man. Tracked runaway slaves, and brought 'em back, beaten, hog-tied, and barely alive. Took me two days to find her," he paused in recollection, "just a flash of vermillion on a palomino mare. She could ride faster than most men. Maybe too fast, as she weaved around sweetgum trees. Made a sharp turn, overcorrected, and flew into a thatch of weeds. She was pulling burrs from threads of frizzled, golden hair when I come up on her, calm like, hands outstretched.

George hollered, "Can I come back to the fire, now?"

"Keep on the lookout!" Frank grumbled with an icy disdain at Arthur's shiny harmonica. "Continue, Tye."

"She peered up and panicked," he recalled. "Pulled a derringer from her cleavage and waved it with dainty hands. Her voice cried, 'come any closer and I'll put a hole in your chest.' I didn't have the heart to tell her that at that range the bullet would more than likely skip across the ground. I assured her that I wasn't there to harm her...just bring her back to her husband. That he promised he'd change his philandering ways with other women. She cried back, 'and the men'?"

"Good God!" Arthur said in disgust.

Tye nodded. "My jaw must have fallen three feet. Her face was sprinkled with dirt and tears, and I just felt for the woman, who said she was treated like a showpiece...a porcelain figurine to be admired, but never touched. I wanted to take her out of the state, but ended up escorting her to the county courthouse so she could make the matter legal. She wanted to fight for her land. Get the dirty scoundrel off her plantation. I didn't stick around after that. If anybody believed her, in that county, he'd also be lynched for fornication with other men. I've seen my share of lynchings, so I bid her farewell."

Frank handed Tye a hand-drawn picture of Amanda Wilkes.

"After we deal with Thomas, I want you to find her. Father's been missing her something terrible."

"Pretty woman."

Frank nodded.

"Need to know why I'm tracking her. Won't be taking her back to any mistreatment."

"She's chasing after a dead man," Frank spoke crisply. "It's time for her to go home."

"Let's find your man, first. Then we'll see if there's anything left in me to go on."

Arthur took his harmonica to task until Frank warned, "You blow into that thing and you'll be shitting it out with your morning oats! George!" he bellowed. "Time's expired. Arthur's raring to go!"

Arthur leaned against the pale bark of a pine, tattered blanket covering his rifle and aching knees; and the camp went quiet, the night sky weighing heavily on his tired shoulders as eyelids flitted, fighting sleep. Something delicate brushed against his cheek, but he easily waved the pesky insect away.

When he lifted his head, a noose tightened around his throat, lifting him, suspending him, just inches from the ground. The more he struggled, the harder it was to breathe.

Tye appeared and knifed at the noose until Arthur was freed, and no longer flailing like a dying fish. On the other side of the tree was Arthur's horse, licking at sugar crystals scattered amongst dried needles, pulling a rope that hung frayed over a sturdy limb.

The next day, the posse trekked north just hours from the border, when metal glistened like a ray from the mid-day sun. Driving toward it, Tye eyed his saddle perched against a rotting stump. George was quick off his horse, marching toward it when steel claws clamped around his leg. He gripped the trap, cussing up a storm, when Frank and Tye rushed over.

"Jesus, Frank, get it off! Get it off!" he begged.

"Hold still!" Frank commanded as he worked at releasing the steel trap.

"Does it look bad?" George asked Tye with desperate eyes.

"I've seen worse. Knew of a Blackfoot boy who had to cut his own foot off to survive. I do believe that was also a bear trap." Tye spoke with honesty until he recognized panic in George's blue eyes. "He's just fine now. Walks on a peg."

George went pale and screamed until Frank stuffed a branch in his mouth. "I'll work faster at freeing you if you're quiet!"

Arthur rushed to the men with a rag, and rushed away as the metal teeth were pried from George's mangled flesh. He sidled over to Tye's saddle and found shoved into the stirrup a strip of bark, smudged scribbles on the inner side.

"Strap on your saddle, then skedaddle!" he recited loudly. "If you move too slow, duck real low!"

Tye lifted his pistol and moved stealthily around the lofty trees, his heart palpitating much like those he often preyed upon.

After Arthur and Frank switched the saddles, they perched George's shaky body atop his black gelding.

Figuring the danger was gone, Tye mounted his horse and scanned the rugged northern abyss, his view quickly hampered when a blast sent his hat clear off his head. When another bullet grazed his shirt, he jumped amidst a cover of green foliage.

Frank and Arthur spurred their horses towards the firing gun, leaving Tye to scrounge for his hat and pride, while George risked life and limb, staring languidly into open spaces, as blood filled the empty spaces of his boot.

More bullets rang out, silencing the birds; but the breeze blew strong, throwing shadows and light from every direction.

Tye felt like he was being watched as his own eyes shifted through the moving trees and flickering leaves.

Frank and Arthur reappeared.

"We're riding into Canada," Frank announced.

The yellow leaf of an aspen tree flew into Tye's chest. "I hear the Scarlett Jackets run the roost in those parts. Let them have a go at Thomas. Besides, weather's changing men. There ain't a town with a warm bed or a watering hole for miles. I have my hat off to this Thomas," he said, fingering the hole, "and my life for another day."

"I'm with Tye," George mumbled weakly.

Frank glared at Arthur, who was rubbing his neck.

"I should get George back safely," he rambled nervously. "Besides, I ain't been swallowing right the whole day." His adam's apple moved with a face full of grimace.

"Fine," Frank scowled. "I'll go after him myself! Tye, you see to it these….these poorly, injured men get to Helena safely," his voice hissed with displeasure.

Tye nodded as he mounted his horse. With hat firm over white hair, he wheeled his thoroughbred south of the barren, wilderness land.

Chapter 12

Two springs had passed before the Sullivan ranch was bursting with mustangs again. I was leaning on the fence with Pa, observing the horses move freely through the growing, green fields.

"When will you break the black stud?" I asked.

"May be too wild," Pa replied as the stallion lunged at the fence, kicking and leaping.

"Why don't you release him?"

"He'll never leave the herd, Patrick."

"And what if he's too ornery?"

Pa shot me a glance. "Then we put him down. Trey should have a go at him, soon."

"Maybe he should work the bay mare with the lone white sock. She keeps biting and kicking the other horses."

Bill watched as the aggressive horse whirled and nipped at another's neck, chasing after her, threatening to wound.

"Dominance versus submissiveness," Pa said quite plainly as the assailed horse's cry filled the pasture. "It's very natural with herds," he paused and turned to me, "but it's time she be tamed."

A small smile crept at the corners of my mouth. I desperately wanted to break that black stud and had to start tonight if I was going to accomplish it.

I was very confident, almost cocky, that I could take on that ornery horse despite Pa's repeated words to stay away from the stud. I would show him and everybody on our ranch I was capable of breaking any horse I wanted to.

Late that night, I ran the stud into the corral with the snap of my whip called 'gentle persuasion' against the damp ground. Once within the wooden rails, my swinging loop caught more air than it did stud's neck; but I kept at it. His slick back flickered in the full moon's light to an explosive nature that kept me on my toes and away from the walls of the corral.

Filthy, choking on dirt, and tuckered out, I gave up on the first night; but I did rope him on the second night. A few days later, that stud was trotting around the corral at a steady pace while I held a taut line.

I felt fully confident I could ride that horse without a saddle the next day…...

Trey was yawning as he meandered to the door of the bunkhouse scratching the hairs of his bare chest. Opening it, the sight of me lying on the back of the black stallion must have shaken the last bit of sleep from his head.

"What the hell! Son of a…Patrick's mounting the stud!" he hollered back, grabbing his shirt.

"He's breaking the stud?" Andy asked, so astonished, the coffee he was pouring pooled onto the wooden floor.

"No, he's just taking a nap on him!" Trey snapped.

They bolted out the door at the same time.

"Bet you five dollars he's bucked off before we get to the corral!" Trey spat out.

"You're on," Andy muttered.

Meanwhile, in the kitchen, Bill was kissing the top of Mary's head as he did every morning. While reaching around her small frame for the coffeepot, he glimpsed my quiet bedroom.

"Patrick still in bed?" he asked

"No, I think he's outside with those wild horses," Mary answered.

Bill slammed his mug against the table as his heart panged with worry.

I always had breakfast before I went out to the horses…always.

Rushing out of the house, his breath caught in his chest at the sight of the black stud in the corral. He didn't yell or shout for fear it would spook the horse and send me tumbling to the ground.

The mustang bucked as I moved him into a trot; however, the kinks appeared worked out when the pace quickened to a lope. I couldn't hide my huge smile as the powerfully small stallion moved smoothly around the corral.

Trey was fuming as he handed Andy his money. "How the hell'd he get that horse so tame?"

Just as the words left Trey's mouth, my reins ushered the horse in the opposite direction, and he hastily bucked, then bucked again. I jerked around in the saddle, legs struggling to straddle, while he whirled and corkscrewed towards the fence.

Andy and Trey were screaming and flailing their arms when the stud rammed the side of the split rails.

"That's gonna leave a mark!" Andy grimaced.

I hung on until the horse double kicked, doing it with such great flair, I flipped in the air. Dusted, I felt I might have dented the mercilessly firm ground.

"Patrick get up!" Andy and Trey bellowed as the horse reared too close to my dazed and dopey body.

While shaking the dizziness from my head, I struggled to lift my heavy torso. Turning, horse hooves lunged at me, until Pa's strong arms yanked me away. The black horse bolted through the open gate and that's how he aptly got his name, Bolt.

"Patrick!" Bill cried fretfully. "You hurt?"

I held the arm that got jammed into the fence, wincing in pain.

"Your arm, is it broken?"

"No, it's just sore," I moaned, rubbing it. "I know what a broken arm feels like. It's not broken."

I was so frightened, so disappointed, so worried about what Pa was going to do. He just kept staring at me in alarm as I peered at him nervously. What he did next took me by surprise.

"Good!" he ranted, grabbing that sore arm and pulling me off through the cow pasture, along the fence where the wildflowers grew, to the five lonely stones.

"Said it wasn't broken!" I wailed, trying to rub the pain away. "Never said it didn't hurt!"

"I never told you how my son, Oliver, died. Suppose I should have told you sooner," he said bleakly, his relief turning to regret, then undeniable grief.

Pausing, Pa seemed to be in such a bad way, he struggled to breathe, panting, "He decided he would tame a stud alone. I was in Fort Benton with the men and didn't know it, but his best friend, Trey, had a foolish two dollar bet with Oliver over who would tame him first. I guess you don't know it, but Trey's been with us since he was a boy."

He hesitated again, walking a stride or two, obviously still disturbed by the haunting images that flooded his mind. "It would've been a horrific sight for Mary, finding her only son being trampled by this wild and uncontrollable creature. When I left that day, I looked at Oliver for the last time and told him to stay away from that horse. He just smiled his confident smile waving me away."

Spinning around, Pa mumbled, "Should have taken him with me. Mary shot the horse and did the best she could to care for Oliver. He never woke up, though. Died a few days later….just thirteen years old."

His sigh was heavy, expressing without words how close he believed it was to happening again. "There was a lot of forgiveness to be done in that house. Our lives changed in an instant, and that's all it takes, an instant; and your life can change forever."

I was still rubbing my arm, trying to take in what Pa had been through, what he was going through. I heard everything around me: the tremble in his voice, a crow cackling high atop the tree, the breeze's slow movement through its leafy branches. I felt Pa's sorrow. I felt everything around me and was deeply saddened.

"These horses are wild," he said. "Don't ever forget that. No two are alike."

Grabbing my arms, he gave them a little shake. "You must have patience with them. Follow the stages I've taught you and never rush it. If the horse remains unpredictable, erratic, it doesn't mean you're a failure. It means the horse cannot be tamed. It happens!"

"What if I want to break 'em like Trey does?" I asked boldly.

He exhaled loudly, "Then this is where you'll be buried, alongside your mother. The choice is ultimately yours. But the risks are much greater the way Trey works his horses. And in the end, I don't believe the horse is ever truly tamed that way."

He eyed my torn pants. "Whatever you decide, you won't enter that corral and tame another mustang until you've more protection on those legs."

I nodded and hugged Pa, feeling so badly for his loss, my mistake, his sadness, and my impetuous risk. Peering at Oliver's gravestone, I felt grateful to be alive.

As we walked back to the house, Pa kept his arm around me, his weight unusually heavy on my shoulders.

Ma ran from the porch and wrapped her arm around me until I limped into the kitchen.

"Patrick, take those trousers off so that we can clean the cut."

As I did, Ma got the whisky and some boiled water and clean cloth.

Pa was pouring coffee while rubbing his head, appearing rather pale and weary.

"Sit down!" she commanded. "We have to clean all the dirt out so this may hurt a bit."

I peered at the whisky, wondering when I was gonna get a drink to ease the pain as she dabbed the cloth in water.

"How's it looking, Mary?" Bill asked, concerned.

"Just a scrape, but I'll add a dab of whisky so it's nice and clean."

He nodded tiredly, proceeding to the front door.

I watched as he paused with his hand on the knob. Something wasn't right with him and I hoped it was because of what had happened in the corral.

"Patrick, this may sting a bit," she said, dabbing the whisky soaked cloth on my leg.

When the alcohol reached my cut, she got my full attention.

"Hold the cloth still a minute while I look at these trousers."

She spent more time inspecting the rip in my pants than doctoring to my leg. As she left the room, pants in hand, I snatched the whisky and took a big swig. I coughed and she briskly re-entered the kitchen with a sympathetic eye.

Reaching for a shot glass, she prescribed, "One glass, Patrick Sullivan. That's all you're going to get and not a drop more!"

I smiled sheepishly thinking that's all I should need to keep me more than happy.

Ma left me in the kitchen again and I got to thinking about how strangely Pa seemed. I slid on clean trousers and searched the stable for him, but found Trey instead.

"How's your body, Patrick? Still in one piece!" his eyes blazed.

"It's fine. Thanks for your warm concern," I replied guardedly.

"What the hell you doin' breakin' my stud? You know you're only supposed to handle the mares," he said in a belittling tone.

"I'll handle any horse I want to!"

"Don't touch the studs! They'll break you 'fore you break 'em!" he spat out, digging his finger into my chest.

I shoved it away.

He forced my hand away, and before we knew it, we had our hands grabbing at each other as we swung out the stable door.

"Get your hands off me!" I roared.

"Not 'till you tell me you're sorry for bein' such a Yokel who don't know a horse's ass from its head!" he blurted viciously, slapping me in the face.

I broke my right hand free and swung it back.

Trey paused, waiting for the hit.

I had all of my anger in that fist and couldn't wait to unleash it.

"What's going on here!" Bill barked. "Trey, get back to taming the horses. Patrick, to the house, now!"

As I waited in the kitchen, I scraped that whisky bottle across the table and took a swig for the pain my ears were gonna get when Pa walked through the door.

He entered and sat heavily on the chair. Grabbing the bottle, he poured himself a whisky into my empty shot glass with shaking hands, his breathing heavy.

"Patrick, what are you doing fighting Trey? You know better than to raise your fist in anger."

"I just…I just don't like being smacked around," I whined irritably.

"It didn't appear like that. I saw someone," he shook his head, stumbling for the right choice of words, "something in you that gave me grave concern."

"I have to fight back or I'll never get left alone!" my voice cried in desperation, despite that I was hung up on that someone Pa said he saw in me.

"Then you're no better than the one who started it. Anger and violent behaviour only cause more angry violent behaviour."

I confronted Pa with something that had been nagging me for some time.

"If you believe that so much, why were you giving the Sioux boxes of ammunition because we all know that rifles cause more violence than my fist ever could?"

The kitchen filled with silence as he took his time to respond. "I gave the Sioux ammunition so they could defend themselves. I do believe a man should be able to defend himself. You know as well as I do that they've been pushed from their lands, lands that they've been promised. They're not looking to start a fight. They're looking to protect what's legally and morally theirs."

"Well then, you must believe me when I say I was defending myself."

Pa stared squarely at me as my nervous foot shook the plank floor. I scratched the back of my neck until it bled. He didn't believe my lie, and neither did I.

I couldn't wait to unleash my fist, to hit back, and it was stifled.

"Nonetheless, Patrick, there's a passage from the Bible that's most appropriate in this situation. I want you to figure out which one it is, and when you've chosen the right one, you can return to taming those horses. In the meantime, finish your chores. Work that anger out of your body."

"Turn the other cheek," I said in arrogant confidence.

"Not that easy."

"There are thousands of passages in the Bible that are appropriate. Can you tell me which part? Romans, Corinthians, Psalms?" I pleaded.

He glared at me, both hands firm on the table. "No! You will not touch those horses until you speak the correct passage to me. I don't care if the seasons change, years pass, or you're the last man standing on this ranch! You will not touch those horses until I hear the correct passage. Are your ears open to my words?"

I defiantly said, "Yes!"

It took me a week before I figured out the correct passage with the help of Ma.

I chased Pa all over the ranch with verses about forgiveness, peace and leading a humble life, feeling completely deflated after seven days of endless searching.

At supper time, Ma asked if I still said the Lord's Prayer before I went to bed.

"I say it every night just like you taught me. Well," I paused, "almost every night."

And then it dawned on me. I was just about to blurt it out when Ma asked me to finish my chores in the stable.

"Go away with you and let your father eat his pie in peace."

She gave me a cold stern 'don't you be messing with this powerful gale' look.

I sent my confused self off to finish my chores.

The next morning, I stomped to Pa, who was kneeling on the roof, and shouted out, "Forgive us our trespasses as we forgive those who trespass against us and lead us not into temptation, but deliver us from evil!"

"I'm sorry, Patrick. I can't hear you. Come up the ladder and bring me a handful of shingles."

I trudged up the ladder and tossed the wooden squares his direction.

"Why don't you take one and put some nails into it right here," he said, pointing to a needy area.

I ranted out the passage over my pounding.

"You speak that prayer every night?" he asked.

I half nodded. "Almost every night."

"Then why don't you try listening to it and feeling it in your heart."

I placed another shingle and nail, ready to hammer, when Pa grabbed my arm.

"A promise is a promise. Go tame another horse," he said, raising dark, bushy eyebrows.

I went off as quick as a shot down the ladder towards the corral. I didn't wait for him to change his mind.

I tamed another mare while Pa broke Bolt. Whenever I looked at that horse, I kept thinking of the boy who would never ride a horse again, never be a man, and never grow old.

It took some time getting over the fear of being thrown, knowing it could have been a lot worse; but I had to get over it if I was going to tame another horse. And in the end, the fear melted away for I loved it.....I loved breaking horses and wouldn't give it up for the world. I tamed four more horses during that hot and dry summer.

I also loved taking the sweatiest horses to the Missouri River to get cooled. It was one of my favourite chores because it meant I would also get relief from the heat.

On one sweltering afternoon, I walked Lincoln to the meandering river bank through the comforting shade of lofty pines. I stopped to hear the crackling of the trees' cones as they split open, spewing their seed over beds of dried brown needles. The sound reminded me of hard corn popping over flame in a lidded pan.

I yanked off my dusty boots, pealed away my sweaty clothes, and smacked Lincoln's haunches to the cool waters through blizzards of mayflies hovering above the river's surface. As I was squeezing water from my cloth over Lincoln's withers, Trey approached with Ginger.

Naturally, he came around, eyes planted on my naked state. I waited gloomily for his big lips to start flapping.

"Patrick, your ass is whiter than Ma's sheets," he said, shielding his eyes.

I turned around rather smugly and crossed my arms. "Is this view better?"

I always considered myself to be a well endowed kid...man, so I felt pretty confident as I stood exposed while the water lapped at my thighs. I'd seen the men wading in the Missouri many times and they always came out looking so small.

Trey studied me through thick clouds of tiny bugs and started laughing. "Look's like Lincoln's got at least a foot over yours. Hope you don't have pecker envy."

"Oh, Lincoln," I muttered under my breath, swatting his haunches and ushering him away as Trey sent in Ginger.

I reached down to soak my cloth while Trey took a tobacco pouch and paper from his pocket. Sitting on a rotting stump, he rolled himself a small cigarette.

While striking a match against the heel of his boot, he mumbled, "Patrick, you know where I'm from?"

"Hell," I murmured.

Trey laughed as smoke puffed out of his mouth. "So I see you do have pecker envy."

My head grumbled, willing him to go away.

"I'm from Mississippi," he proclaimed, inhaling smoke deeply. "It's a small backwater town where kids run 'round with no shoes, lice in their hair, and empty bellies. Starvation so bad a horse dies and the community hovers for a piece of its meat. My father joined the Confederate Army….more for the pay than the glory. Returned without his arm and decided we should get the heck out of the state. Go where land was free…start fresh."

I continued to cool Ginger, wary about Trey's eagerness to share his life story.

"While we were travelling, my mother and sister got sick with cholera. It's one hell of a disease. You're in dire straits when water's the only thing keeping you alive and you can't keep it down. We buried them and continued north to St. Louis, Missouri…..I digress, Patrick. Got to put my mind on the right track."

"I wish you'd take the right track back up that hill to the ranch," I growled, but he continued to speak, spoiling my quiet cooling retreat.

"Before we left our town, I spent one last day with my two friends at the creek cooling ourselves just like you are now. Randy and Charlie were their names. Both boys had cussing mouths, were dull-minded. A moth would take the focus away from their chores, and their father would punish them. These boys had red marks all over their backs and legs. There was no bright sun reflecting off of them."

I stiffened, wishing my clothes had stayed on my back.

"Your marks…your marks remind me of dusty pink ribbons I once saw trailing from the mane of an alabaster horse. Old scars. They are few, but they are long. Must have been pretty deep cuts, and I wonder……wonder what the hell you did to deserve those scars?"

I stood speechless as the images of that night began flooding my mind.

"Come Ginger!" Trey called, clucking his mouth until I was standing alone.

"Soak them scars, Patrick! Soak them scars!"

And that's what I did. As I lay floating on my back, I let the cool river flow through my ears, listening to the silent watery world. I willed the Missouri to wash my scars away, but scars never disappear. I willed the Missouri to wash away my memory of that night, and it did.

Chapter 13

The autumn sun's descent beyond the Rocky Mountain ridge forced darkness to creep over the Sullivan acreage too soon; so I worked faster to get my work done.

When I questioned Pa about his health, he said it was just a part of aging. He seemed to be aging too quickly, so I worked harder to ease his workload.

Despite my interminable chores, I was asked to accompany him when a distant neighbour was in need. Even though I welcomed the break and spending time alone with him, I didn't particularly care for one neighbour because she had a daughter named Cora, who quite simply…annoyed me.

Mrs. Talbot's cows always strayed from their pasture. Pa and I would go and round them up. As we ventured to the Talbot farm, I sensed he had something important to say.

"Patrick, very few of us are born to be leaders like your namesake, or Lincoln, or Wilberforce. Most of us are just ordinary, what I would like to call ordinary heroes. Ordinary heroes offer to help their neighbours, give a kind word, and share a smile. Never be disappointed that you're just an ordinary hero. The world needs us just as much."

When we got to Mrs. Talbot's farm, she would always come running out of the house with sweet tea and pound cake, making us stay for a spell. Pa knew how lonely she was, so he would indulge her. Mrs. Talbot would call Cora to the porch every time I was there.

Cora looked normal. She was very tall and thin, had long blond hair and freckles. It was her mouth that I found very….unattractive. She had these big front teeth that bucked out some. It wouldn't have looked so bad if her mouth wasn't moving the whole time we were there.

I smiled shyly and that seemed to encourage her even more. The quieter I got, the louder she got. I glanced at Pa, and he gave me the 'five more minutes look'.

Cora liked to sit really close and it was fine today for she smelled like lye soap. Other days she reeked of manure, or exuded an oniony smelling sweat, or the odour I dreaded most, the stench of dead animals.

I never smelled like that. I had the Missouri surrounding the ranch and bathed in it as often as I could, even when it would numb my hands and feet 'till I could barely bend them.

Cora obviously had less access to water. She worked hard, so I tried to be compassionate in my thinking since my time with her was probably the only rest the poor girl had. Maybe, that's why she talked so much.

"Patrick, how old is the right age to marry?" she asked, picking at dirt in the nails of her coarse fingers. "I think you can marry as young as fifteen if you find the right person. I think you marry when it's the right time. Patrick, what do you think is the worst chore on a farm? I think it's dealing with them chickens. Wringing them necks has to be the worst job on the farm. I hate that job. Patrick, anyone ever tell you, you have the sweetest smile? I think that smile is the most beautiful thing I ever seen. And your eyes, Patrick…"

She coveted them like rare gems to hang around her neck.

"They're the bluest blue I ever seen. I could just swim in those eyes."

Turning away, I mumbled. "I wish you'd swim in water." One of Mrs. Talbot's ten cats had curled her way under my arm. I started scratching the back of her ears, her noisy purring a distraction from Cora's noisy talking.

"Patrick, I wish you'd touch me the way you touch that cat."

I threw that little cat over the porch like she was rabid and glared menacingly at Cora. "I can be really mean, Cora!"

She smiled, "I like that in a man."

The cat hissed at me before sauntering away.

I peered at Pa, silently begging for mercy.

He shot me a considerate smile before saying it was time to go home.

Another neighbour we helped out from time to time was Clay Crawford. He wanted a new horse to plough his field, so Pa brought along Murphy.

Pa was unusually quiet as we headed toward Crawford's property, so we took in the sounds of the flowing Missouri and the soft breeze that swayed through the fragrant branches of the tall pines.

Veering from the winding river, we slowed to watch the man working his field. He was laying his whip into the plough horse harshly. The sight of it was like black lightening cutting through the air, the sound of it hauntingly ear-piercing, filling the pasture with terror.

Pa didn't take kindly to people beating their horses.

Clay cracked his whip, and I cringed, averting my eyes.

"That man is killing his horse," Pa spoke sharply as the whip whirled and struck the horse's haunches so mercilessly. "See how he holds his head so high. That fierce jerking of the tight reins has probably caused the bit to tear his mouth to pieces."

The horse finally buckled, nearly snapping the man's plough in two.

I choked out the words, "He has no love in his heart."

Pa placed a gentle hand on my shoulder as he guided the horses toward the passageway.

As Clay walked over from his field, I saw my grandpa's scowl and animosity on his face, and if it weren't for Pa's reassuring glance, I would have fled.

"I see you brought me a horse…'bout time. That one there's pretty much done in," he hissed.

Pa wasn't intimidated by his behaviour, though he did keep his hand on his sheathed rifle the entire time we were there.

"Mr. Crawford, your treatment of that horse is appalling! I'll not be giving you one of my horses until you can manage your rage!"

"How I treat my animals is none of your business! Now hand over the horse, or I'll…" His whip raised, the bitter man was abruptly cut off.

"Or you'll bring harm to me or my son?" Bill bellowed. "No, Mr. Crawford. You want one of my horses, you'll control your anger; or you won't have anything to plough that field. You won't plant any crops in the spring. Your wife and five children will hunger and you'll lose this land."

I waited for that whip to uncoil and find its way to me, for temper and anger always released its rage on me.

Clay's eyes blazed over unturned soil before setting on the home where his large family already cried out from a barren pantry and empty table for sustenance.

Pa was unflinchingly fearless, expressing no anger, just resilience that no more of his horses would bear the sting of a whip.

I watched how Clay's face changed from scornful rage, to recognition, to resignation.

"Call on me when you're ready," Pa said. "And I'll help you, help you to train this horse to plough that field without the use of any whip or bad will; and that field will flourish with abundance for your hungry family and for market."

Turning our horses away, he said at me, "Maybe we've gotten to the man's heart through his stomach."

"How's he gonna get to our ranch without a horse?" I asked curiously.

"The walk will do him good."

****

By the descent of winter's first snowflakes, I knew Pa was sick. He was always cold, had very little appetite, and fell asleep every night in the keeping room while Ma and I played softly on the piano.

One night she was singing, 'Then you'll Remember Me' and Pa's snoring was so loud it shook our hands from the piano keys.

We laughed.

I said silently, *I sure will remember you as I try to finish this song with Ma.*

"Should we stop playing?" I whispered. "We might wake him?"

"Nothing will wake him up, son, when he's that deep in sleep," Putting her arm around me, she sang while I caught up with the keys.

I was so cautious around him. It felt like I was walking on rotting fence rails, though one night at supper my mind couldn't control my mouth.

I was stabbing a chunk of stewed beef when Pa cleared his throat. He did that all too often and it always got my undivided attention.

"Your mother and I would like to invite Mrs. Talbot and Cora to supper on Sunday."

"Maybe I could go to town with Trey. Give you more room at this table," I offered quite nicely.

"Patrick, your place is here for Sunday supper," he reminded. "Besides, we would like you to spend more time with Cora."

"Why?" I asked rudely.

"Because she's a nice girl...young woman, and someone your age should be with a nice, young woman."

"I don't want to be with her," I said honestly. "I'd rather be with someone like....like Ma."

She smiled; her cheeks went rosy.

"Ma is kind, a quiet talker, and she...she obeys you."

The smile fell from Ma's face as she turned to Pa quite indignantly. "Bill Sullivan, you tell your son...."

"Now Mary, calm down," he spoke abruptly, but Ma stopped talking; and I liked that about her, though her smoldering glare directed at Pa surprised me.

"If I were to marry Cora, I'd be ordered around like one of her livestock," I said matter-of-factly. "She doesn't read books. Says they're more practical for fly swatting.

She talks so much, I can't hear myself breathe, and that's just not good for a person like me."

I should have stopped talking about Cora, right then and there, for I got a compassionate look from Ma, but my Cora rampage wasn't finished.

"The other day she asked me what letter came after 'j' like I'm dim-witted. I managed to mumble out 'k' before she puckered up pale, thin lips and jutted them in my face. At least that shut her up for a few seconds." I shuddered, "Heck, I'd rather kiss Taffy."

"That's what I'm worried about," Pa said. "You spend more time with those horses than people."

"I live on a ranch surrounded by horses. What do you expect?" I snapped.

"I expect you to be interested in female people," Bill stammered.

"Well, Trey has some female people he wants me to meet in Fort Benton."

Ma fervently shook her head, but I went on.

"He says they're sweet, most forthcoming, quiet talkers and…and they're good riders, too."

Pa purposefully dropped his fork so he could point his finger at me. "Stay away from the women of Fort Benton! They're breeders of disease and filth!"

I shook a doubtful head. "Trey always comes back healthy and clean. Matter of fact, he says it's like a weight's been lifted off him and he's always happy and smiling for at least the next two days."

Ma stood with a noticeable scrap of her chair. "I've heard enough from you, Patrick Sullivan, and not enough from you, Bill Sullivan. You will both clean this kitchen together and discuss why it is, you'll never go to Fort Benton for a woman, Patrick, and why it is, that no married woman should ever have to obey her husband, Bill!"

Before stomping to the keeping room she snatched her freshly baked pumpkin pie and tossed it back in the oven.

"And don't you be touching my pie! There'll be nothing sweet for you, Bill Sullivan, this evening."

We sat in silence, finishing our cold Irish stew. Pa casually turned his eyes Ma's direction.

"What's she doing, Pa?" I asked wistfully.

"Darning my socks," he nodded calmly. "It'd be an entirely different evening for you if she took the scissors to them. Go fill the basin with hot water and put the dishes in to soak."

I sauntered over to the pot of water figuring I would be the one doing the obeying tonight.

While Pa dried the dishes, he explained that Trey was visiting the brothels of Fort Benton for his women. He then told me to strike the word obey from my vocabulary when it came to women, quietly elaborating that they would obey best if they didn't know they were doing it. He pointed out that I must be tactful in getting a woman to do what I wanted.

"Mary, you want me to be putting the dishes away?"

"No, Bill. You always put them in the wrong places. Just leave them on the table."

Bill winked at me, whispering, "That's the way to get a woman to do what you want her to do."

I smiled, passing the last washed plate to Pa. As it smashed against the floor, I turned to see him stumble for a chair.

I called out frantically to Ma while grabbing him from falling to the floor.

We got him to the bed as he struggled for breath.

"Patrick, have the men go for the doctor. Patrick!" she shouted.

I nodded, but couldn't take my eyes from him.

"Now, Patrick!"

Opening the door to the bunkhouse, Andy and Trey were having a drink at the table.

I could mumble out three words, "Pa, Doctor, now!"

And that's all it took before they were saddling their horses and riding away from the ranch.

My time was spent pacing the floor and sitting at the kitchen table chewing my nails, waiting for the doctor to come out of Pa's room. I jumped when he appeared with a somber smile on his face.

As he moved closer, I moved further away, until I was against the cool wall of the stone hearth.

"Patrick, it's been years since I've seen you. You must be keeping well," he said softly.

I always felt uncomfortable around doctors. It felt like they wanted me to stay sick so they wouldn't be out of an occupation.

"Must be the fresh Montana air," I answered anxiously. "How's my pa?

He looked sullen, so I braced myself for the worst possible news.

"He's fine for now. It's his heart, though. It will give out long before the rest of his body does."

"How long?" I asked hoarsely.

"Hard to say," he replied unsurely. "If he takes it easy, maybe a year or two."

"What can I do?" my voice barely audible.

"I think you're already doing it. Bill tells me you're practically running this ranch with the help of those men out there. Other than that, just keep him calm. If he has an attack like tonight, offer him whisky if he can swallow it and come fetch me."

At the door, he swiveled and leaned against it.

"Patrick, what did you tell me you used to do when you suffered an asthma attack?"

"I imagined being weightless, boundless, floating up to the clouds."

"That's right. God's gentle hands bringing you up to the heavens…peaceful thought. Might come in handy for your father."

As the door closed, I clutched the kitchen table wanting to break it in two.

Ma came out of the bedroom.

"Patrick," she said, touching my shoulder gently. "I'm going to tell the men your father's….fine. Please go and sit with him."

I nodded, watching her slowly move in grief. Breathing deeply, I entered his room.

Pa was indomitable to me, but the man lying in the bed was pale and weak.

"Patrick, sit on the bed. Don't be afraid," he said.

"I'm not afraid," I smiled softly. "I'll be here for as long as you want me to be."

He held my hand as tightly as he could.

"You make me very proud," he spoke lightly. "I feel blessed and grateful for you."

I nervously shook my head, speaking honestly, "I find myself more of a bother to you. Can't think of one time I ever made you feel proud."

"Well, how about the first time I took you to church?"

"That was embarrassing to you."

"Not all of it," he spoke truthfully. "You were sitting beside me and the lovely Cora joined us."

"She just got so close to me. Her leg rubbed up against mine and her hand touched my knee. I think that was very inappropriate in the house of the Lord," I said indignantly.

"Uh-huh. So you took it upon yourself to flee to the piano and lead the congregation with the hymns, but you didn't know all of them."

"I knew five….four at the time," I admitted.

"That first song?"

"Shall We Gather At the River."

"It was pretty horrible, choppy, painfully slow. You should've quit after the first verse, but you didn't and half the congregation nearly walked out."

"Yes, I remember quite clearly. That song flowed too quickly. It should have had a slower tempo," I stuttered.

"But you stayed firm and played the next hymn despite the Pastor's prayers that you rest your weary fingers."

"In the Sweet By and By."

"You redeemed yourself playing that hymn. Played it with great soul and spirit, and I was very proud of you. Proud of you for staying at that piano despite the many scowls and sighs, despite your crimson coloured cheeks."

"You said the congregation may not have known me before the service but they definitely knew me by the end of it. You proudly announced me as Patrick Sullivan, your son, I remember."

Pa smiled solemnly as his hand caught the tears streaking my face. I shied away, but he pulled me back.

"Never be afraid to show your love or your sadness. It shows your humanity."

He held me to his chest as it slowly swelled and sank. His beating heart, so full of love but weak in strength, tore at my soul. It was so cruel that the best part about Pa would stop too soon.

****

During the remaining winter months, the tables were turned as Pa spent most of his time in the house and I ventured out as often as I physically could. I relented on afternoons when he was eager to teach a new skill or offer advice.

On one particular afternoon, he was staring out the kitchen window giving me a math problem to solve. He felt I had to strengthen my math skills so I could do the negotiating with the Cavalry.

"Patrick, say we were offered fifty dollars for…"

"Pa, that's not nearly enough?"

"Well, seventy-five dollars a head for let's say twenty mustangs."

"Twenty, that's not nearly worth our time….."

"Twenty-nine mustangs times seventy-five dollars a head" he said abruptly.

Writing the figures down, I soon offered, "How about one hundred dollars a head for thirty mustangs, which would be three thousand dollars!"

His head shook in disapproval

"Nine times five, carry the four…." I mumbled, wishing I could just listen before I spoke.

"Did you do all of your chores today?" he asked.

"Yes, Pa. I have ten chores and ten fingers so it's very easy for me to remember all my chores," I declared, counting down all I had done. "I've fed the horses, milked the cow, cleaned four stables……"

"You should count your fingers again for one of our cows is heading towards the river."

I scurried to the window and offered a contrite face. "I'll go after them?"

He squeezed my arm tightly. "No Patrick, you're not chasing after those cows. We have one sick member of this family. We don't need two. Go tell the men to collect those cows."

Desperate not to upset him, I nodded politely and headed to the bunkhouse.

At that point, large snowflakes were falling and melting almost instantly on my woolen coat, however dampness was in the air. The temperature was rising.

Andy was alone when I entered the room. Jimmy and Mike had been away for the past few months with Jimmy's sister, Kate. Her husband had died that fall so Jimmy and Mike went to help with the farm.

"Where's Trey?" I asked.

"He's off whoring in Fort Benton," Andy announced. "Spending most of his pay, I'm sure."

"I think I left the cows in the pasture with the gate open. Why don't you start rounding them up from the field?"

"I'll get my coat."

"Andy, why does Trey go all the way to Fort Benton? Doesn't Helena have whores?" I asked naively.

"He's banished from those whorehouses."

"Why?"

Andy was buttoning up his coat as he answered, "Well, Patrick, he was seeing this one soiled dove and she had, um….she had a deformity and Trey didn't like it too much."

I looked at him curiously.

"She had three teats."

I looked at him curiously.

Andy put his arm around me as we walked to the door. "A woman has two breasts and two teats, one on each breast. This woman had two teats on one breast."

I faked comprehension, though my mouth still opened in bewilderment, trying to picture it in my mind.

"Trey couldn't concentrate with these two teats staring at him so he asked her to cover up. She took offence, said she couldn't do anything with his, uh…softness. Trey felt insulted so he slapped her. She pulled a knife on him. He pulled a gun on her until Amelia Boudreau stormed in, threatening to blow his brains out. He's not going to Helena anymore and the moral of that story is…..if you're ever with someone who has a deformity, don't point it out. Just sweep that knowledge under the carpet."

I agreed quickly. "We best round up those cows before Pa comes looking for me. I'll get Lincoln and head towards the Missouri. We'll meet back at the barn."

After my horse was bridled and saddled and repeatedly cinched, I moved him along the passageway, which was very· slippery. The snow had turned to ice. It felt like sharp shards of glass stabbing at my face.

By the time I was at the edge of the hill, hail was coming down, causing Lincoln to fretfully toss his head. The last straw was when one massive chunk came thundering from the sky and cut my cheek. I moved us under a pine tree, flung the saddle to the ground, and covered our heads with the blanket.

"I've never seen or felt hail this size before Lincoln," I admitted as the heavy mounds continued to pelt us. "They're like the size of Bolt's…the size of your male parts when you had them."

He fussed as his unprotected body was pummeled by the icy balls.

"Lincoln, you have bad breath," I said, putting my hand to my mouth. "Actually, it's me."

I stretched my hand out to find the hail had turned to rain. Climbing atop Lincoln, I left the saddle and blanket behind, very anxious to get back to the home I promised I wouldn't leave.

After the stray cow was roped and brought back to the barn, I found that two more were still missing.

"I'll head north along the river. You head south, Andy," I ordered, reining my horse away.

The hills surrounding the Missouri were growing taller when I squinted to find our cow moaning and flailing by the river's edge.

Leaving Lincoln, I cautiously made my way down the slippery slope, but fell backwards, sliding until I was finally propelled a few feet from the groaning cow.

"Patches!" I cried, finding his head all torn up, bleeding.

"Patrick!" Andy bellowed from atop the cliff. "Do you want me to come down?"

I looked into hard rain. "Patches can't move, and I can't climb this hill! I'll go around!"

"No you won't! I'll pass you a rope!"

With the support of a Pine, he pulled me up as my boots struggled to grip rock, my knees grinding against jagged edges.

When we arrived at the ranch I was drenched in wet and mud, my cheek blood-stained, as I prepared for the scolding of a lifetime.

"Patrick Sullivan!" Ma growled quietly. "Where've you been and what happened to your face?"

"Do you know there was hail the size of…the size of balls of yarn coming at us? Patches got his head bashed in by…."

"I don't care about Patches," she said, throwing a hand towel at me. "Dry your hair, wipe that cut, and go see your father before he calls for you again."

I did as ordered, moving to the dimly lit room.

As I went for a chair, Pa patted a spot on the bed.

"Are the cows safely in the barn?" he asked while I kept my damaged cheek angled from his gaze.

"All except for Patches. He's in bad shape….can't move," I said sadly.

Pa tilted my face towards him. "That's not what's most important, Patrick. A cow can be replaced. You've got to have common sense when you go after these animals. If it puts your life at risk, then it's not important enough. What happened to your face?"

"I ah..… cut myself shaving, having a rain shower and the blade slipped," I said plainly.

"And your pants?"

I looked at the muddy knees. "Slipped on the way."

"Why do you have to lie so much?"

"I don't lie that much," I lied.

Pa gave me a flabbergasted look.

"I do it to protect myself. I do it to protect others."

"It's a sin, Patrick. That's why I make you pray so much for forgiveness. And one day, those lies will hurt you and maybe even worse."

Weakly, he touched my arm. "Let me rest now."

"Sure Pa," I said solemnly, blowing out the candle as I left the room.

Chapter 14

A warm gust of wind ushered Bill Sullivan through the doors of Callahan's Saloon in Fort Benton. Teetering to the bar, he reached for a stool but stumbled.

Eyeing him through the wide mirror, Sean reached out a hand to steady the man.

"Why, Bill Sullivan," Mollie Callahan said behind the counter with a curious gaze. "It's been a while."

Too weak to utter a word, shivering, and gasping for air, he simply nodded to the big-boned woman.

"Is it that cold out there?" she asked naively. "Why don't I brew you a coffee?"

"No," he managed to say, pointing to the counter. "Whisky."

She quickly poured.

He quickly drank.

"Where's Danny?" he asked.

"He's dead," she announced, tugging a grey curl from her weathered and rosy cheek. "Consumption a few months ago."

Pouring two more whiskies, she slid one to Bill.

Their glasses were raised in a toast.

When Bill's trembling subsided, he turned to Sean, "Thank you."

Sean's eyes swept over Bill to surmise no threat: unarmed, shaking, and most likely the town drunk.

"Where's that boy of yours?" Mollie enquired.

"He's outside, though he's not a boy anymore. Turned seventeen a few weeks ago."

"I know. He was here on his birthday with that other," she hesitated, "boy you took in."

"Trey?"

"Yes, and I don't think he was taking Patrick to church, afterwards."

Bill brought clasped hands to his disapproving face.

"John always sensed a rebellious nature in him," Mollie divulged matter-of-factly. "Said you should've had the good sense to leave him on that ferry..."

"Molly, please," Bill pleaded as his shaking resumed. "I'll have words with him when I return."

"How long have you been this way?" she asked with newfound awareness of Bill's poor constitution.

"Too long."

She covered his frigid hands with hers. "Whatever you need, Bill.....whatever you need."

His appreciative smile turned to Sean, who sat bearded, bedraggled, hunched over a half dozen empty shot glasses.

"Buy you another drink?" he offered.

"Drink's not what I need," Sean grumbled.

"If it's work you're looking for, I could use another hand rounding up mustangs."

"I can't even round up my own horse."

Mollie leaned into Sean. "Cavalry's heading this way."

"One more for the road," he said, with one hand on his glass and the other on his Colt forty-five, as the military man approached.

"My ranch is two days south of here. Minutes from the Missouri," Bill advised.

"You don't want my kind near your place," Sean spoke gruffly.

"Those hands could be put to good use."

Sean tipped his hat and sauntered past the military man whose voice rang out, "Mr. Sullivan?"

"Mollie, would you be kind enough to fetch Patrick for me now?" Bill asked with urgency.

On the boardwalk, Sean was moving away from the mid-day sun when he glanced at a young man sitting in his wagon fidgeting with the reins.

"Look my way," Sean mumbled. "Just once, look my way."

The glance was brief, too brief, as the focus became the mercantile across the street, then back to fiddling with his reins.

Sean turned in time to bump into Katherine, who was just ahead of three Cavalrymen smugly eyeing her swaying figure.

"Why, Mr. Cunningham, it's been a while. You must come this way."

****

Just days before another mustang round-up, the Sullivan ranch was bustling with chores. In the stable, I was pondering how to convince Pa not to go when Trey sauntered in looking anxious.

"Hey Patrick, want to try somethin' different."

I continued shoveling horse muck from Taffy's stall into the wheel barrel. "If by that you mean I can sit back and you can work for a change, sure!"

Trey crossed his arms and wedged himself between me and the wheelbarrow.

"What kind of trouble you want me to get into now?" I asked suspiciously.

"No trouble. Just a friendly wager. Five dollars if you can do it."

"And what do you get if I don't?"

"A piece of your gold."

"You think I'm an idiot. My gold's worth more than five dollars."

"Fine, Mr. smarty pants. How 'bout you clean out my three stalls for the next week?"

"What do I have to do? Race you for it?"

"No, we already know I can't hold a candle to your pace on a horse." Trey feigned a look of admiration, though his arms were stiffly folded. "I was thinking about something a little more challenging."

Trey eyed Ginger as his hand ran from her withers to gleaming haunches. "I want you to stand on the horse's back a few minutes."

"That's the craziest thing I've ever heard."

"Can't do it, just say so," Trey goaded. "You know what they say about you. Sweet Patrick, meek and mild. Sounds like they're describing a girl!"

I scowled at him, shovel still firmly planted in my hands. "I can do anything I want with a horse and choose to hold my temper so I can be an example to your hot head."

"In the real world, away from Bill's protective arms," Trey said, hovering over me, "you'd be used, abused, chewed up, and spit out like a gob o' tobacco. Figure, I'm tryin' to toughen you up."

"By standing on a horse."

"By proving to yourself that you're willing to take risks….that you're brave."

"When do you want me to show this bravery?"

"Now, while Bill and Mary are at Talbot's farm," he urged. "I'll meet you outside with a horse of my choice."

"Just don't pick the stallions," I answered quickly.

After taking wavering steps out to the path between the stable and house, I yanked off my boots and socks. My mind kept repeating how utterly foolish this was; however, my male bravado pushed on, ready to prove how brave I could be.

Trey came out with Shannon, standing well over sixteen hands. She was by far the tallest horse we had on this ranch, but I stayed resiliently steadfast in my decision.

I looked at Shannon.

Her brown eyes looked curiously at me.

Then I glared at Trey. "How the heck am I supposed to get on the horse?"

I thrust my foot into Trey's cupped hands and grabbed Shannon's mane. My slender body slid over her shiny back until I sat upright. Both knees were pulled tightly to my chest while my arms stretched for balance. With my feet nestled into her wide girth, I slowly rose. Kneeling on my haunches, Taffy's whinnying echoed across the pasture, nearly sending me tumbling.

"How long do I stay standing on this horse?"

"Five minutes."

"Five minutes! Are you crazy?"

"Fine," Trey acquiesced. "Two minutes."

I slowly rose and pointed my arms directly outward for balance and stability.

"It's not so hard," I said bravely. "So long as you don't look down. Oh, and thanks for giving me such a big horse."

Trey's deflated face gave me great satisfaction. The two minutes flew by and my pockets already felt heavier.

"You hear that?" he asked.

Horses' hooves thundering along the ground meant my parents would be home sooner than we thought.

There were no other ranches nearby and we weren't expecting visitors.

"I've got to get that horse back in the stable," Trey stammered, clucking his tongue.

Shannon shifted, my balance wavered, and gravity prevailed, messily landing me on a mound of horse turds.

My anger sprung me from the flattened greenish-yellow patties, ready to tear a strip off of Trey after grabbing my boots and socks.

He turned, relaxed, saying I might want to change for I smelled and looked like shit.

"I don't give a rat's ass!"

"What's that I hear, Patrick? Sounds like a Bible verse coming on in about five minutes," Trey drawled smugly as Pa's carriage came up the passageway.

"I hope to see my five dollars, soon!"

"I don't care about the money. I just wondered if you were listening to my voice, again, instead of your own!" he hissed. "Away from this ranch, people gonna be asking you to do foolish things and you got to have the balls to say 'no'."

"So it's not about being brave anymore. It's about being foolish!"

"You looked pretty foolish on Shannon's back. But I think you're just wet behind the ears. Don't do what don't seem right, Patrick. Listen to your own common sense."

What seemed right was that I get out of my dirty clothes before my parents reached the stable. I tore off my ruined shirt and pants, and flung them into Lincoln's dirty stall. I must have looked like a white ghost fleeing the stable in my undergarments.

When they walked into the house, I smiled blithely, laying the book on the kitchen table.

"Why, taking a rest from your chores?" Pa asked.

"Just anxious to hear how Cora's doing," I lied.

Pa gave me a critical glare. "You'll just have to wait to hear about Cora with bated breath. Go and finish your chores," he commanded wearily.

At suppertime, Pa spoke about Cora having a male friend visiting the farm quite frequently.

I wondered how many senses this male friend actually had because I knew I'd gladly give up my sense of smell and hearing around her.

I displayed my boyish grin, saying how lucky for Cora, but thinking how lucky for me.

"Patrick, you do anything different today?" he asked.

I stayed staring at fried ham and baked beans. "Nope."

Pa sniffed blatantly. "You smell that, Mary?"

Mary started sniffing.

I took my nose to my arms and my chest, hoping the flattened horse feces hadn't settled into my skin.

Pa peered down and with the end of his butter knife, lifted my filthy shirt from a burlap bag.

"Mary, do you recognize this?"

"Why…..why it's Patrick's blue cotton shirt," she said, looking absolutely horrified.

I swallowed as Pa's bewildered face turned my way.

"Is this your shirt?"

"Yes."

"And that would be your pants in the bottom of this bag."

I nodded with great hesitation.

"Well, I could pull out the Bible, but I think this time I'll go by the 'Book of Bill'."

"The Book of Bull," I blurted out, shaking my head, "the Book of Bill?"

"It's a book in progress and it gets fatter everyday. The 'Book of Bill' states that thou shalt pay for thine own distraught clothes."

Obviously Pa's book had a Shakespearean flare.

"How much would it cost to purchase another shirt and pair of pants, Mary?"

"Oh, about five dollars, Bill."

"Five dollars?" I stammered.

"I have another rule from the Book of Bill," he stated. "Children should be seen and not heard at the dining table."

"But...."

"Ah...ah...ah," he said, dropping the shirt in the bag. "And also, Patrick, you must understand that we do not throw tattered and dirty clothes away. We boil and wash them, make them into rags for cleaning and carpets, and into bandages for those who repeatedly fall off of horses with scrapes so that they don't get infections and die!"

"Could I...."

"Ah....ah...ah," he replied quickly.

I guess I wasn't going to get any more food, either. The bowls were too far out of my reach, so I grabbed the burlap bag and a bar of soap and headed for the Missouri River.

Before my feet hit the path, I changed direction for the stable to find Trey cleaning out Ginger's stall.

"Why the heck did you do that?" I asked angrily.

"Don't go off half cocked. I'm no tattle tale. I'm in hot water, too," Trey confessed. "I have to go and dig another hole, move the outhouse, and then cover up the crap from the old outhouse. It's the shittiest job on the ranch!"

"Well, I lost my five bucks that you still owe me so I didn't tell."

Just then, Andy came out from around Whitestreak with a toe pick in hand. Only Andy could be behind that horse and not be seen. Everyone else was too tall.

"Howdy boys," he said with a full mouthed grin. "Best you quit beating the devil around the stump and get back to work."

Trey kicked a pile of mucky hay Andy's way. "Damn Canadians. Honest as the day is long."

Eyeing Trey, I lifted the burlap bag, smiling devilishly. "You want to borrow my dirty clothes while you dig a new crap hole."

"Those are boy clothes, Patrick. I'm a man. Go tend to your washin'! Hope your hands don't get too wrinkled!" he barked with a thrust of the shovel into Ginger's stall.

I grabbed the wash pot and laughed all the way to the river, thinking of Trey digging that hole. It was the worst job on the ranch. Swarms of flies would stand on the brown, reeking mound before landing on your sweaty face. I figured I'd pay five dollars just to watch Trey do that job.

As I scrubbed the clothes clean, I thought about how to keep Pa from doing the horse round-up. It was a useless waste of my mental capabilities. I couldn't persuade him to stay home.

"When you get thrown to the ground and kicked in the gut, you've got to get back up, dust yourself off, and keep moving," Pa said in his soft Irish tone. "Besides, the Lord can find me anywhere when he's ready to call me home."

Despite being as tough as nails, he wouldn't be riding his horse on this journey. He'd sit in the chuck wagon alongside Mike.

Since I was now seventeen, I considered myself a man, so we were now six Sagebrush men of the High Plains.

That first night we made camp, Strong Bull appeared, though I now knew there were no magical spirits summoning him to us.

The talk around the campfire quickly turned to the laying of rail track seen in Helena, which would bring more settlers; and more supplies; but would also cut through prime Indian hunting grounds. Pa grumpily complained that most of the tribes had already been forced to reservations, with his final summation being that the cavalry would need fewer of his horses once the last of the few non-conformant bands were rounded up.

The men went awfully quiet when Pa's temper raged so Jimmy lightened the somber mood with his jokes.

"What did one horse say to the other horse?" he asked. "The pace is familiar but I can't remember the mane."

He piped in with another joke. "Patrick and his Pa were walking in the woods when they came across a sign saying, 'Tree Fellers wanted.' His Pa said 'Ye know, it's a shame Mike isn't here. We could have gotten the job'!"

"I've got one," Andy said, glaring directly at Trey. "An American and an Irishman were enjoying a ride in the country when they came upon an old gallows. The American thought he would have a joke on his Irish companion. 'You see that, I reckon' said he to the Irishman, pointing to the gallows. 'And now where would you be if the gallows had its due?' Jimmy replied coolly 'Riding alone'."

Everyone chuckled except for Trey.

Pa went into a coughing fit, so I, along with Jimmy, helped him to his tent. Jimmy stayed with him while I moseyed back to the campfire.

When I returned, Andy was singing a cowboy song called 'The Streets of Helena'. Then he began singing a sad song about an Ottawa girl.

"It's for her I pine, for those sweet lips so fine; I miss my sweet girl from Ottawa."

Trey couldn't help himself. "Is that why you always have your hands under the sheets, Andy?" he chortled, "missing that sweet Ottawa girl. Is she native?"

"Ottawa's a place, not a tribe!" Andy snapped. "It beats spending all of my money on whores!"

Trey eyed me. "I don't know 'bout that. What do you think, Patrick?"

"You said we were going to Fort Benton for a new cowboy hat and candy!"

"Well, you got your hat and something sweet for your mouth," he chucked. "We took the Farting Horse Pass to get to Fort Benton that time."

"The what?" Andy asked, very confused. "You didn't, Trey!"

"Hell, yes I did.....horse needed to be broke. I figured Patrick be the best person to do it."

"That horse bucked me off twice before we got to town," I whined.

Trey snorted. "It took us more 'an two days to get there. Picture this....Patrick's on 'Flick' aptly named so 'cause of the way her tail flicked in the air every time she farted after she coughed. Patrick's on his new saddle. The one he just got for his fifteenth...."

"I'm seventeen, Trey! I see your math's as good as your English," I spoke unabashedly.

"I see your face is as good as smashed in if you use that tone with me again, kid," he threatened. "Patrick's moseying along and all you hear on the quiet trail is squeak, cough, fart.....squeak, cough, fart, and Flick; well

Flick gets so frightened by her own bodily noises that she bucks and bucks again."

Andy was howling so much, I thought I saw tears running from his eyes.

"Patrick," he gasped through his chortling fits. "That saddle still creaks!"

"Pa says it'll creak 'til it's paid for," I mumbled unhappily.

"Anyhow, I digress," Trey said.

"I wish you'd regress back to infancy and not know how to speak," I hissed.

Trey cracked his knuckles as he scowled at me. "We were in Fort Benton and just happened to stumble into Lady Katherine's house of personal gratification."

I blushed as the thoughts of that afternoon flooded my mind. I was in the room with a fair, curly haired plump woman named Clara. We had just sat on the squeaky bed when another woman stormed in, seething with anger. She lunged at Clara, telling her to go to her own room.

Clara whimpered, "My bed's….not ready." She didn't want to confess that it had itchy bugs. "Katherine told me to use your bed."

"You liar! Get out of my room, you dirty harlot!" Ophelia raged, yanking Clara from the bed while she held tightly to my arm.

"Oh no, you don't! This one's in my room so he stays with me!"

"We'll see about that, you old nag!" Clara cried.

"Clara, go and take a bath! You smell like moldy cheese!" Ophelia hollered, slamming the door in her face.

I was nervously staring at the floorboards when I felt the woman's dark eyes upon me.

"Well, you're a young one."

She loved the young ones. They never took too long to spill their seed and sometimes all it took was a sultry glance. This shy one, however, was more fascinated with the floorboards.

"What's your name?" Ophelia asked gently sitting beside me.

"It's Patrick," I stuttered.

"Well, Patrick," she said, easing delicate fingers through my hair.

I hastily turned away.

"This is going to be tricky if you don't like to be touched."

"What's your name?" I asked timidly.

"It's Ophelia."

I quoted.....

> "Too much of water hast thou, poor Ophelia,
>   And therefore I forbid my tears;
>   But yet it is our trick,
>   Nature her custom holds,
>   Let shame say what it will...."

"From Hamlet," she replied.

I peered at Ophelia. "You know Shakespeare?"

"Oh, yes. I've been to every Shakespearean play in Helena."

My tense shoulders eased a little. "Do you...do we have to? I could lie. I'm a good liar."

"Why'd you come here, Patrick?"

"It's my birthday, today. My friend dragged me here."

"Well, happy birthday. April fifteenth. What a prodigious day! Your friend will know if you don't do anything. He'll know."

She eyed me scrupulously. "How old are you?"

"I'm seventeen."

"Is this your first time?"

Awkwardly, I said yes, but that I had someone special in mind, and just hadn't gotten around to doing it, yet. I spoke truthfully even though I hadn't actually found her, yet.

"Well, we don't have to do that. There are other things we can do and because it's your first time, we can do away with the inspection."

"It's fine! Everything's fine down there!" I assured, scratching the back of my neck.

Her curious eyes made me very uncomfortable.

"I haven't seen you around Fort Benton, Patrick….."

If she thought I was going to give her my last name, she was dead wrong.

"It's Patrick, just Patrick!" I glared at my hands unable to shake the thought of my Pa and how disgusted he would be. Stiffening, I felt Ophelia's displeasure. Her peculiar stare remained until she finally stood and searched a drawer for something.

I perused the book she handed me titled 'Romeo and Juliet'.

"We could just read if you prefer," she offered. "It's your dollar."

As I leafed through the acts, she moved in closer and unbuttoned my shirt while peaking at the pages.

She was adept with those hands: jacket tossed aside, suspenders eased off, us lying on that bed in mere seconds.

"You just let me know if you want me to stop and I will," she smiled sweetly.

I didn't mind her touch. She had long, slender fingers and their silky softness sent a warm glow through my body. I didn't put up a fuss as her smooth and moist red lips started kissing my tightly chiseled chest.

While my eyes never left Shakespeare's poetic words, I felt she was really keen on kissing me; so I didn't want to hurt her feelings.

"Read me a passage," she whispered delicately, her warm puffs of breath tingling my skin.

My voice came out amplified, rushed…..

"The dancing being done,
Romeo watched the place where the lady stood;
And under favour of his masking habit,
Which might seem to excuse in part the liberty,
He presumed in the gentlest manner
To take her by the hand,
Calling it a shrine."

She continued kissing the concave of my stomach while running her fingers under the seam of my buttoned pants.

As if a hindrance, all of my clothing was discreetly pushed away. Every muscle in my body was relaxed except one. I should have stopped her tender kisses along my sensitive inner thighs…her firm hands along my muscular outer thighs. But I didn't. I was a slave to her touch: her hands, her lips, her warm, wet mouth! I tried to say no, but it came out sounding like a deep moan, a grinding groan, and finally, a small, small cry. My body betrayed me.

Ophelia was already off of the bed, standing at her bedside table. She clasped something from the small drawer and returned completely naked. Facing me, head propped on her arm, she chewed a mint leaf in a seductive manner. The book got tossed to the floor as she looked hungrily into my eyes.

"Is there anything else you would like to do, Patrick, just Patrick?"

Grinning at her, I couldn't deny her alluring smile with that pouty red lower lip, or the sultry curve of her smooth white hip, her full breasts round and heaving, or how she was beckoning me for more, I was no longer eager to be leaving.

Ophelia recognized the familiar smile, though full of youthful vitality and boyish sweetness. Her probing eyes roamed beyond the lean torso to something uniquely similar.

"Patrick! Patrick!" Trey shouted, snapping his fingers in my face.

I looked at Trey and the rest of the men licking their lips for a vicariously lurid experience.

"She had such a way of…," I hesitated, "tickling my chest with her wavy, dark hair."

"Is that all you can remember?" Trey yawped. "Hell, you must've been in there an hour! Cost me five dollars!"

"Good men don't boast, and call our debts cleared!" I replied in an urbane way. "However, I don't believe she remembers you. Amidst her insatiable desire to know all about me, she asked quite clearly, 'Who's Trey'?"

The men howled while Trey scowled.

"How much you spend on that dark haired harlot and she can't remember you?" Andy chuckled.

"I wonder if that Ottawa girl remember you the way you remember her," Trey smirked.

Andy dropped his tin cup and walked away.

"I'll give you half an hour, Andy, 'fore I get in that tent. Then I want you still as a dead horse!"

Chapter 15

Before we arrived in Big Horn, we passed the newly laid rail track that ran along the Yellowstone River. My mind wandered to the places I could see, the speed I could travel, and the comfort of a long bench, until my horse whinnied, unhappy with the rolling hills I urged him up and down.

When I took in the Big Horn River, the emptiness surrounding its bank was eerie. There were no Sioux camps this time. I wondered if they….if Nawaji had made it up to Canada.

Moving into the mountains, we made a quick camp, and took an even quicker inspection of the corral. We were eager to begin rounding up horses on account of Pa's failing health. Jimmy stayed with him while the rest of us followed a ravine, and soon found a band of them drinking from the shallow waters.

I would follow Andy and Trey as they pursued the horses along the water's edge through the path of evergreens toward our wooden enclosure.

As my heart quickened, I plunged my fingers into leather gloves, uncoiled the whip in my right hand while my left held the slack reins.

I tensely waited.

Trey turned, smiled and hollered, "YAH!"

We heeled our horses and cracked our whips, scaring the mustangs into a chase. Our galloping pace continued as we ushered these quick and resilient ponies through our cleverly planned chute with the corral coming quickly into sight.

The sounds: one stride, one breath; one stride, one breath; as they moved. The sights: manes and tails gracefully lifting and falling with each powerful leap, would always be awesome, breathtaking to behold.

Trey jumped off his horse and fastened the gate, trapping the mustangs within the six foot wooden rails.

He wanted to go mustanging for the few horses that lingered by the bank of the water.

I glanced at the camp and while I didn't see Pa, the rest of the men seemed quietly calm so I eagerly agreed.

Trey chased after a frisky mare, the colour of chalkboard slate, while I aimed my sights on a deep choc-olate brown distinguished by a brilliant, round patch of white between very alert eyes.

We spurred our horses into lightening speed, kicking up Montana dirt.

Whirling my lariat in the air, I blissfully looped the mare's high-spirited head. Rearing and whirling, she tried to break free, but my firm grip wouldn't release. I'd rather chew gravel than let go of that bucking horse.

When she finally settled, I turned to Trey with a cocky smile; however, he had already snagged his intended horse, looking exceedingly smug.

As we added these horses to the twenty or so that were in the corral, I glanced at the tents raring to share my triumph with Pa.

My huge grin vanished when I saw their solemn faces. My heart panged and my stomach lurched.

"Patrick, yer father's gone, son," Jimmy spoke grimly.

"What?" I glared at everyone in disbelief. I shook away his lying words, rushing to the tent as Jimmy tried to hold me back. Callously, I pushed him away.

"You're not gonna stop me from seeing him," I cried, bolting to the tent.

He was so still, so pale. I shook my head in denial, the gravity of his death still incomprehensible. Out of sheer desperation, I searched for his heartbeat, wanting desperately to hear his voice one final time….wanting to tell him I loved him.

"I'm not ready to lose you, Pa. What do I do now? What do I do now!" I wailed, touching his skin, still warm, soft. Shaking in grief, the tears streamed down my cheeks into the softness of his shirt as I clutched at his strong arms tightly.

It was Strong Bull who effortlessly pulled me from the tent. I felt empty, depleted, and full of such sadness that I had no memory of getting home.

Andy said it was Strong Bull's persistence that kept me warm with blankets, eating, drinking, and home healthy to Ma.

She was devastated.

We held and comforted each other those first few days without him. Our home was so lonely and quiet without him.

Angela and Edward would be arriving any day. I didn't want to see Edward. I didn't want to see anyone, so I went to Helena for a week. The town was a busy place for anyone who wanted to be alone, so I kept moving like Pa said.

I walked to a saloon and tacked to a board by the swinging doors was a poster of Sean Thomas, offering a three thousand dollar reward, dead or alive.

Memories of him brought curious thoughts of Colleen and Ethan, and mixed feelings about my grandpa.

After a few lonely drinks, I decided it was time to go back to Virginia City. It was time to see the family I left nine years ago. I was ready to face my grandpa, feeling that he couldn't hurt me anymore. While I never would forget what he did, I did not fear or hate him.

With a heavy heart, I meandered home. Ma was in the middle of making cornbread when I entered the warm kitchen. She hastily dropped the sugar from her hands to give me a tight squeeze.

I offered to help her, grabbing a bowl off the shelf.

"How was your time in Helena?" she asked.

"It's a busy town, but I stayed pretty quiet."

"Pass me the flour."

"Ma, I have family in Virginia City and plan to see them."

She stopped whisking, her emerald eyes sad, curious. "When?"

Despite my hesitant demeanor, I replied, "After the mustangs are tamed."

Nodding, she resumed her stirring.

"Will you come back?" her voice quivered.

Peering out of the window, Edward was trying to coax a horse back to the stable.

"I don't know, Ma. Don't know where I fit anymore."

She shot me a hurtful glare. "You're my son. You belong here, on this ranch, and you have a place here!" she said with a small hand to her heart.

I grasped her other hand with a smile of gratitude. "I know, Ma. And I'll never forget that, never forget you, and never forget all that you've taught me."

Taking the spoon, I turned the wet and dry ingredients into batter while she watched, watched me so intently, I knew she was taking it to memory as if it was the last time.

She knew she couldn't change my mind. Despite her heavy sadness, I would leave in the fall after the mustangs were given to the Calvary.

While I broke horses, timid Edward was lured into the corral once. I introduced him to the dark brown mare, lone white spot atop her silky head, I aptly named 'Domino'. As I was lunging the horse, I asked Edward to try it. Domino was trotting in smooth circles when a nearby horse whinnied, jolting her into a thundering gallop.

Edward hopped out of the corral like a hunted rabbit, and I looked like the fool trying to catch the rope as it snaked across the gritty dirt.

Trey appeared and we cornered the high-spirited mare, relieving her of the rope and setting her free to graze on the tender green grasses.

As we were walking back, Trey suggested I break the stallion.

My eyes swept over the docile horses.

"If you're looking for the Prairie mustang, you won't find him. I want you to break that stallion" he said, pointing at the half-thoroughbred range horse.

"What'd you do with the wild stud?"

He squinted into the mid-day sun. "We don't need any more mustangs. These half-breeds are less ornery and have just as much gumption and stamina."

"How do you want me to break him?" I asked warily.

He glared at the stallion. "You break him any way you want to."

I started the next day choosing to take my time with the bay horse, standing erect as a lodgepole pine at six-teen hands. He was still part mustang, so I was sure he had enough ornery blood to throw me to the ground. I called him 'Big Red' because he stood so tall, powerful, and confident when he wasn't being chased by a slender man with a lasso.

When I finally roped him, he reared and spun, pounding the copper ground as I held my firm grip with the hope that Edward was watching. Once the stud's willful ways gave in to mine, I moved my gentle hand along his proud face and under the strands of his long black mane. He whinnied but didn't try to pull away.

I would continue breaking him my way, leaving the saddle to wait in the stable for a week.

The night before I was set to ride Big Red, shots echoed across the pastures. I bolted out of bed, pants barely clinging to my waist as I grabbed my shirt and bow and arrows before storming into the kitchen.

Ma was standing by the hearth clutching a rifle.

I snatched my boots and headed for the door.

"Patrick, be careful, son!" she cried.

Outside, lamplight illuminated Jimmy and Mike's sullen figures while the stable pasture was eerily silent.

"Where's Trey and Andy?"

"Tey be chasing after horse tieves," Jimmy replied, his face full of dread.

I swiftly turned, ready to walk away, when Mike grasped my arm and swung me back. For the first time, I understood him.

"No!"

Yanking my arm loose, I took one step toward the stable when he pushed me into the corral fence.

"No!"

I was about to protest when horse hooves stormed the passageway. Our horses loped through the open gate with Trey and Andy closely behind.

When Andy dismounted, he faltered.

"He's been shot!" Trey bellowed. "Let's get him inside!"

When we entered the darkened room, I tripped over a disheveled pair of pants, the floor still covered in clothes.

Jimmy pulled away Andy's jacket and shirt while Mike searched for whisky and a towel. Trey nervously lit a cigarette.

"How's it look," Andy mumbled, sweating profusely.

"Bullet grazed yer arm. Deep tear, will need stitches. We'll wrap it tight 'till morning."

"I'm goin' out front," Trey growled, "see if there's anymore sons of bitches to shoot."

"I'll go with you," I said, moving for the door.

A distinct 'click, click, click, click' filled the room as I reached for the knob.

"Take another step and the only thing you'll ever mount again is a chair," Trey hissed.

"Easy, Trey….easy," Andy stuttered.

I swung around and stared through the barrel of his pistol. "I'm willing to fight to defend our ranch and property!" I cried.

Trey glanced at my weaponry with disdain. "Maybe if they's just waving pistols, you'd be useful. But they're carrying rifles and rifles don't miss, do they Andy?"

Andy wearily shook his head.

"Your pa's still warm in his grave, and your ma was just a somber shadow after Oliver died. Then you came 'round. Take your sticks and go to bed!" Trey commanded like I was an insolent little boy.

"Talk is," Andy stammered, "Granville Stuart's forming a vigilance posse to get these horse stealers. We shouldn't have to go chasing after them, soon. Until then, go protect Mary," he pleaded.

I stood unflinching until a blast from Trey's Colt sent me vaulting for the door.

"Rats," Trey snarled.

I followed his glare to the bloody creature splayed on the floor. Shaking with fury, I stomped out of the room.

****

A few hours later, I was putting the blanket and saddle on Big Red for the first time. As I was cinching him, I glanced at Edward nervously watching, his hands clutching the top rail like a tornado was expected to brush down any second. I hoped he was taking notes because I planned to be gone in two days.

After mounting Big Red, I purposefully reined him Edward's direction, my timing impeccably callous as the horse bucked right over his fearful head. I never saw a man gravitate to the ground so quickly.

"You still there, Edward?" I called, figuring he might be crawling back to the house. While grinning from ear to ear, I calmed Big Red and spurred him into a smooth lope.

Edward was still dusting off his pants when I demanded he open the gate.

He pathetically limped over despite that his butt should have taken the brunt of the fall. Clearing the way for me to move Big Red into a gallop, I tore him through the passageway and around the pasture of idle longhorns.

As I neared the low fence, I decided to go for one last jump. Nobody would stop me from doing what I wanted to do this time. I leaned forward, tightening the reins, but my cues were ignored.

Big Red stopped suddenly and I kept moving.

When I flew over the horse's head, I heard cows' frantic mooing as my unwelcomed body landed hard, interrupting their grazing, the grasses doing little to cushion my sudden thud.

I panicked.

Trey could be heard shouting, but my voice was sucked along with any air. My lungs sagged empty as I desperately tried to fill them.

"Patrick!" Trey shouted, sliding to the ground and slowly turning me around. "You hurt? How's your head?"

"Got the wind knocked out of me," I gasped. "Can't move my left arm."

"Let's just walk it off," Trey insisted, taking my right arm and flinging it over his hunched shoulder.

"How's Big Red?" I wheezed.

"Mike's checkin' on him. Don't you worry. Just keep breathin'."

"I heard…snap Trey. Hope it was…fence."

He nodded. "I hope so too."

"Ma'll be pleased….chaps saved my pants."

"Shut up, Patrick," Trey eyed me with a petrified grimace. "Your face looks whiter than your ass."

Trey was such a compassionate man. I would have walked alone if I could have, but every bit of my energy was spent getting oxygen into refusing lungs. The only sound we could hear was my raspy breathing. I hoped it was a good sign for Big Red.

I tried to turn my head but Trey's firm grip was relentless.

"Don't worry about the bloody horse!"

"Mary?" he called out.

She appeared from the keeping room and rushed to me. "What happened? Your shirt's torn up? Are you hurt, Patrick?" she fretted.

I wagged my head, trembling, trying to hide my agonizing face and control the wheezing that escaped my droopy mouth.

Trey walked me to my bedroom. Blessed mercy came when he released his clawing hold and walked out of my room.

"What happened?" she asked anxiously.

"Mary, he tried a jump with Big Red and took a good fall. He's having trouble breathing. His arm's beat up, too!" Trey spoke too loudly.

I think he was trying to drown out my pathetic sounds. "I'm fine now, Ma," I whimpered.

"Then give me your shirt and I'll mend it."

Trey peaked in on me as I painfully removed it.

"Pass it to me, Patrick," he said while gawking at my left arm.

I nodded in agony, easing myself onto the bed.

"Mary," Trey spoke softly. "I think his arm's out of joint. We'll fix it tonight at the campfire. Let him rest now. I'll come get him when it's time."

Mary agreed. "Thank you, Trey. I'll keep watch of him."

With steps moving briskly to my bedroom, Ma found my chest heaving and sagging to the rhythm of my wheezing, my right arm slung over a sweaty forehead.

There wasn't a way to hide my trouble breathing. It took every fibre of my being to stay calm, feel weightless, and pray for quick relief.

She was easing me up, stuffing pillows behind my head, disappearing, reappearing with a glass of water in her shaky hand.

"Want me to stay?" she offered, stroking my arm.

"No, Ma. Just need peace," I mumbled incoherently.

The front door creaked open. Soft footsteps and a welcoming breeze of fall air entered my room as Angela peered at us.

"Mother, is he…." her voice quivered.

"He'll be fine, Angela. Go back to the vegetable garden."

I tried to reassure her, but Ma quickly hushed me. "Patrick needs quiet and rest. Go away with you now."

Angela tiptoed away.

"I'll be in the kitchen, son, should you need me."

When Trey reappeared, I was putting the last mouthfuls of Ma's flaky steak and kidney pie into my mouth.

"Patrick, you just about ready?" he asked.

I shook my head pessimistically. "I'm not up for it."

"Buck up! This is your farewell party. We have something special for you," he enticed.

I looked at Ma, who gave me a concerned smile.

Edward's eyes stayed firm on his plate. Supposedly, he saw me fall and promptly spewed out his breakfast in the cow pasture. His appetite must have returned for he was already into his second meat pie, eating fervently without so much as a glance my way.

Angela just kept shooting me pitiful eyes like I was at death's door.

Slowly ambling out of my chair, I leaned into Trey's ear. "If this surprise happens to be Cora, I'll tear a strip off you 'cause I'm in no mood for miss lips moving faster than the tumbleweeds off the plains."

"Hey, I never said your surprise was a person," Trey spoke as cool as a cucumber while giving Mary a re-assuring wink.

Once we were outside under a clear starry sky, I admitted my arm was hurting so much, it might be broken.

"We'll get Jimmy to look at it. He can fix anything."

"Sure, if you're a four legged animal. I'm just happy you didn't ask Edward out to this. He might have hurled Ma's meat pies if he saw how much pain I was in."

"Oh, I asked him, but he's just too tired after cutting the hay."

"Didn't you tell him we have a machine for that?"

"No. He seemed quite happy to swing a scythe around all afternoon. Besides, it wore the crap out of him. I can't wait to watch him bale hay by hand tomorrow. Just kind of forget we have a reaper for that, too."

Our laughter filled the night air.

It was a good fifteen minute walk through the freshly cut hayfield, the sweet aroma quickly changing to burning pine as the billowing smoke clouds came into view.

Beyond the Sullivan ranch, the roaring flames cast long shadows of the men and made the evergreen trees look ominously brooding. Andy and Jimmy were already rosy cheeked, either from the burning embers or whisky swishing in their tin cups.

"Patrick, how ye feeling lad?" Jimmy asked with worry. "Tat was quite a fall ye took from Big Red?"

"I'm fine. Just a little sore. Keep your knife away from me," I stuttered nervously. "Andy, how's the arm?"

"I'll survive. Doc stitched it up real good."

"And Big Red?" I asked hesitantly.

"Was splintered," Jimmy answered. "I pulled it out and cleaned te wound. I'll keep a close eye on him."

"Speaking of wounds, I have something that will ease yours, Patrick," Trey declared.

"What's this?" I asked, looking at the thin rolled up paper in his hand. "Is this one of those smokes Pa used to calm his heart?"

Trey smiled sharply. "They were actually meant for you in case you had a......."

"I get it. Will this make me loopy like it did Pa?"

"Let's find out," he said, raising his brows.

The men watched as Trey's match lit the cigarette while I inhaled from it.

"Patrick, you have to suck in deeply so it can reach your lungs." Trey spoke in a patronizing tone, tapping my chest.

"Get your hands off me or I'll burn you with it!" I warned.

"Gonna see family in Virginia City?" Andy asked.

"Yep. Gonna see the good, the bad, and the surly."

"Who'd the bad be? The one that marked your back," Trey spoke boldly.

"No, that'd be the surly…my grandpa," I said, feeling the smoke doing nothing but burning my throat. "He wasn't all that bad. Taught me how to hold my breath underwater for thirty seconds."

"We all got family like that," Andy said. "I think its 'cause of all the inbreeding."

"I've never even met the bad. Likes to kill people for a living," I said in earnest.

"Saint Patrick's got a killer in the family, and I was raised by angry wolves," Trey said with much amusement.

I was ready to lay into him when excruciating pain had me doubled over. "Can I have some of that whisky? This smoke's doing nothing for me."

"Oh, Patrick, I feel your pain," Andy sympathized with a wince.

"I've broken my arm and been kicked in the head at least twice," Trey confessed.

"That explains it," I muttered. The forest filled with laughter until the searing pain returned. "Fill this tin cup to the top, Jimmy, before I punch Trey."

I've popped my arm out my socket twice, cracked three ribs," Andy admitted. "Mike's been impaled by a fence rail."

"Worst time I got hurt was a year before Bill scooped you up from the ground," Trey muttered with a cigarette between his two fat lips.

I glowered at his insensitivity.

Smoke blew from his crooked grin into the black sky as we quietly waited for those lips to start flapping again.

"I was currying the kinks out of this stallion and he bucked and spun his head at the same time. Horse buckled and fell on my chest. I was taken to the kitchen table. Mary was shrieking 'don't let him die or I'll never eat off this table again.' Doc took one look and said 'I don't know where to begin'."

Andy mumbled too softly, "Not the way I recollect it happening."

"Didn't know it but my organs and lower ribs was tossed around, and I just kept saying 'do what you have to so's I can get back on my hoss.' Didn't take any painkillers when he cut me open and pushed his way inside," Trey expressed with hands in the air, "looked like he was stuffing a turkey."

"Trey, you did so....."

"Shut up, Andy!"

"I dare say it put Bill in a fretful state of mind. After all, Oliver only been dead two years. Horse falls on you, get the thousand pound animal off you quick and avoid getting kicked in the head. To Oliver," Trey toasted, raising his tin cup. "Best friend I ever had."

We drank eagerly to Oliver's memory.

After the smoke was chased down with a gulp of whisky, I asked Jimmy if he'd ever been hurt aside from the wounds I witnessed.

"Jimmy gets saddle sores," Trey snorted.

"Oh Trey, ye be such an ass," Jimmy moaned.

"No Jimmy, it's your ass we're talkin' 'bout right now," Trey snorted.

"Can we stop talking about asses, broken bones, family," I cried out in frustration.

There was a long pause at the campfire. Moving my arm slowly, I started to feel a welcoming numbness.

"Patrick, the danger on this ranch is nothin' compared to the danger out there," Trey asserted, puffing on his cigarette until its ash burning brightly. "I just wonder if you can weather that storm. Your mind and body are both weak."

"I'm not weak! I can take anything comes my way!"

"You hear that, Andy?" Trey asked. "Time to put your money where your mouth is, Patrick."

He stamped out his smoke while Andy moseyed over and pulled me so close, I thought he was gonna kiss me.

"No, I'm just gonna hold you tight while Trey pops your arm back in. Trust me, it's safer this way."

"What?" I asked confused, turning to Trey who was smiling sadistically when he twisted my arm and POP was back in its socket.

"Sugar, honey and spice!" I screamed, to my knees.

"Patrick, you bakin' a pie?" Trey laughed. "What happened to shuck? Am I not gonna hear a shuck out o' your mouth, Mr. I can take anything?"

I growled at Trey as shock still rocked my brain. "It's a portmanteau, you dumb ox!"

"It's a portman what?" Trey asked.

"A portmanteau!" I hollered. "When you put two words together to make a new word! Don't you read?"

"All I want to do is get drunk as a skunk. Is that a potmanhole?"

"No, that's a rhyme you fool, not a portmanteau!" I spat out. "It's like putting gigantic and enormous together. It becomes ginormous like your head."

"I'm gonna give you a ginormous smack to the head and kick the shucking daylights out of you! How's that for using your portmanholes!" Trey roared.

"Let's have a toast to Patrick," Andy chirped in. "We can just forget about the language lesson right now, boys. Oh, that reminds me….here."

Andy passed me a book.

"What's this?" I asked, my vision blurry.

"It's 'Jules Vernes - Journey to the Centre of the Earth'."

"You mean you had an English copy all along!"

Andy nodded with a full mouthed grin. "I think it sounds better in French, though. Besides, there was no way I was giving up my warm and cozy job of teaching you French during those icy days when you could freeze the balls off a brass monkey."

"Merci."

"De rien."

"Would you two shut up?" Trey drawled. "There'd be only one language that matters."

"What language is that, hayseed?" Andy taunted.

"American," Trey replied.

I coughed the weed right out of my mouth while everyone chuckled. Trey went searching for the small nub.

"Andy, could you teach me that language?" I asked in a mocking tone.

He hiked up his pants. "I reckon I could just so's I could see Trey's look of stupor again."

Trey stood, fist raised. "You say another word and my fist'll find your teeth. You'll be talking like Mike."

"Speaking of Mike, where is he?" I asked.

"Toot ache" Jimmy replied. "All of tose tree teet be rotten."

"But he refuses to let us pull 'em," Trey began. "I say we pull 'em after we're all liquored up. Speaking of liquor, pass Patrick more whisky. We all need a drink, cheer us up. This is a farewell party!" he spoke blithely. "Besides, I need to get so drunk I don't hear Andy moaning in his sheets, Mike chewing on his toothless gums, and Jimmy….Jimmy you make the most unhuman sounds and smells, I can't hardly sleep a wink."

"Trey, ye know me have te stomach ailment."

"No Jimmy, you have the over-eating ailment which causes the gassy ailment, followed by the stenchy air ailment, causing me to gag ailment."

"You know, Trey, you'd look a lot smarter if you didn't speak," I articulated fearlessly.

Trey smiled grimly at me. He couldn't wait to pounce on me like a playful cat over a timorous mouse.

I swallowed, thinking I'd been through enough pain despite that I wasn't feeling any pain right now. I was so dizzy and numb I licked my lips and couldn't feel them anymore.

"Patrick, ye ill lad?" Jimmy asked, while I swayed like a creaky branch in a windstorm.

At one point, I fell off the log thinking the flames were leaping at me.

"To Patrick!" Trey announced. "May he forget his way to Virginia City!"

We all drank to that. Then I offered a toast to Pa.

"Oh hell, he's gonna say a poem," Trey cringed.

I ignored his big mouth, staggering to my feet.

"To my pa, Bill, who had the audacity to care about a, what'd you call me, Trey? Oh yeah, a runt." I wavered some more. "Who had the audacity to take in a runt and give me a home. Give me a home so I wouldn't have to roam, north."

"North is that way, Patrick." Andy kindly corrected my direction.

I turned my entire body north, mumbling incoherently, "So I wouldn't have to roam north in search of 'The Bad' who I wish I never had for a father."

Trey looked at me oddly. "Bill had the audacity to take you in 'cause he'd have two more hands to work his ranch."

I was staring blankly at Trey when my feet gave way. Andy swiftly caught me, cringed in pain, then dropped me like a hot stone.

"What did Patrick say?" Jimmy asked.

"I don't know. I'm just glad he didn't hear what Trey said," Andy groaned.

"Can't figure what kind of language he was saying," Trey slurred. "I'll drink to it anyway."

****

I was being shaken and could hear Ma's voice as I struggled to open groggy eyes.

"Patrick, wake up son," she spoke softly.

"What is it, Ma?" I asked rubbing my aching head.

"You were yelling and moaning. I was deeply worried. Are you in pain?"

"No, I just had a weird dream," I mumbled.

"Did that Trey give you too much too drink?"

"No, I'm afraid I did this to myself. He can be a real pain in the….Ma something's been gnawing at me for a while."

"What is it?"

"If Trey's been here since he was young, why doesn't he live in this house?"

"Your pa and Trey didn't see from eye to the eye."

"Was it breaking horses, reading books……."

"Religion, Patrick. Trey lost his faith in God a long time ago. Bill tried to help him, but he refused to listen. Finally, Trey moved to the bunkhouse but Bill never had the heart to force him from the ranch."

I barely nodded, my head so full of thick and hazy fog I thought it'd come out my nose.

"Please don't leave, Patrick. Not like this."

"Ma, my mind is set. I have to go while the wind is at my back."

"Don't ever forget where your home is," she cried.

I hugged her as tightly as I could considering all numbing effects from the alcohol and smoke had warn off, leaving me in dreadful pain with a splitting headache.

****

In the morning, the men were all awake to see me leave for Helena.

Jimmy made a sling for my arm which helped to keep it from aching so much.

Andy gave me a big smile and wished me luck.

Trey glared grimly at me. "Stay safe, little brother."

Cruelly, he squeezed my sore arm, whispering, "Mustangin' won't be the same without you, and neither will my visits to Fort Benton."

I gave Angela a warm hug, followed by a pleasant enough nod to Edward, who said to my surprise that I was welcome back anytime, and he seemed sincere.

Ma gave me a lingering embrace, hoping I would come home safe and soon. Then she proceeded to ask if I had packed my bedroll and warm clothes, including the grey sweater that she had woven for me, books, pemmican, water, and the tent she wouldn't let me leave without. She also tied my winter boots by their laces to the horn of my saddle, her intuition screaming that I would run into wintery weather. It was only August.

"I have everything I need, Ma. If I put anymore on Taffy's back, I won't be going anywhere but the stable pasture."

"Please just come back to me safely," she cried as tears flowed freely from her watery green eyes.

I would be riding Taffy. Lincoln had injured his leg the week previous and was unable to accompany me on my journey.

My first stop would be Helena.

As I entered the town, I struggled with thoughts of making a hasty exit, but as I was getting more provisions and changing some of my gold into currency, I saw the theatre was playing Shakespeare's 'Romeo and Juliet'.

I stayed for the play and supper. Momma would have loved it; Ophelia would have loved it, too. I had to shake the image of her out of my mind in order to concentrate on Shakespeare's poetic play. I got to thinking about the words, how they rolled off of the actors' tongues so eloquently, and then I got to thinking about Ophelia's tongue. I chastised myself, but was relieved that she conducted her trade in a northern town.

Heading south the next day, I played Shakespeare's words in my mind.

> "O, here will I set up my everlasting rest,
> And shake the yoke of inauspicious stars
> From this world-wearied flesh.
> Eyes, look your last!
> Arms, take your last embrace!
> And, lips, O you.
> The doors of breath seal with a righteous kiss
> A dateless bargain to engrossing death…."

I would be making all of my decisions from now on and decided to ride like a bat out of hell until Taffy's breathing told me otherwise. As we traveled away from the Missouri River, I kept her moving at a swift gallop until we were caked in sweat and dust.

When I stopped to make camp, it was the Madison River that would cool and cleanse our hot and sticky bodies.

Trout were splashing out of the water and I slowly slithered my way to an unsuspecting jumper, snagging the speckled slippery fish for an early supper.

I made a fire, and by the time it was blazing hot, the fish had been shaved of its scales, sliced open, cleaned, and ready for the frying pan. My arm still throbbed, so I took out one of those smokes, eying it carefully. Half, just half, I agreed upon, without any alcohol; so I could still have my wits about me to carry on to Virginia City the next morning.

After a speedy breakfast of hard boiled eggs, bacon and coffee, Taffy was fed her oats and a bruised apple, groomed, saddled and ready to venture south to my birthplace.

As I entered the valley of farmland surrounding Virginia City, the sun had already set but the sky was a brilliant red against the jagged, rocky cliffs. I continued a slow walk into the town that held very few memories but would always be an everlasting place where my mother, father, and so many others came for a new life, a better life, a richer life.

The day was now done and darkness was falling over my shoulders like a heavy blanket. The lamplights gleaming from the town, no brighter than the night stars, did little to change my somber mood. Such a feeling of sadness came over me I considered a hasty return to the Sullivan homestead. I shook off the emotion as my horse continued her unwavering walk into the sleepy town.

Virginia City was much smaller in size than Helena but once had the distinction of being the capital of Montana. That title was taken away as quickly as the gold was taken away. Once the stream ran dry of golden nuggets and dust, the prospectors that flooded Wallace Street took their empty pockets to other promising streams leaving a wake of empty buildings.

I approached a hotel that was similar to one Momma pointed out many years ago when my broken arm throbbed painfully, not so different from the agony I felt now, so much so that I shuddered at the familiarity.

Even though the name had changed to Grosvener Hotel, the white-washed building looked like it was preserved in time. I found an available room and slowly climbed the spiral stairs, my long exhaustive journey finally catching up to me.

Chapter 16

Sleep came quickly and so did the brightness of the morning's sun through my tiny window. Glancing at my reflection, combing fingers through short dark hair, I decided not to shave today or any other day. I wanted to look as old and mature as I could in my new life, alone. I saw Momma's eyes in my own and her round lips that my face had eventually grown around.

Though I tried, I could never totally shake that intense, wistful look that Momma said was inherently from her mother's side of the family. Well at least it wasn't the stern, angry look I could have inherited from my grandpa's side. I smiled, trying to imagine my father through it, but too many years apart made that impossible.

While eating breakfast, I glimpsed the piano. Before leaving the room, I wandered over and placed my fingers on the keys, hoping to feel something.

I said silently, *walking in Momma's footsteps is not in the cards, today.*

After collecting my horse from the livery, I proceeded northwest to the Wilkes ranch, taking in the scenery of mountains and green lofty hills as if it were the first time. Pausing, I committed it to memory like one of the photographs on Pa's wall. I figured I wouldn't be this way ever again.

As I tugged on the reins, the ranch came into view and looked much smaller than when I was a child. Grandpa's barn seemed to pale from its former glory in size, and I questioned whether it had indeed been the same one. I rode through the front pasture where cattle used to graze freely. Now, only a handful of Herefords dotted the fenced property.

It was eerily quiet and I wondered if Grandpa still owned the ranch. I dismounted and slowly headed for the front door, ready to knock when a familiar voice called over.

"Can I help you?" he asked.

Instantly, I identified it to be Jacob's voice. He was middle aged now and had spread out some, though I now caught up to him in height. I could tell by his blank stare that he didn't recognize me.

"Jacob, it's me," I swallowed, and the name I vowed never to be called again, "Henry Jr."

"Henry Jr.!" Jacob cried. "Oh my God!"

He came over and gave my sore shoulder a tight squeeze.

"It's been so long! Where've you been?"

His face was a mix of surprise and curiosity.

I smiled through pain and was just about to answer when Mable caught my eye. She came around the corner with a basket of fall vegetables and stopped, a look of breathless wonder across her face.

"Henry Jr.?" she asked.

I smiled warmly.

"Oh my Lord!" she cried, dropping her basket and hugging me.

I hugged back, fighting tears gathering in my eyes.

"I prayed you and Miss Mandy was all right and here you is, all growed up and strong. So hansome like your father!"

Upon hearing Momma's name, I couldn't hide the sadness in my face.

"Where's Grandpa?" I asked solemnly, hoping to get through the toughest part of this reunion.

Mable turned sad. "Oh Henry, your grandpa's dead. Died two years ago. Come inside. I'll give you some coffee and we can talk."

I helped Mable scoop up the loose vegetables before walking over the creaky step and along the porch where Momma and I would sit on the wooden swing, she rocking us, reading, while the warm summer's breeze tickled my hair.

Jacob opened the door, and I felt eight years old as I entered that hallway. I glimpsed Momma's piano as we moved to the kitchen and my forgotten memories began playing in my mind: Momma turning from the stove stirring sweet sticky huckleberry jam, Grandma bringing out hidden treats from behind china bowls, and Grandpa sitting at the head of the table, shoulders forward as his fork dug madly at food.

At one point, I could hear so clearly his footsteps stomping through the hallway, I shuddered.

Mable interrupted my thoughts, asking whether I took anything in my coffee.

I shook my head, observing the dining room, noting it hadn't changed much. Maybe just fresh paint as I stared at the wall that took so much abuse from Grandpa's angry supper plate.

Jacob offered a chair and sat across from me.

"Henry was never the same after you left." His eyes expressed sorrow.

Mable brought over the strong brew, its steam wafting over the rim of the large mug.

She divulged, "One night in da barn he knocked a lamp over. Da hay caught fire and Henry was badly burnt. Jacob pulled him out but couldn't save da barn. He rebuilt it last year. It's smaller but suffices. Your grandpa lingered for two weeks in agony and pain….didn't speak much during dat time."

I nodded, figuring just as well for I truly felt nothing for the man: no hatred, no love, no sadness, and no happiness. I felt absolutely nothing, and my countenance remained distant, maybe even cold.

"Even dough we was no longer slaves, he wrote down on a piece of paper dat we was free," Mable continued. "He also willed da property and livestock to us. Now we know you're alive, dat all changes. Dis is yours," she cried, taking my hands.

"No, no," my head shook adamantly. "I don't want it. It's rightfully yours. He wanted you to have it and it's yours," I said emphatically.

Her face expressed great surprise.

"Mable, this place holds wonderful memories of you, Momma, and Jacob; but it also brings me much sadness," I paused. "Just came here to make peace with Grandpa. Then I want to see my cousins."

Sipping my coffee, I welcomed the short silence.

"Henry, where's your momma?" Mable asked with trepidation.

"She's been gone now nine years. Died on the way to Helena. We were stopped by Indians, and there was a…. a fight and Momma was killed. I was rescued by a good man. He, along with his kind wife, raised me in a loving home."

I spoke about growing up just north of Helena, the horse round ups, ranch life, but mostly about my adoptive parents.

Finally, I told them about wanting to see my cousins, whom I hoped were still southwest of Virginia City. Mable and Jacob confirmed my belief, keeping in touch with them from time to time.

I felt the need to make tracks while my will was still strong and the day was still young. My chair reminiscently squeaked across the wide planked floor.

Mable gave me a tight embrace before pressing her sweet hands on my face. "You come back to us anytime, Henry Jr., anytime."

Her voice was so unchanged by time, her eyes staring sympathetically, I felt like that lost and little boy again, and had to feign an optimistic attitude.

Jacob accompanied me to the big willow tree.

We meandered through the pasture, the Herefords undisturbed, lazily chewing on fall grasses.

The gravesites of Grandma and Grandpa came into view. The two lonely crosses seemed so tiny under the huge canopy of the tree.

Jacob shook my hand and walked away so I could have privacy to say my last goodbyes.

Removing my hat, I took a pensive breath.

"I forgive you for what you did, though I'll never forget how you treated us." An odd sense of comfort was sweeping over me, knowing he'd never lay an angry hand on me again. I imagined the flames, violent, raging, raging against rage itself. I imagined them engulfing my horrible memories of him.

"My stepfather taught me that a heart can be broken, but that it can heal and be even stronger than it was before. That hands were meant to hold love ones, not hurt them, and that through the grace of God, love can truly conquer all."

I lingered a while under the shade of the tree, feeling serenity in the gentle easterly wind coming off the Plains.

While heading to my horse, I took a long and lingering gaze at the ranch in this valley protected by sheer rock, feeling a sense of peace and closure.

My duty bound journey continued to Colleen and Ethan's home. The sun was still high in the deep blue sky as the forest of my happiest childhood memories came into view.

The quiet stillness of the home unsettled me for some reason. I was partway to the wraparound porch when I hesitated, considering this reunion for another time.

A little girl suddenly appeared and gently took my hand. She led me through the front door and into the quiet hallway.

Colleen stared into my eyes and recognition was immediate. Her face expressed surprise, relief, and sadness. She couldn't believe she was staring at a young man who had Mandy's sensitive blue eyes and Sean's handsome smile, and it ached at her heart.

She wouldn't stop crying, her voice still beautiful even though frenzied, almost shrill. Her hands longingly touched my rosy face.

I was overwhelmed by a flood of memories.

So was she, welling up. Finally forced to face a flower papered wall, she fanned her tearful face while ordering her son, Matthew, to get Ethan from the mill.

I was told that Patricia had gotten married and was now living in Butte. The rest of the children were still at home. Colleen also mentioned having some miscarriages and decided not to have any more children after her sixth child, Amanda, was born. She wanted to wait for Ethan before she heard about my life after leaving Virginia City, seeming hesitant with a hand on her heart.

When Ethan came flying through the door, he appeared overwhelmed, embracing me like I was a ghost ready to vanish into thin air.

"I just can't believe you're here, and you look so….so healthy and strong," his laugh trembled. "Please sit, Henry. I'm anxious to here about you and where you've been these past, oh..nine years."

I informed them about what happened after we left their home. Tears filled Colleen's saddened eyes and flooded her cheeks upon hearing of Momma's death.

Ethan was quick to offer his handkerchief while I silently prayed I'd never have to tell that story again.

Then I spoke about Bill and Mary Sullivan with love and admiration. Colleen and Ethan glanced at each other, appearing comforted and relieved to hear I had been so well taken care of. I reticently told them my name was now Patrick Sullivan.

The kitchen filled with the silence of a long pause, which was finally broken by Ethan.

"That's just fine, Patrick….just fine," he said with a somber smile.

Colleen felt it hard to conceal both her sadness for Mandy and a tinge of betrayal that her only son would forsake his name for another.

Reaching across the table, I grasped her hand.

"Colleen, I've had nine years to overcome my past and build a new life. This must me so much for you all at once. I wish I could've come to you sooner, but I wasn't ready."

She squeezed my hand. "I'm going to get supper ready. Hope you'll stay so you can meet…you can see the children," she said, her voice shaky.

"Why don't we get some air in that magical forest you spent so many hours in?" Ethan offered lightly.

We passed two of the children as they chased each other through the thickly treed field. The leaves of the aspen trees were turning yellow, falling, coating the ground in softness.

"I feel I have to apologize for something I did just before you left for Helena." He turned to me, his face full of regret. "I asked your mother not to leave for I truly felt Henry just had a bad day and you got in the way. I liked him. He was a hard worker and many in Virginia City spoke fondly of him."

Ethan leaned against a tree and watched me intently.

"You don't speak of him at all. How horrible it must have been for you to feel you had to ignore your family and become part of another one, and change your name."

I nodded with uncomfortable sorrow. "I don't feel anything for him, anymore. I know that he treated me poorly and I didn't deserve that. Neither did Momma or my poor grandma. I just feel disappointed and unhappy that they didn't get to live within a loving family like I did."

Ethan nodded solemnly, winding his arm around my shoulders.

"I have to tell you one more thing, Patrick. It's about your father, Sean Thomas," he said, as we began walking. "He's alive and I know where he is."

Ethan glanced at my lack of emotion.

"Sean came looking for your mother a year after you left Virginia City. You were a surprise to him. He was," Ethan paused, "he was in a bad state. The years have been unkind to him. Constantly on the run from the O'Flaherty men and the Vigilante Committee, he couldn't settle anywhere for too long. Come to think of it, I think Frank

O'Flaherty would go after him in a heartbeat if he knew where he was."

I listened to all of this intently but showed little feeling for the man I never knew.

"Your father is up in Canada living with a widow on a farm. I think he still hopes to see you one day," he sighed. "If seeing him brings you any unhappy thoughts, don't go. You don't owe him anything. He made his choice many years ago. You get to make your own decisions now without the weight of any guilt or obligation. The man I see before me is strong, confident, a good man named Patrick Sullivan. That sad, little lost boy is gone, and I don't want anyone to bring him back."

Ethan slid an envelope from his jacket pocket.

"It's your choice. Tear it up or read it, but make the decision in your best interest."

I peered at the letter from the man I once despised for starting a chain of events that led me to a dark hole. At this moment in time, I felt the letter would remain unopened, like my momma's, for all eternity. Let both letters burn at the same time, for their only connection had a new life; and it was much more promising if it was lived without obligation, regret, or guilt.

After a very noisy supper with the family of seven and several tears shed by Colleen, I returned to Virginia City, exhausted and somehow.....free.

Walking into the hotel, my steps moved to the bar for a drink, or two, or three. I smiled, figuring I had so much family now, but just wanted to be silent and alone.

While ordering another whisky, I heard a woman at the piano playing a popular Stephen Foster song called 'Beautiful Dreamer' and for one tiny moment, I imagined my father sitting here listening to Momma play for the first time.

I took out the envelope that threatened my inner peace and asked for a few more whiskies, but they only strengthened my courage to look inside.

At first glance, I noted the letter was neatly written. I could see the man could spell.

He wrote that all hope of meeting the son he never knew was a fading glimmer, but didn't want it to be because he couldn't be found. He wasn't running anymore. He found a woman who cared for him deeply, no matter how distant he was.

Sean used other words in his letter, like trying to move on, living with regret and disappointment.

I felt a twinge of sympathy, even curiosity about the man who Momma loved so much she swore she would never love another.

I should have had more to drink for I started thinking that maybe I could help this man like Pa helped me, to get past my demons and build a better life. My head shook at such foolish thoughts. Sean Thomas was probably set in his ways as an outlaw: most likely untouchable. And then there was that letter, Momma wrote so long ago.

Why not go on an adventure with no expectations? I'd be just a man exploring the great north with just a casual bump into this man.

I whispered, "Why not?" Smiling at the woman playing the piano, I climbed the winding staircase to my room.

There was plenty of time for women in my life. I wanted to see more of Montana, alone; and then head across that border to see how the people in the Dominion of Canada lived.

****

The next day, I procured extra blankets, food, and a long coat as a cooler than usual autumn had arrived.

As I walked along the quiet street, a parched throat sent me searching for a beer. The saloon was sparsely filled with Irish men, that manner of speaking distinctly familiar. I also saw a piano in the corner and wondered if I might play one of those drinking songs Ma had taught me.

I asked the bartender about playing a tune, and Ned looked up, smiling, uttering he'd give me another beer if I could play something to encourage more drinking.

I grinned, replying I'd try.

"Here we go," I said softly, my fingers touching the worn black and white keys. The song was 'Finnegan's Wake' and even though there were just a handful of drinkers, they sang it.

"Go on, lad! Play another!" they cheered.

I played 'Wild Rover' and imagined Pa watching and smiling from the corner of the room with Sergeant Jones. When I finished, I was called over to a table of five men playing poker.

"I say, that be fine Irish tunes ye played, what's yer name?" The burly man with wispy white hair asked while motioning me to a chair.

"My name's Patrick…Patrick Sullivan."

"Oh Patrick, what a strong Irish name ye got. Ye want to play?"

"Ah, what's the buy in?" I asked hesitantly.

"What's the buy in, Frank?"

Eyes on his cards, he mumbled, "A dollar."

"Well, how would ye like to join in next round?"

Peering across the table at the man with the deep knife scar under his left eye, I swallowed, "That's a bit too steep for me. I just play for small change."

"Well then, how 'bout a drink to quench yer thirst?"

I agreed.

The burly man was named Paddy Brett. To his left sat Michael Tate, who had long salt and pepper hair and a thick beard my envious eyes figured would never sprout from my face. Beside him sat Frank....Frank O'Flaherty.

I was introduced to two other men, but was too immersed in my father's nemesis, now eyeing me with sharp, black eyes. He had a prominent forehead and a prominent chin which went well with his prominent attitude. A fat cigar nestled between thick lips until he hoisted it in the air with a heavy hand.

Surprising me with a crooked smile, he asked, "How old are you, kid?"

"I'm seventeen, sir," I answered as plainly as I could.

"Well, there's plenty of time to play cards, ain't that right, Paddy," he said, glancing his way.

My beer came and it was dark and thick. I knew Jimmy and Mike would have loved it, but I felt like spitting it out. I forced it down while the men continued playing.

"I've not seen ye before. Where ye from, Patrick?" Paddy asked.

"I'm from a ranch north of Helena. My pa was a horse breeder. He died a few months ago."

"Oh lad, I'm sorry. Ned, get Patrick another beer to drown his sorrows!"

Before I had a chance to refuse, another pint of the thick brew was in front of me.

"Thank you, Paddy," I smiled grimly before shifting my wary eyes to Frank, who had a furtive glare.

"What's your business in Virginia City?"

"I'm visiting family. Plan on heading east tomorrow, though."

Frank nodded, shuffling the cards, catching me off guard when he asked, "What's east?"

"Nothing much, really," I spoke nonchalantly, "just good hunting grounds, wild horses."

Frank groaned, stretching out his right leg.

"That leg still bothering you?" Michael asked.

"When does it never bother me?" Frank snarled.

"Who gave you that limp?" Michael asked naively.

None of us were prepared for Frank's response as he madly flung a knife Mike's direction, narrowly missing his hand.

"Who the hell'd you think shot me in the leg and left me for dead? You want another hint, 'cause my Colt forty-five's ready to answer the call!"

"Patrick, you want a cigar?" the player on my right offered nervously. "To go with the beer you haven't touched, yet."

I nodded, my eyes never leaving Frank's face as he leered at Michael Tate.

"I've never had this beer, before," I said, attempting to cut the tension in the room. "It's different."

A big draw of the cigar sent me coughing embarrassingly.

Paddy patted my back. "It seems he's never puffed on cigars before, either," he teased.

The men released a low chuckle at my expense.

After polishing off the two thick beers and cigar, my skin felt a pale shade of green. I politely excused myself, offering my thanks to everyone at the table and taking one last glimpse at Frank O'Flaherty before hurrying myself out of there.

Finding a quiet alley, I aired my paunch. I would stay in town another night, but I didn't bother going back to the saloon. My instincts told me to stay clear of Frank O'Flaherty.

Meanwhile, Frank spent the rest of that day trying to figure out why my smile seemed so familiar. Then it dawned on him who smiled the same way back in Helena many years ago.

Frank was with a whore named Anna Mae at Ms. Amelia Boudreau's hurdy gurdy house when the cold-blooded killer 'Sean Thomas' came in silently with pistol in hand. Frank was in the throws of passion while Anna Mae straddled him. Something cold pressed against his temple, and his eyes opened to Sean's arrogant smile.

"Anna Mae, you might want to move away from Frank, otherwise his brain matter's gonna be all over your face," Sean suggested brashly.

"Not today, Mr. Thomas, and not in my brothel!" Amelia bellowed, holding a pocket twenty-two pistol quickly snatched from her garter belt. "You shoot Frank and Anna Mae's gonna have more than his brain matter to clean up. Besides, you ain't messing up this bed! Anna Mae's got another customer in twenty minutes. You both take it outside, now!"

"Ms. Amelia, from what I hear, Frank take's a long time to come. I'll be long gone by the time he's finished with Anna Mae."

Sean lowered his gun and made a hasty exit around her and out the front door.

By the time Frank got pants over his hardness and left the room, Sean was long gone.

"I hope you don't expect to leave without paying!" Amelia snapped.

"I could throw you and your whores out of this house!"

"I own this house, Frank! Got the deeds to most of the buildings in this town!"

"No doubt paid for by the riffraff in this territory."

"And the lawmen who get more than their share of time getting off in my girls!"

He angrily threw money at her, seething that Thomas was in his grasp; and that he could have ended the ten year manhunt for the elusive outlaw.

Many years had passed and bullets had flown in both directions since that last encounter, and he still chased after the man. He shook his head irritably and decided right then and there that it was time to put Sean Thomas in his grave. He would have to travel to the Dominion of Canada and contend with the Red Coats, but it was worth it if he could put a bullet in the man's skull.

Then his thoughts turned to the kid. He had to be Amanda's boy. And if he was in town, maybe Amanda was, too. He stiffly mounted his horse and headed northwest to the Wilkes ranch.

His slow move up the dirt passageway didn't catch sight of anything different from his last visit to the ranch in early spring: a few measly cattle still grazing on fall grass, Jacob tending to his chores, and dark smoke billowing from the chimney.

When he reached the black farmer, he was swinging bales of hay onto his wagon.

"Hello, Jacob," Frank said, still atop his horse.

Jacob squinted at the darkness of Frank's massive presence amid the blazing sun. "Hello, Mr. O'Flaherty."

The saddle creaked as Frank shifted his weight.

"Come now, ain't it 'bout time you just called me Frank?"

"I'm sorry, Frank. Don't have time to talk. Takin' this delivery of hay to the livery in Virginia City," he replied, wiping sweat from his creased forehead.

"I'm surprised you're doing this all by yourself considering Henry Jr.'s back it town."

All emotion left Jacob's face. "I don't know what you're talkin' about. How many times I got to go through this! Henry Jr.'s been gone some nine years. Ain't seen no hair of him since he left with his momma."

"Then you don't mind me going into the house and having a look around."

"Suit yourself!" Jacob answered. "But don't expect Mable to set a place at the supper table!"

Frank laughed. "Fine, Jacob. Another time, then. Best get that hay to the livery. Don't want Mr. Sykes to go getting it from someone else, now do you?"

Jacob waited for Frank to trudge off his path before he contemplated whether to warn Henry Jr. of his unsettling visit. He shook off the decision to find him, though, figuring it best to keep his distance. Besides, Henry Jr. was a man now. That boy was long gone. With the swing of another bale of hay, Jacob resumed his chores, clearing his mind of doubt.

Chapter 17

On my last morning in Virginia City, I lingered, hands behind my head, watching the dust twinkle and dance in the warm sun. When I did rise, the bed did its usual creak as my feet hit the worn wooden floor. I stared at my too youthful complexion, touching smooth skin. If I was going to Canada, I'd have to give my face time to age. And I'd do it in the wilderness of Montana.

I heard church bells chiming this first Sunday of September and felt it fitting to take in an hourly service with the religious folk of the town.

As I was stepping off the hotel porch, a newspaper ruffled and behind it, Frank O'Flaherty peered up.

"Thought I might find you here. Where you off to this morning?" he asked.

I kept my glance pointed the direction of the Methodist church for my cheeks burned hotter than the sun.

"I was, uh, just going off to Sunday service," I swallowed.

"I thought you was, uh, going east into the plains."

"That's right. Then home."

"To the Wilkes ranch?"

"To the Sullivan ranch," I answered without skipping a beat. "Best be on my way before the weather changes."

"Where'd your father come from anyway?"

"Cork."

"Slán abhaile, Mr. Sullivan" he said grimly before flipping the newspaper up to his face.

"I hope it's a safe journey home, too," I replied, ever grateful Mike refused to speak English.

Frank creased the paper in his fisted hands. Even though a shadow of doubt filled his mind, he fought every urge to lift his pistol and send the kid to his grave. But would that bring Thomas to him? As far as Frank understood it, Thomas didn't know his kin was alive.

While deliberating his move, north or east, Frank lifted his da's pocket watch from his pocket. He'd have an hour and half to pack and move out.

After the Preacher's sermon, hymns, and my quick prayer to keep O'Flaherty away, I moved east to the High Plains. I felt eyes on my back, leaving the quiet town; but once I moved into open spaces, the sounds of Taffy's movements were all that could be heard. I didn't know how long I'd be gone. For the first time in my life, I would make all of the choices and decisions, and my first one would be to take my time and go at my own pace.

It had only been months since I was last at Big Horn and the mountains.

After four days of travelling, I saw the Crow Indian reservation in the distance and thought of Nawaji. I wondered if the Lakota Sioux were still in Canada, and that gave me more incentive to head north after my sojourn.

I found a spot among the pines and Douglas firs, not far from a small creek, and built a lean-to with my canvas tent so I could watch the stars and keep a close eye on possible predators.

My perishable food was eaten first, and when that dwindled, I went hunting and fishing. I searched out small game and whittled a spear from a branch, plunging it into trout streaming through the shallow waters.

At night, I wrote in my journal while puffing on cigars as the flaming logs crackled and slowly turned to powdery ash. I enjoyed my quiet and solitude living so much, I thought about staying here, forever.

This was my life and I could do whatever I wanted. The thought of meeting my father felt daunting at times. Did I really want a relationship with this man?

I considered throwing the letters in the fire: letting them perish like her dream of seeing him again. Who would know if I didn't fulfill Momma's promise?

"Anybody care if I burn these letters?"

Taffy peered at me and shook her light-brown head.

"Oh I see….well who you gonna tell? Who's gonna understand you anyway?"

It might be time to go back to people. I was having a conversation with my horse.

That night, laying on my bedroll, I could hear wolves howling in the distance, the tranquility of bubbling water just steps away, and the hoot of an owl perched on the branch of a Douglas fir. I could just make out the reflection of the quarter moon in its eyes. Now if that bird would have hooted once or twice, it would have been a perfect sound to nature's harmony. But that was not so. That annoying owl just kept hooting and hooting.

"For goodness sake, you shucking hooty bird, shut up!" I hollered, my voice echoing throughout the still forest, feeling doomed never to get a good's night's sleep.

I lingered in this area another two weeks despite my not so wise owl's decision to stay and hoot, until I aimed arrows at it. I must say that there isn't much meat on an owl considering its wing span is about six feet, but I did get my peaceful nights' sleep back.

My biggest thrill was waking up to find ten or so mustangs hovering at the bank of the creek just a few feet from my camp. I figured it a sign to try mustanging, alone.

"Well, Taffy, it's time you got some exercise."

I got my lariat ready, and pulled on my tan leather gloves and chaps before moving like the wind off the Plains towards those wild ponies. My chase thinned them out until I focused on a brown with black points. We kept a close pace galloping along a thin path besieged by watchful evergreens.

With each leap, head held high, her mane gracefully rose and fell. As I reached out, my wide loop soared, making contact. But she turned, daring to squeeze between trees, while my horse ran straight, the rope sagging empty.

"Next time, you won't be so lucky!" I called out, laughing.

I wouldn't see her again, for I decided to move north the next morning. The timing felt right for me to find my father before the weather turned cold. The nights were already turning chilly and the daylight hours were becoming shorter and shorter. It wouldn't be long before temperatures could drop below thirty-two degrees.

I took out my journal for the last time in front of a blazing fire and wrote about visiting Little Big Horn just hours earlier while the sun still shone brightly in the indigo sky. The day was eerily still as I walked past the tombstones of Custer's seventh cavalry. I tried to imagine what it was like on that June day of 1876 as my hand swayed through the sharp green grasses that peaked between the rows of white slabs.

I wondered what was in the hearts and minds of the two hundred and fifty soldiers as they faced thousands of

Lakota, Cheyenne and Arapaho Indians armed with rifles, bows and war clubs. I tried to listen to their spirits in the wind tell the tale about suffering and loss. How the river turned bloody, and the peaceful land became deadly as horses screamed, guns crackled, and men cried out.

I heard Strong Bull say that the battle took no longer than it takes a white man to eat his breakfast. How they fought the painted men with bravery and determination.

My sadness for the loss of these Cavalrymen was mixed with a twinge of contentment because this would be the only victory for the Lakota Sioux. I understood that Custer's enemy was just a man, a painted man who finally fought fear, ignorance, greed, and won. How, on one day, he would have claimed many coups with the strike of his weapons and scalped many heads to fringe his clothing.

In the morning, I took one final wash at the creek, staring at my reflection in the clear rippling waters, the stubble starting to take away some of my youthfulness.

I still didn't know how I would approach my father....if at all. If I didn't like him, I wanted the option of getting the heck out of there without being shot.

Ethan said I was shorter than him by a couple of inches, leaner too. I thought that maybe this measly beard would hide the fact that I was his long lost son. I didn't need a father anymore, anyway. I'd just get to know him, give him some advice like my Pa gave me, and see the rest of Canada on my own.

****

I decided to continue my journey north. Breathing in the peaceful tranquility one final time, all of nature was hushed except for a lonely hawk triumphantly crying as it soared through its cerulean domain.

Moving along an army supply trail, I entered the Yellowstone valley and a town called Billings by nightfall the next day. Trey called it the Magic City because it grew so magically as a railroad town since its founding in March. The glint in his eyes indicated that he magically visited one of the town's hurdy gurdy houses.

Treading quickly along the dusty road, I picked up supplies, enjoyed a warm meal, and mailed a letter to Ma.

I prayed I was charting a good course as Taffy moved away from the land of forests and rivers.

The Missouri river remained too distant, so I prayed for a small stream or creek along the way. As the hours of the days ticked away, the temperature started to drop.

By the time this night had fallen, my breath was puffing out in misty clouds. I was very thankful for my canvas tent, set up beside the only landmark among the flat and never-ending grassland, a sagebrush bush.

Taffy was groomed after everything was removed, including her bridle. We had clocked sixty miles into this barren land, and without a tree to tie her to, I hoped she'd still be here in the morning for another day of travelling. She got her oats and cool water while I survived on apples, pemmican, and my woolen clothes for warmth.

I awoke too early in the morning to the sounds of rain running off my pointed roof, thankful that all of my belongings, including the saddle, were within my dry confounds. My sleep resumed peacefully until I was awoken by something nudging my arm.

I was too tired to move, grumbling, "Go away!" But the constant nudging persisted until I tried to shake it away. That's when I panicked for my arms were pinned to my bedroll. My eyes opened wide to find I was in a canvas tomb. My breathing, already shallow, became even shorter quick gasps as I frantically wriggled to free my body from the cold, heavy cover.

"Taffy!" I howled.

My arm finally broke free to pull back the canvas flap. Sucking in the crisp, cold air, I crawled out to get the shock of a lifetime.

"Good God!" I cried, staring at endless hard packed snow, three feet deep, and it was just the start of October.

I realized then how difficult life could be and how easily death could come.

Taffy nudged my shoulder again. I stroked her head in gratitude, sighing in relief until my legs became uncomfortably wet and numb. I didn't linger in the snow.

After I found my boots, I packed everything on Taffy's back. Turning in circles, I tried to determine which direction was north. The snow seemed to go on forever as it glistened in the sun. I felt lost until I recalled the sagebrush tree completely buried under the heavy flakes.

I followed my instincts, heading west towards the Missouri River, hoping for warmer weather and even warmer friendly farmers. I made quick tracks, biting hungrily into my last apple.

Though I wouldn't get warmer weather, it only took a day to find that friendly farmer. He was swinging his axe making a sturdy wall of firewood when he looked up and waved me over.

His huge grin was soon replaced by a curious glare as my face cleared through drifts of snow.

"Hello," he said. "Where you headed in this blizzard?"

"I'm headed north a ways," I said vaguely, rubbing my numb fingers to life.

"Come in," he said adamantly. "Warm yourself."

"Thank you, kindly," I replied.

As the door opened to a tiny room, a small woman with greying hair peered up from her sewing.

"Martha Joan," Elijah Lancaster said. "This is Patrick Sullivan. He's heading north in this mess. Thought he was our boy for a moment there. Told him to get warm by the fire and thaw out his bones."

"Much obliged, Ma'am," I spoke most appreciatively.

"I'll take the saddle and blanket off your horse," Elijah offered.

I was about to object when the man's hands went up.

"Now, now, you won't go far in this storm and neither will your horse without a rest."

"Please sit," Martha Joan smiled affably, offering a chair by the hearth."

She had a soup cooking in a cast iron pot over the burning logs.

My stomach must have done the obeying as I was soon hunched over that cauldron licking my lips.

"You're welcome to supper," she said. "Can't imagine you've been able to cook up much in this weather."

"No, Ma'am," I said. "Soup smells good."

"Porridge. Peas porridge hot, peas porridge cold."

I interrupted, "Peas porridge in the pot nine days old."

She laughed softly. "Do a lot of reading, do you?"

"It helps to pass the time during these interminable, grueling winters. But…. my grandma read me that rhyme," as the memory of her flipping pages in the rocking chair came into focus. "I'm sure that old book is still in the Wilkes house somewhere. I guess it's the stories and sayings that remain."

Elijah walked in with a sudden gust of wind, threatening to turn the flame to smoke.

"Be quick with you, Elijah. You're letting out the heat!"

He forced the door closed with his solid stature.

"I've never seen the likes of this weather in years," he said, brushing white flakes from his silver hair. "I predict it'll be the longest winter we've see in these parts. You best stay the night if you know what's good for you."

"I don't want to be any trouble."

"No trouble. We have a loft," he said, pointed up.

Martha Joan ladled out soup while Elijah stacked the damp wood neatly by the fire.

Turning my chair a hair, I was now seated at the kitchen table.

Elijah gave me an odd stare, glancing up from the fire.

You see that picture behind you?" he asked. "Wind must've spun it. Can you make it level?"

I pivoted into the small corner and swung the stitched crosswork of two doves framed and suspended on a nail, to give it what I thought, was horizontal perfection.

"A little to the right," Elijah suggested.

I nodded, making the slight adjustment.

"Just a smidgen to the left," he directed.

"Oh, Elijah, let the boy eat before his porridge gets so thick he won't be able to scrape it with his spoon!" Martha Joan cried while slicing bread.

"By George, he's got it anyhow, Joanie!"

"My name is Patrick," I corrected.

"I know, son. It's just a saying. Can't rightly tell you who said it first, though Joanie could."

"I believe it was Shakespeare's Henry V," she said unwaveringly with eyes darting to a cabinet of books.

"My Joanie has a mind as sharp as a steel trap. She knows those books inside out."

"Helps to pass the time during these interminable, grueling winters," she winked. "How far north are you going?"

"I'm going to the Dominion of Canada."

"Canada?" Elijah asked with surprise. "In this weather, I'd recommend Texas."

Chuckling, I said I had family to see.

"Have a map?"

"Nope."

"A compass?"

"Nope."

"Well Joanie, the man has no map or compass. What do you think of that?"

"I think he's going to get lost."

"I planned on using the sun and the Missouri to guide me through my travels," I said plainly.

"That's all fair and well when the sun isn't hidden behind grey clouds and the Missouri isn't two hundred and fifty miles away."

"Two hundred and fifty miles!" I said with disbelief.

"Stay a night or two," Elijah said with finality. "I'll make you a map for your travels with the rivers and mountains you'll see along the way."

"Don't forget Round Butte and Square Butte."

"I won't, Joanie. Their butteyful landmarks."

We laughed as the fire crackled and took the chill from our bones.

Sometime in the night, the chill returned to my bones despite the layers of sheets and quilts I was wrapped in. I quietly descended the ladder and added logs to the smoldering embers. Opening the cabinet, I reached for the Shakespearean play and opted to keep the fire going.

Lighting a candle at the table, it swayed as the heat took the frigid breeze away.

The next thing I felt was a small hand to my shoulder.

"Morning," Martha Joan spoke mildly.

I glanced up, eyes half shut.

"I tell you, some evenings I feel the eternal sleep coming on," she spoke gloomily. "Much appreciate you keeping us warm."

"I should be on my way," I said, trying to expunge the feeling like I was being adopted to care for aging kin.

Elijah stepped in with more wood. "Day's brighter, warmer too."

"I'll whip up breakfast," Martha Joan said.

"Patrick, our son is coming from Fort Benton. He's a Cavalryman. Should be here any day to take us to stay with him. Take my compass," he insisted, outstretching his hand.

Feeing remorseful, I said, "No, you may need it."

"Patrick, this blizzard hits again, you won't know north from your south or east from your west."

Pushing it into my hand, he squeezed it shut.

After a hasty breakfast of scrambled eggs and bacon, I said good bye to the mature couple and moved away. But I couldn't stop thinking about the Lancasters as I stared at the compass. The thought of them having one of those eternal sleeps kept flooding my mind.

I charged back to the small homestead and offered to escort them to the town. Despite that the wagon was hurriedly loaded of their meager food, clothing, and logs of dry wood, the travel west would be a slow one, adding another week to my journey; but we would arrive safely and soundly.

Memories of us huddled under a dark sky in the Conestoga wagon, draped in its canvas and my canvas, swaddled like babies in heavy blankets, still shivering, would never be forgotten. But we did rise every morning, despite the freezing temperatures and the lingering drowsy effects of my smokes that I lit, unbeknownst to them, to keep the wagon silent of my ragged breathing.

The potent leaves put Martha Joan into such hysterical fits of laughter, she even giggled in her sleep.

One night, I dreamt of Momma. The canvas was flapping wildly to the beat of a strong breeze when I turned to find her sleeping peacefully beside me.

"Momma," I whispered into the frosty air. "Momma, we should go home. It's not safe."

"Tomorrow," she whispered back. "Tomorrow."

Her slender fingers reached out and warmed my cheek. I clutched her tightly, not wanting to let her go.

Of course, by morning, she was gone.

When we reached the Missouri River, I considered crossing the winding waters that flowed low this time of year and heading home, just a two day ride away.

As Taffy trekked across the icy water, I drowned my instincts and common sense. Moving north, it would take me a week before I was in the Dominion of Canada.

By the end of this journey, with at least fifty slow miles travelled each day in this dry iciness, I became wretchedly familiar with saddle sores.

When I walked, I commanded a great pace of one mile per hour to get relief from the leather that chafed me raw and to give my horse a rest. I even carried my personals, longing to know what a pack horse really felt like. I was glad Taffy didn't have spurs.

Acknowledgements

Deepest thanks to my spouse for encouraging me to write this story. It is with warmest gratitude to my mother, children, and cover designer/editor Theresa Leonard for encouraging me to send it out into the world. I've been inspired by talented writers Guy Vanderhaeghe and Jeannette Walls.

I wish to thank Ajax Public Library. I've trudged through the aisles gathering everything from DVDs titled 'Wild Horse Redemption' and 'Saint Patrick' to books about North American Aboriginals; their history and culture during mid to late 19th century.

What I found most valuable was a dusty collection of Time Life Books, titled 'The Old West' that I discovered in my mother's basement. These books, leather bound and ornately etched with western motifs, were priceless in their historical accounts using language and expressions of that era, complimentary with portraits and paintings.

In remembrance of the late Deanna Durbin for singing the Stephen Foster songs mentioned in my book, particularly Old Folks at Home. Her voice will never be forgotten. And to the poets, Shakespeare, Emerson and Elizabeth Barrett Browning, whose words will never be forgotten.

And finally, a thank you to Joy Anderson and a woman named Margot, for teaching me how to ride and care for horses. Their guidance and patience have been invaluable.

About the Author

A graduate of Ryerson University, the author was also born in Toronto, Ontario, to a Sicilian father and a Canadian mother with English, Irish, and Scottish heritage. This novel is written under the name of Alek Leslie. The author's maternal Great-Grandfather was born in Assiginack, Manitoulin Island, Ontario, in 1880, and was raised by an unforgettable Ojibwe woman while his parents, immigrants from Donegal, Ireland, ran a hotel. This published story is part of a trilogy. The journey continues with:

Montana Son – A New Country